The Chronicles of Sanat Kumara

I Am Ready

Martina Violetta Jung

The Chronicles of SANAT KUMARA

Volume 1
I Am Ready

Copyright © Martina Violetta Jung

All rights reserved.
Paperback first published in January 2021 on Amazon
www.drmartinaviolettajung.com

ISBN: 9798582804284

German original 'Die Chroniken des SANAT KUMARA,
Band 1, Ich bin bereit', September 2020.
Copyright © Martina Violetta Jung

Translated into English by Martina Violetta Jung
Edited by George Frederick Takis
Cover design: Kirsten Lenz

DEDICATION

The Chronicles of Sanat Kumara
are dedicated to all those
who hear the call in their heart
to recognise and to serve
that which we call holy truth.

ACKNOWLEDGMENTS

The experiences and conversations with some inter- and multidimensional light and energy workers and healers have helped me enormously in writing this first volume of the seven-part novel series *The Chronicles of SANAT KUMARA*. The same applies to the books and private notes of some of them. I thank you all from the bottom of my heart and look forward to our further cooperation.

RECEPTION IN SHAMBALA

Chronicle time 18.761.997 - 01.01

I am TRUSIAN. My team and I are to lead the human family back to its destiny in the cosmic plan. All others in the team are already incarnated on Earth. However, I still have three years of training ahead of me so that I can live and act meaningfully in a land-dweller's body. On 5 January 2000 I will be born as a mixed-breed baby named Lucia in Kinshasa and will begin my ministry on Earth. But today SANAT KUMARA will first officially introduce me to the spiritual hierarchy of the Earth in the Great Hall of Shambala. About a thousand light beings have accepted his invitation. They stand quietly side by side in their garments of light, glowing radiantly in the different colours of the rainbow, waiting for the Lord of the World to address us all.

The Great Hall of Shambala is impressive, even for someone like me who has known large parts of the cosmos for millions of years. The hall is built of white shining, filigree processed stone, which flatters my sense of vibration. Carefully I touch the floor with my hand. He swings in. I feel the high-energy connection of the golden dome of the hall with the cosmos. On the walls geometric shapes are reproduced with diamonds, emeralds, rubies and many other precious stones. I especially like the whirls and spirals. They attract or emit cosmic energy, depending on the direction of flow. Here it is like in the cosmos; everything is constantly in motion, attracting or repulsing, narrowing or expanding. A light-being in a bright green robe about fifty steps away uses the time before the official beginning to address me telepathically. The deep voice inside my head is not familiar to me, but who or what is already familiar to me here, on these vibrational levels which are low by my standards?

Welcome, TRUSIAN. My name is GUNAH. Thank you to you and your team for making this sacrifice for the human family. Forgive my curiosity but may I ask how you got this Command to Travel to Earth?

Greetings, GUNAH. SANAT KUMARA sent a request for help to the Galactic Council through the Stellar Council, and the Galactic Council, with the approval of the Cosmic Council, asked the leadership of our constellation to let me leave my leadership duties to assist Earth with a strong team.

Do you have experience in dense matter?

None. We usually vibrate in the eighth dimension.

And yet you volunteered to accept this mission in the drama of the third dimension?

If only one percent of the stories that are told in the galaxy about the activities of the land-dwellers on Earth are true... Don't you find it bizarre that the land-dwellers think that they and the Earth are the crown of creation, while they alone are by far the most underdeveloped planet in this solar system?

It will be hard for you and your team, TRUSIAN, very hard.

SANAT KUMARA certainly thought carefully about why he wanted us.

In a land-dweller's body you lose most of your present consciousness. You will think that your body, your knowledge, your money and your power over people, resources and countries are the benchmark. How do you want to do your usual leadership work? Do you know how many people before you have failed in thousands of years?

We are experienced in training beings to blend into the unity of all life. The Kingdom of Servers sends us its people from all over the cosmos to train them.

I truly do not envy you and your task and wish you success with all my heart. We all urgently need it.

Will you tell me who you are, GUNAH?

I will also be on your team if the going gets rough.

Then he focuses his thoughts again on the Lord of the World. Who is he really? Does he want me to reconsider, or is he already so marked by his earthly experiences that he hardly knows hope?

A few earth-souls begin a mental chat, audible to all present. Obviously they want to be noticed. Strange. NÃO, my Deva-Chaperone, who is standing right next to me, says that they are former poets and thinkers from different eras and cultures of the People on Earth. They all made a remarkable impact on *The Chronicles of SANAT KUMARA*. I feel in my energy field their frustration at how few people have actually understood their messages and live by them. It is certainly useful to listen to their wealth of experience until SANAT KUMARA officially opens the Assembly.

One says: *In hell, purgatory, paradise: three times I referred to the stars, each time with the last word I praised their power over man and earth. Not even the scholars have understood this hint. My pictorial description of hell, the spectacular, the punishments and screams. Why the devil are they fascinated only by the pain-distorted face? But here today in Shambala, I am delighted by a joyful fresh light.*

He probably means me. I have to smile.

Another one says: *Yes, yes, my friend. A few centuries later I was no better. Man is mistaken as long as he strives to recognise what our world in the cosmos interweaves with divine law and holds together at its core.*

Another one switches on: *In the Song of the Spirit, my warrior Arjuna dared to fight long before you. In the midst of the battlefield, he united with the power of his soul and confronted his own flesh and blood.*

These men do not seem to know real dialogue. The stories that people in the galaxy tell each other about self-absorbed land-dwellers seem to have a basis in reality ...

The next one says: *I left the Chinese in 81 verses the path of the middle, how action and non-action unite. In meaning and life there is harmony and peace. Everyone should know how to achieve them and how they manifest themselves as leaders: great light knows no adornment, great life does not shine, a great jewel has a rough shell.*

If this description is accurate our team is made for this mission.

Yes, yes, colleague, yesterday I was smart too: I wanted to change the world. Today I am wise: I want to change myself.

The land-dwellers amongst the humans are the core of our problem. They create famine even out of rich abundance.

One of the gentlemen fixes me with his gaze and says: *Look, look, look ... she is clothed in the radiant white robe of cosmic consciousness, sealed with the rainbow ray of the seven chakras that merge with the white light.*

GUAN YIN is rolling her eyes. I have to smile. She looks at me, almost as if she wants to apologise for proposing our team for this mission. Her purple light robe shines and in this way signals SANAT KUMARA to speak out, to make his mark and to take the lead. He follows the hint of his chief diplomat and majestically raises the staff of his power. The staff is, so my expert eye informs me, made of Orichalcum, with two skilfully shaped conical diamonds at the shining ends. SANAT KUMARA illuminates its flaming figure of light, and I am, as in our first encounter, overwhelmed by the light, the peace and the love it radiates. A young man with shoulder-length, full, blonde hair and bright blue eyes, he is wrapped in a flowing, soft-pink-shimmering robe with subtle embroidery. In this floor-length robe, he looks like an Asian prince but for his blonde hair and blue eyes. All those present are now looking at him. All ears hear the spherical sounds of his energies. Even the former poets and thinkers fall silent. Almost everyone present yearns to reach his level of development.

BUDDHA, KRISHNA, ABRAHAM, MOSES, YESHUA, MOHAMMED *and a few more demonstrated the laws of the divine cosmic order to the people by their deeds. But their opponents twisted, their followers diluted and betrayed what they taught. To this day the land dwellers refuse to recognise these men for what they are and were: teachers of the path of the soul, which everyone must follow within themselves. Our great women, MOTHER MARY, GUAN YIN, OMSTARA and LADY NADA, to name but a few ... all their female abilities have been mocked, ignored, pushed aside, deliberately misinterpreted, belittled and slowed down. The Earth has to regain its balance to take its true place in the cosmic structure. What is happening on Earth is dreadful.*

I hear a murmur of agreement in the minds.

I have invited you today to the Great Hall to give the official starting signal for the 'Let there be light' mission. Welcome, TRUSLAN!

Applause fills the hall.

We are so far behind the plan for human family and Earth that we had to ask our galactic friends for help. The frequency jump forward has begun. And as the frequency of the Earth expands, a consciousness expansion of all its beings becomes possible. But the majority of land-dwellers resist this necessary change and the adjustments of their way of life.

Broad approval streams through the heads of the assembled. I think they all know exactly what the Lord of the World is talking about. I do not know it in detail yet.

The condition of the human family, the representative from Mars in the Stellar Council recently told me, is like a lump of metal against the feather of Ma'at. What is happening on Earth is cold-hearted and greedy; it is unworthy of the souls who before their incarnation promised to fill their bodies with godlike life forces. They are right, my stellar colleagues. And that only makes my position there even more difficult. Inexpertly and thoughtlessly, the land-dwellers have frustrated the plans of the entire solar system. If we had not always watched over them here in Shambala with great effort, Earth would already be a destroyed planet and the human family would be on its way in the galaxy as a stream of refugees.

The assenting thoughts of the assembled beings become louder.

It is high time, with the help of our galactic friends, to raise the human family to the level of the updated divine plan and to make the frequency jump possible through various measures. The multidimensional nature and vitality of the Earth is fundamental to the fulfilment of our mission in the Galaxy. And the human family has finally to fit into this divine order!

SANAT KUMARA illuminates his light-robe once again and sends a mental sign to NÃO and me. We immediately vibrate higher, also illuminating our light-robe for this unique moment.

Esteemed Assembly, TRUSIAN has been at the forefront of the training of members of the Kingdom of Servers for 104,000 years and is valued and known far beyond our galaxy. She has truly not pressed for this Earth mission. Power and fame do not interest her. This is one of the reasons why she and all in her team were the first choice for LORD BUDDHA, LORD MAITREYA, WISEONE and me.

A wave of applause and flashes of light fill the whole hall.

TRUSIAN will now move into the white pyramid for material and physical training. A team of several human families under the leadership of YESHUA, SAINT GERMAIN and Devas under the leadership of WISEONE will give her and the whole team guidance and protection during the mission. They all face a dominant group of fierce and treacherous defenders of the old ways, the power of people who create darkness with their free will. TRUSIAN will begin her mission in the Democratic Republic of Congo. The country was handed over to darkness by the Belgian King Leopold II more than 200 years ago with a white-skinned male delusion of superiority.

So far, our team only suspects what we have gotten ourselves into. SANAT KUMARA has avoided mentioning details.

Two experienced human souls, SOLAS and THEODAR, have taken it upon themselves to anchor TRUSIAN in the earthly business world and make it her home. THEODAR will also support her as a father and advisor. The line of TRUSIAN's female ancestors is provided by our Off Earth Allies.

HONGYETSEE, in the white light robe with blue sash of the Kingdom of Servers, has a question for SANAT KUMARA. If I interpret his thoughts correctly, he doubts whether this can work.

Lord of the World, with all due respect, if the land-dwellers with their free will once again trample on the divine will and cosmic laws as they have done up to now, don't we have to provide far more souls for this mission? Have we really done everything so that Lucia can say 'I am ready'?

LORD BUDDHA, the right hand of SANAT KUMARA for all operational issues, illuminates his light. *We have gathered a team of twelve around TRUSIAN. The cosmic significance of the number in the Deva Kingdom should be familiar to all. This includes NÃO, who will lead TRUSIAN as Chaperone in the Deva Kingdom. The wounds of mistrust due to the atrocities of the land-dwellers must be healed so that the human family can be united and the Earth with all its kingdoms can return to the divine plan.*

WISEONE and numerous Devas at his side applaud. NÃO next to me is happy about this; her energy field raises its frequency higher than before, oscillating into mine. WISEONE, head of the Deva Kingdom on Earth, had a long introductory talk with us. Also present were the Devas responsible for the oceans and those of Africa and Europe. Shy and reserved beings, these earthly Devas. Land-dwellers must have inflicted unimaginable suffering on them. In our home, the Devas are kind and open-minded team players. We work together at eye level and with much respect for each other.

On the front line, however, SANAT KUMARA continues, tearing me away from my thoughts, *the spiritual teachers of all times and religions will soon return to Earth, this time walking side by side with our Off Earth Allies. No one will be able to separate them for his own purposes and dogmas and twist their teachings again. They are already leading the network of all light and energy workers worldwide. And, of course, in battles we can always intuitively give the right ideas to those who are working to fulfil the divine plan.*

HONGYETSEE does not yet seem convinced to me. His thoughts are circling, his head is bowed. SANAT KUMARA thinks the question has been sufficiently answered and wants to continue. But HONYETSEE takes it up.

With respect, SANAT KUMARA, are your Chronicles not full of records of failures? You came to Earth 18.76 million years ago, and everyone knew that it would be a long dark night of the soul for you. Humans have turned away from their Creator of their own free will and filled their world with unconscious dark creatures.

The facts are what they are, HONGYETSEE. Yes, human beings have set in motion millions of catastrophic causal factors throughout the Earth.

The Great Being ZONCRIET is now visibly weakened by this, but will now let people bear the effects of its actions. Storms, floods, unknown weather phenomena - Poseidon will rage. Earthquakes, volcanic eruptions, conflagrations - the dragons will spit out fire. Viruses, plagues and pandemics will raise the land-dwellers to unity. They will plead with Goethe's words: 'Lord, the need is great! The spirits I summoned up I now cannot rid myself of.' But Goethe cannot help them there either ...

Laughter in the hall for the first time.

The veil of earthly-material amnesia will now continue to lift with each passing year. The self-appointed earthly elites cannot stop this with money, power and technology. In their minds, some are already on their way in a spaceship to new habitats on Mars. But those who live today as on the Aniara, rudderlessly enjoying themselves, lying, cheating and suppressing the truth, will not be granted insight and access on Mars. You know that the Martians are headstrong about all development-aid issues.

A smile wafts through the Great Hall. They probably know what SANAT KUMARA is talking about in his thoughts when he says *Aniara*. I don't know, but we in the team are familiar with the secrets of the White Trees, the Devas and Elementals, the Conrees, Dragons, Elves, Angels and ...

Divide and conquer leads everyone, including the elites themselves, to apocalyptic doom. Either all return together to the path of light, or all stumble. TRUSLAN and her team know exactly which task they have to fulfil until the end of the 21st century.

Another murmur goes through the hall. Their hope for our team is justified. The movements and laws of the cosmos have been familiar to us for eons.

The seventh ray, now increasing daily, will help unite matter and spirit. For open-minded land-dwellers this is the necessary soul-lift; for the anxiously matter-attached it is pure poison.

I am ready, just as my team has been for some time. While I am thinking that thought, I receive a lightning insight into life on Earth. Just at this moment, a young man is being shouted at by his father and chastised with the slap of his flat hand in the face. He admonishes the son that he is first and foremost a German and an engineer. This is the only reason why he stands high above the others and can secure his future. The scene is earthly reality, it is true, and it also concerns our team ... somehow.

LIER, 12 DECEMBER 2019

My life is scratching and biting ... this is really not how I imagined the evening before my 20th birthday to be. Robin has been ordered to Singapore by his father from one moment to the next. No romantic evening for two in his student flat in Aachen. Instead of celebrating with my other friends Dimitri and Tasha, I dutifully went home to my family. Now I'm sitting with my parents, Dad's twin brother Luc, Mum's work colleague Raymond and my godmother Tilly at a round table in a fully booked, bourgeois Belgian restaurant on the Grote Markt in Lier. The air is stuffy in here and the chatter is loud. Why is it that I never get things going the way they should?

I poke around in my salad without appetite, spoon the last drop of tomato soup, drink from my water and finally pick a cold French fry with a pinch of mayo from my plate. My thoughts are with Robin. His father has never done anything like this before, he assured me. While I think about our future together, the others discuss cheese croquettes, foie gras and grilled beef tenderloin, Belgian EU policy, upcoming ski holidays in Ischgl and a cultural trip to Rajasthan. Except for Tilly and me, everyone is already heavily intoxicated by Trappist beer and red wine from large goblets. Tonight I am just the excuse they need to stuff themselves and get pissed. If I hadn't come, they would have found another excuse.

'As if to confirm this, my uncle, the priest Luc - thin as a stick, narrow face, yellow teeth and circular hair loss - teases from diagonally over the round table: 'She is of a different kind, our Lucia.' At the same time he looks at me with narrowed eyes in a challenging way.

'Which I'm sure everyone who knows a little more about tha, Uncle Luc, will say as well,' I return as if fired from a gun.

'Excuse me? Your Uncle Luc of a different kind? How can you say such a thing?' hisses Mum, sitting right opposite me, and looks at me punitively. Then she turns around, wants to make sure that no one has heard. It's a good thing her bob haircut, fixed with hairspray, and her strict glasses are a perfect match for all this. Mum's German-Belgian family honour is lucky this time. At the neighbouring tables, too, the chattering noise of the varicose vein squadron surges in line with the alcohol level. 'If it were up to you, Lucia, we'd have to eat our meat standing outside on the street with the smokers.' At the same time she looks at me scornfully, saying I am the eternal disturber of peace.

'She certainly doesn't mean it,' Daddy interjects on my left, his nose crimson from red wine. What else can he say? He only has a say on his bench in the Justice Palace in Antwerp when he judges petty drug dealers. Here at the table, with his frayed purple and white striped Beerschot fan scarf around his neck, he gives a pathetic picture of man, just like his identical brother. If he wouldn't wear horn-rimmed glasses and Luc contact lenses, tha couldn't tell them apart in their plaid shirts with a dark blue jumper.

'Why are you so prickly today, my dear child?' Dad looks at me lovingly and puts his arm around my shoulders.

I didn't start it, and I'm not his dear child either. I have milk chocolate brown skin and black Afro curls. Mum always tried hard with chemicals to smooth them down so that I looked halfway like a Western European. Tha want to hide the fact that I was born in the Congo, in the town of Kolwezi. Everything around it is mysterious and dark. All my questions never got an answer. The only answer Mum allows is my Belgian passport. Everyone at the table has one, that's fine. But Mum and Luc pretend to be better people. Tha think I don't know about your mistakes. Tha think I don't know what the blasphemers in our neighbourhood are constantly chewing on.

'How's school, Lucia?' Raymond comes to my rescue.

'Fine,' I reply with a friendly smile.

'Too bad you don't go to my school anymore. A headmaster likes to show off his best student.'

Somehow I like this good-looking mid-fifties guy who always looks like a fashion conscious intellectual in his tweed jackets with pocket squares and corduroy trousers in bright colours. 'On Monday I'm going to see my professor at the university to discuss the topic for my Bachelor's thesis. I've already prepared a paper to convince him of my idea. I would like to write about the Anthropocene, the age of the Earth Destroyers, because that's what we humans are. I think he lets me do what I enjoy doing. I do not need to go abroad for that. But he has hinted that he could get another projec for me in a company in Switzerland, and there would be good money for that too.'

'Thou shalt not swallow the endings of words. It's *project:* t, t!' Mama sparks in between again. Then she winks at Raymond on the right next to her. 'With your intelligence, you'd think you're doing this just to annoy me. Such educational blunders are unforgivable.'

'You like your professor, don't you?'

'Yeah, Raymond, a really cool guy, professionally mega and not as dusty as his colleagues. I think he likes me too, I mean the way I get involved. He said to me in the corridor after the lecture the other day: "Tha are the most brilliant person I have ever seen in this programme."'

'Thou shalt not use slang words like "tha". It's "you", not "tha". With your intelligence, you should not use that Yorkshire slang anymore. The time when you went to school in York is long past. Don't embarrass your mother in such a way. I am a respectable language teacher.'

'Your Professor is just like me.' Raymond raises his glass

and says, 'To our Lucia.' Everyone toasts to me. Even Mom feels obliged to join in when Raymond raises his glass.

'And after the Bachelor degree, what are you going to do?' he wants to know. But it won't come to that.

'Bachelor in What-Was-That-Again?' Uncle Luc splutters in between, gesticulating in inebriation.

'Geo-Resource-Management,' I say slowly so he can hear. Understanding is rather unlikely, remembering even less, and he isn't actually stupid. When he became a priest he once told Dad that he was only doing this because he didn't want to strain himself and work.

'And what do you do with it?' Luc doesn't let up, but at the same time puts his beer glass back to his mouth and drinks, as if he doesn't really care about the answer.

But he'll get it anyway. 'Carefully evaluate and control the use and intervention in the Earth's resources. Energy relevant raw materials, geothermal energy, water resources, metals, minerals ... protec human habitats and natural balances on land and in water ... Replace ignorance with knowledge and hopefully, in time, greed with brains. Yeah, I think that's a good summary.'

'Uh-huh, and where do you work with it, then?'

'On the computer, in the laboratory, in mines, in the wild, in the deep sea, in the Arctic, in disaster areas.'

'Brrr ... that doesn't sound cosy. What about a boyfriend? Still none?', he turns to his favourite subject with a broad grin, puts down the beer glass and stares at me. 'Come on, don't tell me you haven't got one. The boys must be keen on you, beautiful as you are.'

Not like that, Luc. Not that again. In the past I used to argue with the subject, now I'm not in the mood for it any more. I just shrug my shoulders. Yeah, the boys are after me, but most of them only see what Luc sees - a beautiful young woman. But what clever woman wants a boyfriend like that? Tha and your limited world view are simply embarrassing.

'Watch out,' Luc adds, 'that you don't end up a spinster.'

I cut a grimace and he gives himself over to the Trappist beer again.

'She never tells me anything either,' complains Mum loudly, nudges Raymond with her elbow and gives him another wink. She stood in front of the mirror for ages this evening, styling her bob endlessly with a hairdryer, adding make-up over and over again. She wanted to know from me whether she should wear her nickel glasses or the black designer plastic model with the new woolen skirt with twinset, which were necessary because she gained weight again. Before we left, she also sprayed herself from top to bottom with this horribly sweet perfume.

'Now leave Lucia alone at last. Before you know it, lightning will strike your tower', Tilly says to the right of me for the first and probably only time this evening. Tilly is an ivory, petite person with a grey bubble head and brightly coloured, cheeky glasses. Today they are circular and squeaky yellow. Her outfit is like Tilly, she doesn't fit in the picture, just like me.

'The Astronomical Clock Tower and all the other towers in Lier are public buildings and therefore have a lightning conductor. So don't talk bollocks, Tilly.'

'Just wait for ... the truth to come.'

'From the way you look and eat, a yellow famine is approaching.'

When I was little, Tilly used to argue with Mum endlessly. At some point she could not be bothered any longer. 'You can hardly explain the colour spectrum to a black and white viewer,' she once said to me. Now she only comes from Brussels to Lier when I'm there. She hardly speaks, except when giving one of her oracular sayings, as Mum calls them. Tilly is amused that the others smile condescendingly at her and that their comments are limited to superficialities. Apart from her and me, nobody at the table knows that the tower stands for 16/7 and what that means. Mum only calls her 'Silly Tilly'. She used to call Tilly 'Spectacled Cobra'. But Tilly is the most intelligent of all, chief mathematician of a large insurance company. Tilly has such wonderfully soft features and blue eyes that sparkle like stars behind her sun-yellow round glasses. I can discuss all mathematical questions with her. She knows everything about numbers, including what tha don't get taught at school and university. Simply ingenious. She also provides me with everything that Mum doesn't allow, and that gives her and me mischievous pleasure.

'Thank God Lucia at least brings home excellent marks,' Mum lectures in her head-teacherly tone. While she continues to puff herself up and make beautiful eyes at Raymond, Tilly discreetly hands me an envelope under the table. I put it in my small shoulder bag, invisible to the others, and wink at Tilly to thank her.

'With a little more good conduct, the world would be open to my Lucia. Oh, what am I saying? A villa, not here in Lier, no, in Tervuren or in Brasschaat, would then be no problem. But what does she do? Teases wherever she can, as if we were all blind or deaf. You've just experienced it yourself.'

Right, for once tha've got it right. Blind and deaf, and that's why it takes fact lovers like me. Why did Spirit punish me with these totally crazy middle-class parents?

A 'ping' sounds it in my shoulder bag. I carefully pull out the smartphone and hold it below the edge of the table. 10:46 pm, another message from Robin. Later in the morning he will find out why his father has summoned him to Singapore. I am restless; he probably is too. I think about him every minute and he probably thinks about me too.

'Who wants dessert?' Dad asks aloud and brings my thoughts back to the table. To signal that he wants dessert, he raises his hand like a five-year-old. Everyone else wants one; only I shake my head. The waiter is summoned wordily; crêpe Suzette, five times.

I just want to get out of here and be alone at midnight, in my bed, all alone with myself, if I can't be with Robin. The waiter comes and clears the plates of the main course. I get up and walk towards the toilets in the dark back of the restaurant. I can't stand it right now. I grew up here. I was baptised Roman Catholic. I joined the Scouts. Everything as it should be. But I am not a Pallieter-Land child. I am not one of them and I will never become one. I am not... but, who am I? I will be twenty in a little more than an hours, and I still don't know ... who I am and where I belong. Nobody has asked me: 'Where would you like to go for dinner on your 20th birthday on 13 December?' No, because nobody wants to hear the answer: 'To one of the cool vegan restaurants in Antwerp'. My neck is tied up in anger, a tear is running from the corner of my eye and there is nobody there in the dark to give me a hug. I have to get out of here and into my room under the roof. I wait by the toilets, invisible in the dark, for an opportune moment of distraction in order to scurry past them. Until then I stand in front of a big mirror and tug at my olive green wool dress. I feel as comfortable in it as in a cocoon. Thanks to Spirit the opportunity comes sooner than I had hoped. At the table next to ours they are already flambéing Crêpe Suzette, probably a Christmas party among colleagues. It smells of orange liqueur; the sparks fly, it hisses, and all eyes turn to it. Now is the chance to get out. I inconspicuously grab my brown flight jacket, give Tilly a loving kiss on her hair, say in my thoughts 'Tha're wonderful,' and in a flash I'm past them and out on the cobblestones of the Grote Markt in the cold night.

Walking home through frost and fog, still better than being constantly babbled to. My steps echo amid the silence of the square. At the height of the historic sandstone town hall with its little tower, I turn right and pass the Astronomical Clock Tower, which, at the hour before midnight, wishes me a good walk with its melodic starry play. At least something to love. In the Itterbek the water whispers good night to me until it flows into the river Nete which I follow downstream leaving the city southwards on the dike. The wide meadows sway in the wind, my heart rises, my courage to face life comes back. I still put my cap over my curls and deep into my face. How many hours have I spent alone here looking at and listening to wild geese, herons and swallows? How often did I wish I could fly with them? Have I looked into the air and seen a stallion in the clouds coming towards me at full gallop? How many times have I roamed the meadows with cows and horses, stroking and comforting them? And now the government wants to cut down trees, demolish the farm and turn the meadows around the Nete into a flood plain. The storms are piling up, the water is looking for its place and has none. Too bad, tha morons. But first of all, it's at the expense of animals and nature, which are already shaken enough. Why don't tha tear up a few paved roads so that the water can seep away? I continue to run across the dike towards southwards and hum along my way.

Mum and Dad never understood me, my love for the earth, for the stones, for the animals; my longing to be connected to everything that lives. Mum regularly calls me a will-o'-the-wisp. She only calls me Lucia when she is about to rebuke or punish me. She wants me to have a career. Wants me to be classified as a child of educated people. She wants me to move up the social ladder. She wants me to earn more money than a teacher and a judge. I should be better off than them in the future. But what does that mean? She doesn't really care about me. It's about herself, her reputation, her status, her truth ... So far only one person has understood me completely, Grandmother Mepi ... She *read* me from top to bottom when we first met here on the dike.

I'll be home soon. Before I leave the dike and go down into our neighbourhood, I pull the bottle out of my shoulder bag and pour the remaining daisy water onto a young, ailing tree. I also give it a Reiki treatment. Then I say good night to the ravens, doves, foxes, rabbits, mice, cows and horses and turn right into the Waterschransweg. My path goes past the villas behind high hedges and finally to the right into the settlement full of terraced and semi-detached houses. Our small house lies there quiet and dark. Five steps from the pavement to the front door on stone slabs, framed by carefully manicured box trees. I unlock the door, take off my calf-high, brown lace-up boots and knock the rubber soles against each other in front of the door to make sure no dirt gets into the house. The rough stone tiles under my feet in the tiny hall are freezing cold. I hang my jacket neatly on the hanger in the coat rack and go up the spiral staircase in need of repair to my room. The stairs creak with every step, but Dad has two left hands and craftsmen are too expensive for Mum. Why is it that the truth of my adoptive family is blowing in my face tonight?

In my room under the roof, I turn on the big salt stone lamp; immediately its cosy glow spreads. The sky is starry, the moon is laughing. My eyes wander across the sky. Tears roll, and my heart aches. I light an incense stick with the scent of lavender and pull my smartphone out of my shoulder bag. Nothing new from Robin. After washing my face and brushing my teeth, I toss and turn in bed, stare at the time display, count the seconds until midnight. I wait for something to happen, but nothing happens. Only something has changed since the night I turned sixteen. That's when I heard that kind, loving voice in my head, telling me calmly that everything was okay and that my new life would soon begin. Well, since my studies in Aachen started I have been surrounded by fewer little minds. I do what I find interesting, have a small circle of friends from all over the world: my Robin from Singapore; the bearded strong and tall Dimitri, the Russian Sami from the Barents Sea; and Tasha, the beautiful South American with Mayan ancestors from Lake Titicaca. The three of them see what I see, perceive what I perceive - mostly anyway, sometimes quite differently. We are all studying Geo-Resource-Management in Aachen for the same reason. We love the earth, the stones, the oceans, the animals; and we want to preserve them, protect them from the crazy people for all people.

But is this supposed to have been the breakthrough that the voice spoke of? Grandmother Mepi says *no*. I should be patient; what is be *mine* will come to me. If Spirit would listen to me now, then he would give me patience ... but immediately.

When I am woken up by a 'ping' after a restless sleep, my pillow is wet with tears. Below, the loud voices of Mum and Dad quarrel... quarrelling over me again, I guess. I look at my smartphone, finally, a text message from Robin. I feel a warm shiver running through me. I remember when we first met at the university in Aachen. Our eyes intertwined and I felt it in my whole body.

Happy Birthday, my Darling! We are so far apart, the longing breaks my heart. Forever yours, Robin

HUMANITY LOG

Chronicle time 18.762.019 - 12.13
Project: *Let there be light*
Avidya Moha (aspect of SOLAS) and Dr. Thomas Müller (aspect of THEODAR)
Located 47° 27' 29.578' N   8° 33' 19.714' E

As Avidya Moha steps through the passenger lock with the stream of arrivals into the crowded arrivals hall of Zurich Airport, his gaze looks for Thomas - in vain. They are all taller than him and block his view. He walks a few steps into the hall, and a woman with two small children makes him stumble. But Thomas is already on the spot, and at the last moment his strong grip saves him from a fall. 'You're OK, Pops?'

The woman goes on with her children without caring.

'Disgusting, all these people. Let's get out of here,' says Avidya in his usual Indian-English singsong.

The handsome Thomas in suit and tie with elegantly coiffed dark blond hair and rimless glasses over his blue-green eyes first embraces the shivering, tireless seventy-five-year-old.

'Welcome to Switzerland, Pops!'

'Everyone was coughing and spluttering. Even in Business Class; full to the last seat, disgusting.'

'How nice to see you before Christmas. David will be happy that you attend his eighteenth birthday. What a wonderful surprise.'

'I am cold. Let's go ...'

'Yes, icy, that slush. But the fire is already crackling in the fireplace and the housekeeper has made the guest room cosy for you. It smells of cedar, just like you love it. I am surprised ... delighted ... How long are you staying, Pops?'

'Two nights, till Sunday morning, to be exact, then you and I will have talked it all over.'

Thomas looks at him questioningly. He knows that Avidya detests the cold because of his Indian descent and hates travelling in the cold even more. He shields the little old man in a suit, winter coat and thinning grey hair with his full height and wide outstretched arms against the crowds. But a group of Chinese businessmen obstructs their direct route to the waiting limousine, and Thomas is forced to choose another exit. When Thomas' chauffeur sees them coming, he jumps out dutifully of the car, takes Avidya's briefcase, sneezes and apologises. Thomas opens Avidya's car door behind the chauffeur, says 'Take us home' to the driver, walks around the car, gets in and lets the soundproof glass pane rise between passengers and driver. The leather in the well-heated limousine still smells fresh and reminds Avidya that Thomas only recently received this brand new black S-Class Mercedes with cognac-coloured interior and safety equipment. He was desperate to have this special model, and so Avidya gave in after more than a year of insistence. Avidya waits a moment until the car was immersed in the morning traffic before getting down to business.

'What about the sale of the Kolwezi cobalt mine?'

'By 31 March 2020, everything should be nailed down and the ink dry. We are selling to the European giant of the raw materials trading industry, group headquarters three streets away from us in Zug ... you know who ...'

Avidya nods.

'They buy the company, a transaction on paper here in Switzerland. The local management remains. No one will notice anything, and the local management is sworn to silence. We only have a small annoyance with the Congolese tax assessment for this year. Apart from that, we are in agreement on the purchase price, value according to the usual formula plus ten percent.'

'What about the tax assessment?'

'Corresponds to the legal percentage, as always. Our new local manager just hasn't figured out how to deal with the minister responsible for issuing a new notice with a tax rate of only three per cent.'

'What kind of idiot pays statutory taxes in the Congo?'

'At least no foreign company that I know of.'

'Then fly down first thing next week to sort it out, Thomas.' Avidya looks Thomas straight in the eye to see what he thinks. Thomas remains silent.

Their car comes to a sudden stop. The chauffeur had to brake hard because a black limousine with diplomatic license plate switched lanes without flashers. The driver raises his hand in a threatening gesture as he overtakes the other car on the left by stepping on the accelerator. The diplomatic limousine is driven by a Chinese driver.

'Those Chinese again. Acting like they already own the world.' Thomas' voice suddenly sounds irritable.

'Let it go, my boy.' Avidya shakes himself and resumes his conversation. 'How did you arrange the deal?'

'Their CEO's villa is located less than three hundred yards from mine on the slopes of Rüschlikon. We meet occasionally for a coffee with cognac and cigar. When the weather is bad, it's quite pleasant in front of the crackling open fire with a view of Lake Zurich. When the sun shines we drink a bottle of wine on the terrace.'

'I see - a cultivated exchange between gentlemen.'

'I'll be relieved when we get rid of this mine and make a profit as well ... and all that in discreet silence.'

'Never mind, my boy, criticism of how cobalt is mined ends up in the media from time to time. They swear arrogantly, shake their heads scornfully, wriggle loudly, but then it's quiet again.'

'It's a good thing that the mining and supply chain of cobalt is opaque from start to finish.'

'Western consumers don't give a damn about any chocolate-brown cobalt filth, about how the metal gets into the high-performance batteries of their smartphones, computers, electric cars and whatever other electrical goods. Do you think that even one single smartphone user would still mock the business practices in the Congo if his favourite toy no longer fitted in his pocket? And the Chinese are even less interested.'

Thomas presses his lips together and shakes his head. Avidya concludes that they are in agreement.

'The world needs what the Congo has, my boy,' he tries to reassure Thomas once again. 'Shiva be praised; the Chinese do the cobalt business mainly with the poor wretches who dig for it on their own with pick and shovel, have accidents or otherwise inhale death itself. It is more inhumane than our industrial mining.' Avidya often sees pictures of these hapless victims before his eyes at night. They rob him of his sleep, but he has become tough enough not to be distracted from his goals. 'It is not our job to bring order into this. It's up to the powerful in the Democratic Republic of Congo to sort it out.'

Thomas shakes his head. 'Yes, Pops, you're right, but ... you know they won't. Of the twenty families that rule the country, a third are in power to meet their own needs, a third are in prison, and a third have fled into exile to protect themselves and their assets. Only a few upright intellectuals are fighting a hopeless battle.'

'Leave it alone, we pay the workers according to local conditions, we can't and don't have to do more.'

'The company has ...'

'Let it go. Everyone must first look after themselves. Don't forget how many charitable foundations we support in England, Lebanon, India and also in Switzerland.'

'Yeah, but ... '

'Let it go. It isn't because of the mine in the Congo that I made the journey from London to Zurich ... nor for David's birthday.'

Thomas looks into his face and raises his eyebrows. 'I had already wondered what was so important. We talk on the phone almost every day ... '

'It's something serious, and it's taken me too long to be open to hearing it at l.'

'Is something wrong with your health? You look tired and - excuse me for saying so - haggard.' Thomas' forehead wrinkles into high waves and deep valleys. His neck muscles tense up as he waits for Avidya to respond.

'It's curtains for me. The doctors give me a maximum of three more months.'

'What are you saying?'

'Don't look so horrified, it makes it twice as hard for me to leave. Pancreatic cancer ... advanced. Pritha comes to the same conclusion. I don't want to die, but Shiva leaves me no choice.'

A shiver of horror overflows Thomas from head to stomach, which suddenly cramps up. Tears come to his eyes.

Avidya is touched and thinks: *Why is he not my son?*

'I ... I,' Thomas stammers, 'I can't tell you how much it hurts me ... Pops ... I don't want this to happen. Is there no possibility of a cure?' He pulls a bright white, starched handkerchief out of his pocket, puts the glasses in his hair and dries his eyes from tears and pain.

'Thanks, my boy, I appreciate it.' Avidya puts his right hand on his forearm and exhales deeply. 'The show must go on without me. I need to transfer my powers before a disaster happens and the Vijay Group falls apart. I have spoken with my Amal. Her two sons from her first marriage cannot run the Group. The network of companies, their tax structures across countries and continents, longer-term strategic thinking; that is not their cup of tea. Ibrahim is an extremely capable and shrewd metal trader, always finds the right balance between long and short selling, but he is far too hot-headed to make big decisions that have to last. And Ismael has always been the financier, calculating prudently and avoiding strategic risks. He lacks a feeling for future developments and interpersonal sensitivity. But it's not possible without those qualities. Amal has to understand that. Her sons are not up to it, and neither are our two daughters.'

Thomas twitches noticeably, continues to dry his tears. Avidya also starts to cry. He does not want to die! Especially not now, now that he has made it. Now that he has power. Now that he is a rich man, has his box at the Grand Slam finals in Wimbledon, eats strawberries with whipped cream and drinks champagne with the native Brits during the breaks. Now that they not only have to pay attention to him, but also respect him. What has he not sacrificed for this? Avidya Moha, the bastard from Mumbai. They had never taken him seriously, and now even stuck-up English aristocrats with their Oxford English have to bow before his Indian-English singsong.

'But Amal's sons will want the power, Pops. They ... ' He pauses and puts his handkerchief back in his pocket.

Avidya also dries a tear with a paper handkerchief. 'Yes, my boy, they certainly will. But Amal will tell them that this is the best way, even though she would love to see one of her sons in the big boss's chair. Don't get her wrong, she is a caring mother, and if her first husband hadn't died ...'

'Yes, it's tragic ...'

Avidya wants to chase away the thought in his head, but it arises nonetheless - and maybe Thomas suspects it too. He clears his throat. 'You, my boy, will do it. You alone are capable of running Vijay Group, and hopefully later on your son David.'

Thomas presses his lips together and grasps his throat with one hand. After a moment of reflection, he replies quietly: 'They can throw me out at any time. Do you know that?'

'You can rely on my promise. I will transfer shares to you in my will. Amal, her two sons, our daughters Pritha and Maya would then have to join forces to remove you from the executive chair. You know that the Arabs and Hindus in our family are not on good terms. That gives you extra protection.' Avidya breathes with audible difficulty, his facial skin becomes blotchy red. Of course this means a precarious perch on the volcano for the rest of Thomas' life. They will all want to have their say and always have objections. They will constantly pretend that they can hold a candle to him.

'They won't want me in charge, Pops. You know it.'

'Bollocks. They all lack the imagination for the really big things. That's why you and I have to tie up everything before I go. That's why I'm here.'

'Why did you tell me alone and not with Maya and David present?'

'Maya can't keep anything to herself, and David is too young.'

'He comes of age today, looks like me when I was young. His whiskers are sprouting. He's already had two girlfriends, both from good families, I pay attention to that. Since he recently started to study information technology, he has really blossomed. I am very proud of him, you know? He found his thing early, and on his own ... not like me ...'

Avidya curls his lips. He loves his only grandson, but he never knows how old he is, when his birthday is and what he does. 'David is a capable boy, takes after his father, Shiva be praised.'

Thomas blushes, embarrassed by this surge of fatherly enthusiasm occasioned by incipient demise. Then he gets a grip on himself. 'And what does Pritha say? As your doctor, she is sworn to secrecy.'

'Pritha is wise. She limits herself to her role as a doctor. She, Amal, and you, and that's where we leave things. Everyone else will hear it together when you and I present the new direction and the new rules to the family.'

'And Amal is really on board? I mean ... '

'She is insightful about the true abilities of her sons.'

'Isn't there any other solution, Pops?' He looks at Avidya with his eyes narrowed, almost as if something was hurting him.

'Sell ... is it that what you mean? No way! Don't you have the guts?'

Thomas stretches. 'Haven't I proved I can do it?'

'Yes, you have, you have. You're tough when you have to be tough, a skilled tactician, farsighted, smart, and popular throughout the industry. And you have what I don't have: handsome looks, a striking, melodious male voice, white skin, light brown hair, a German surname with a doctorate in engineering; and yet, for the entire world, you are the charming Canadian.'

'But so far you've kept peace and order in the patchwork family, Pops. You always put your foot down when Ibrahim and Ismael rebel. I do not have such authority. Amal's sons will make my job a living hell.'

Avidya remains silent and blows his nose into his wet paper handkerchief.

LIER, 13 DECEMBER 2019

When I wake up I have birthday wishes from Dimitri and Tasha with smiley face, kisses, cake and flowers on my smartphone. A new moment of happiness. I hum to myself, write back quickly and look forward insanely to celebrating with them in my dormitory in Aachen. I also open the letter from Tilly. A card, in front a picture of the winter starry sky. She has written on the back: *Your imprisonment in the tower of the blinded is over. Now you will see the stars. You are an 8, still a 3 in a², but already on the way to the 9. Draw your strength from it. Always there for you, your Tilly.* She has also put two hundred Euros into the envelope. How sweet of her. I'll quickly send her a thank-you SMS with kisses. When I get back to university, I'll thank her with a parcel from the finest Aachener Printen, the world famous biscuits she loves so much.

As I come down the creaking stairs into the hallway, it smells of roasted pork. Mum knows that the smell makes me sick. Another subtle punishment. She clatters with dishes in her kitchen, which means that there's a rant coming. But first the doorbell rings. Mum calls out in a croaky voice in her commanding tone of the head teacher: 'Open up ... Dad has forgotten his key again.' I grab the door handle to open, unsure how he will greet me. Will he congratulate me lovingly or be angry from last night because I ran away, or is he still angry from the fight with Mum?

But there is no Dad at the door. In front of me stands a

middle-aged woman ... she looks almost like me, Afro curly hair, head and body shape like mine, but dark brown skin colour. I am running out of breath, I have to swallow, pull my hand over my mouth ... my knees are trembling.

'Happy birthday, Lucia,' she says in French with a clear and warmhearted voice.

I take my hand off my mouth. 'Who are tha?' I can barely make it audible.

'My name is Walikia Keita, I am the sister of your biological mother and indescribably happy to finally stand before you.'

'What's going on here?' Mum echoes from behind like a bugle against a massed wall of pupils' voices, and from the front I see Dad coming towards me with a paper bag of rolls in his hand and his frayed Beerschot fan scarf around his neck. But nothing more happens; time stands still for a moment. Dad walks silently around us both and says to Mum: 'Come in, leave her alone.' The front door slams shut. I don't know how long we stand like this, she and I. Eventually, I reach out my hand to greet her, but I don't know what to say.

'I'm sorry to surprise you like this. I would like to introduce myself properly and present you with something from your mother and our family. May I come in?'

Awkward minutes go by. I leave her outside the door, explain to Mum and Dad that my biological mother's sister is there. Mum's features immediately become hard, as if petrified. Daddy goes with me to the front door, I introduce them to each other, and Daddy politely invites Mrs. Keita in for a coffee. Mum does not shake hands with Mrs. Keita. Dad overlooks this, asks our guest to join us at the dining table with a freshly starched white tablecloth, on which a red birthday candle is burning and books in gift-wrapping paper are awaiting me. Mum comes with an extra cup and saucer of the Sunday dishes in her hand and places both of them with a reluctant gesture on the free place at the table next to mine. We sit down. Mum sits there stiff and rigid. Dad pours coffee clumsily, spills it and immediately catches a nasty look from Mum. A bizarre spectacle. Mrs. Keita smiles, 'Walikia' she said; but I'm not sure if I listened well enough, I'm just overwhelmed. She sits to my left, Mum opposite her, with her arms crossed, close to her body, like a protective shield. Dad looks at me lovingly.

'I'm sorry to show up unannounced, but I thought it was the best.'

'Welcome. Please have a some coffee and then tell us why you came.' Dad smiles at her friendlily. He means what he says.

'I would appreciate it if you could tell us what the theatre is all about and why you are disturbing us today.' Mum leaves no doubt about how she sees it.

'My name is Walikia Keita, I am the sister of Lucia's mother and I came from Kinshasa.'

'*I* am Lucia's mother!' cries Mum angrily from across the table as she flashes her armour and stretches her hands across towards me, as if she had to save her chick from a menacing wolf. Mrs. Keita does not lose her temper and continues smiling.

'My sister Amaike and our mother Shaira, Lucia's grandmother, were murdered in the open street twenty years ago today. Miraculously, the doctors at the hospital in Kolwezi managed to save Lucia's life. As she was dying, my mother ordered that the child Lucia be baptised and given up for adoption in Belgium, but to guard the bond of the soul for all eternity.'

My throat contracts again, I want to ask what ... how ... but I can't get any sound out and instead just knead my hands. Dad reaches for Mum's left hand and holds it in his, shyly.

'Our family walked this path with bleeding hearts and trembling hands. We lost three women in the family in one fell swoop, but we knew that we could not let Lucia become a target too. If someone went so far as to shoot defenceless women in the street, there are powerful interests behind it.'

'Whose target?' asks Dad and rubs his left hand nervously across his face.

'We Keitas are rebellious, resisting the exploitation of our country by foreign companies, corrupt politicians and provincial officials. We are used to influential people making our lives difficult ... but nobody had ever shot at us before.'

'Who fired?' Dad breathes deeply as if it were the hardest question ever.

'Guards at a cobalt mine.'

'They're just the henchmen.'

'Yes, Mr. Peeters, we agree.'

Daddy turns pale white around the nose.

'Kolwezi is located in the very south of the Congo. This is where around sixty percent of the world's available cobalt deposits are located. This is where the big money is made and then put into very few pockets. The Congo is one of the richest countries in the world in terms of mineral resources, but its population is one of the poorest.'

'Were the perpetrators identified and brought to justice?'

'No.'

Dad's nostrils tremble. Mum gets wet eyes. I stop trembling, turn more towards Walikia Keita.

'How do you know that Lucia is my daughter? How do you know where we live? We were assured the adoption would be anonymous.' Mum's eyebrows are raised, her eyes are wide open, her pupils are fixed and her voice is distorted in rage.

'In one of the most corrupt countries in the world, money can also buy a name from the adoption agency. We found out the rest ourselves here in Belgium.'

'We don't want to associate with criminals ...' Mum points to the front door with her open hand.

'"Criminal" is what you call it when you want to protect the life of your own family and still want to know where the child is and how she is doing? Interesting. If that is your verdict on the Congolese, Mrs. Peeters, then let's look at the whole picture. The wealth of Belgium is largely due to the exploitation of my homeland and the murder of my people since the times of King Leopold II.'

'That's where it all ends!'

Mrs. Keita lets her eyes wander for a moment over Mum and Dad's books on the shelves in the living dining room. 'You seem to be an educated family. But what you don't want to see or know exists anyway. If you want to get excited, you have to start with King Leopold II. He first took the land from the tribes of my homeland, who had no idea of private property and their own great culture, under the guise of wanting to civilise barbarians and spread charity. He made them work on his rubber plantations and in his factories, and those who did not keep up, those who did not meet the production quotas, had their hands chopped off, were allowed to die miserably. If King Leopold II and later the Belgian state had not treated the Congolese like subhuman beings, who knows, perhaps we would be prosperous today, free from corruption, free from gang wars over coltan in the eastern part of the country, free from exploitation and child labour in the cobalt and gold mines. Then we would not have to protect our children by adoption from cold-blooded murderers and bloody power struggles over natural resources.'

Mum opens her mouth wide, wants to strike back, wants to be right, as always, but Dad gets in her way, completely against his habit.

'Calm down and listen, Elizabeth. It's all about Lucia now, just Lucia.'

Mrs. Keita breathes out slowly and continues speaking gently. 'When Amaike became pregnant, our mother told her that the child's soul was destined for great things.'

'What kind of hocus pocus is this?' Mum snorts angrily across the table and stands up demonstratively. 'This is a civilised country! Lucia was brought up properly!'

Before Mrs. Keita can continue, Dad intervenes in a more determined way: 'Please sit down, Elizabeth, and just listen.'

'I understand how your wife feels.'

'No, you don't understand,' says Mum angrily from above over the table and points her index finger like a pistol at Mrs. Keita. 'You just barge in here like that, trying to make me feel guilty, only to take my child away from me and expose her to hocus-pocus and charlatans. I won't let you do that.'

'Elizabeth, Lucia has a right to know where she came from and what really happened back then. We could never give her answers to these questions. Listen now or leave the room until Mrs. Keita has finished her visit!'

Mrs. Keita reaches with her left hand into her handbag, which is standing next to her on the floor, and takes out two parcels wrapped in brightly coloured cloths. 'Here,' she says and hands me the large cloth with fire-coloured rays, 'are photos of your mother Amaike, your grandmother Shaira, your grandfather Elyas and members of the whole family. Take a look at them at your leisure whenever you want.'

I take the parcel and press it against me, think for a moment and decide to open it when I am alone in my room. Mum stares at me with narrowed but flashing eyes. I lay it down on my lap, embarrassed. I don't want to hurt her even more.

'And this is the ring of your mother Amaike.' She gives me a tiny green and purple bundle, inside which I find a square velvet box. I open it too, and a delicate gold ring shines towards me. A snake that winds around the finger and bites its tail with its head. The snake's head has tiny eyes made of a ruby red and an emerald green stone. I take it out and put it on the ring finger of my right hand. It fits like a glove. I stretch out my hand, hold it in the timid morning sun that falls through the windows of the conservatory so that everyone can see my ring. 'What a fantastic birthday present. It goes wonderfully with the earrings Tilly gave me for graduation.'

Mum steps back jerkily, her chair flings backwards and falls with a bang on the stone tiles. She runs through the kitchen and out into the hall. We hear every staccato step she takes on the stairs, then a door slams at the top.

'Please excuse me and my wife. That's a bit much all at once,' says Dad, who gets up, puts Mum's chair back in place, nods to me and goes after Mum.

'I really don't want to mess up your life.'

'This has been messed up since I can remember. I am a stranger here. Just look.' I point to the birthday presents on the dining room table. 'I get books every year. Half of the titles I get to wish for myself, the other half is still chosen by Mum. She tries every day to make me a copy of herself. Isn't that crass? I am a grown woman, aren't I? And a blind man can see that I'm different.'

Mrs. Keita turns all the way to me in her chair. 'Your grandfather Elyas has asked me to be here today. He has suffered unspeakably from not having you with him, from not being able to educate you himself. But it would have been irresponsible to keep you in the Congo. I don't expect you to believe or understand this, but I assure you, we were with you all these years.'

I raise my eyebrows questioningly.

'Today is not the first time I've seen you.'

'What?' I blurt out. I can't believe it.

'Every two years I came to Belgium. First I found out the address, then I watched you too, in the schoolyard, on the way home, on the dike and in the meadows by the river. I saw how you talked to plants and animals, how you read while sitting in the sun, always looking at the water and the sky.'

'How come tha never talked to me?'

'We didn't dare to make your growing up any more complicated than it already was. I would have loved to run towards you, hug you and kiss you, hold you lovingly for hours and hours ... but wouldn't have been wise. I had to watch in silence and drive home in tears. At least I could tell your grandfather that you are doing well, according to the circumstances: you love nature and animals and are connected to them in your loneliness.'

'Why only now? I came of age at eighteen. Why didn't tha come two years ago?'

'It was with a heavy heart that your grandfather decided this. He invites you to visit him, me and the whole family in Kinshasa whenever you want. A direct flight from Brussels to Kinshasa should be easy to get. The flight time is just over eight hours. We will pay for the flight and then pick you up at the airport.'

I am confused, and yet I can hardly wait. 'Tomorrow... No, I can't ... over Christmas ...' I think about Mum and Dad. 'No, I can't do that either. Right after Christmas ... Right after Christmas. This year, right after Christmas. Is that possible?'

'Of course, whenever you want.'

'But... I'm paying for CO_2 emissions compensation.'

'Agreed ... We are all looking forward to seeing you so much. We've been waiting longer than you have.' She smiles lovingly at me.

I briefly put my hands in front of my face and have to swallow. Tears roll from the corners of my eyes and I just let them roll. I am not even ashamed. She leans towards me and hugs me, strokes my hair. How good that feels. I can't remember the last time Mum did that, if she ever did it at all.

'Please call me Walikia, Aunt Walikia.' Then she lets go of me and I'll be all right, but I need a moment before I can speak again. She too has tears in her eyes.

'Do tha know who ... who my father is?'

'We know, and we don't know.'

'Tha can't ... It's illogical.'

'With your grandmother's approval, your mother had a love affair with a German engineer working on his doctoral thesis on industrial mining in the Congo. They met in January 1999 at a demonstration at the mine in Kolwezi.'

'Why do tha say *with approval*, Aunt Walikia? It sounds so funny. What's there to approve?'

'In Congo, a girl marries early and has many children. Educated people like us wait. There are hardly any contraceptives, and HIV is omnipresent. But your grandmother was a shaman, like all the women in our family. We can feel, sense, intuit things, read the subtleties. Your grandmother knew that Amaike should leave the Congo with this man and that together they would have a daughter who would serve a great cause.'

'Can't tha be more specific?'

'Revelations speak a different language than research.'

'Oh, well ...' I say, but I don't understand.

'At the end of July 1999, the young German engineer suddenly disappeared, without a word, without a message. Amaike desperately searched for your father, but never found him until she died.'

'But he knows I exist?'

'She told him she was expecting a child by him.'

'What's his name?'

'Adam.'

'First or last name?'

'First name.'

'Adam is the name of tens of thousands of men all over the world,' I say with a twinge in my heart. I want clarity at last, not new riddles.

'It also remains in the dark who was so afraid of Mother and Amaike that he let them shoot at them.'

'I imagined everything, why I was given up for adoption, but not this. I dreamt ... yeah, I dreamt hundreds of times of a hospital room, I screamed and only saw crying dark faces around me.'

She smiles. 'Memories ... Memories of your birth.'

'Tha really think so?'

'Very likely.'

'But my father?'

'We have no photos. If we had one, believe me, we would have found him long ago.'

I cramp my hands around the little bundle with the pictures in my lap.

'We have nothing that could put us on his trail. But I know deep inside me that you two will find each other, because you belong together.'

'Tha talk like Grandmother Mepi.'

'Like who?'

'The only one here, together with her husband Ilanato Campita, who really, really understands me. An Indian woman, a healer, a wise, mighty woman. "Grandmother Mepi" is name and title at the same time and was given to her when she led the tribe of the Rainbow Colours from Russia across the Bering Strait to Nevada centuries ago. In her present incarnation she did not live out her abilities and life's work as Maria until White Bull reminded and challenged her to do so in 2012 and renewed the title of Grandmother Mepi.'

'Sounds like hocus-pocus to your adoptive parents' ears.'

'Yeah, but I keep it a secret from them. Their real names are

Maria and Wouter; that's how the neighbours know them, but I call them by their real names.'

'Then you are not alone, and that reassures us. I think, Lucia, I'd better go now. Once I'm out of the house, it will be easier for your adoptive parents.'

'But first, let me show tha my room.'

'Do you think they'll be able to handle me going up the stairs to the roof with you?'

'How do tha know where my room is?'

'You once hummed to yourself on the dike, over your pad under the roof and that the moon and the stars always smile through the window there.'

I get up and hug Aunt Walikia. It feels so familiar. Walikia takes off her shoes on the stairs and we float as silently as possible over the wooden stairs into my 'dragon's lair', as Mum always calls my kingdom pejorative.

Walikia looks around attentively.

'So tidy and clean, always?'

'Mum is better than a German staff sergeant when it comes to education for cleanliness and order.'

'Wow!' she gently exclaims. 'May I?'

'Sure.'

She first approaches my collection of minerals and stones on the shelf and then on the round side table next to the bed, where I also make my daisy water. She picks up the best pieces of my collection one by one, the large grey-blue over beige, reddish to brown sparkling agate dragon head, the purple amethyst druse, the petrified grey-blue snail shell, the tree ghost head made of petrified light brown wood, the collection of the four small dragon heads made of amazonite, rose quartz, rhodonite and lapis lazuli.

Afterwards she strokes her fingers almost tenderly over the spines of the books in the bookcase while she looks at the titles at length. Finally, she gazes out of the window over my laptop, tablet, smartphone and desk and across the long, narrow garden towards the meadows in front of the dike.

'The strength of the soul is the most powerful force,' she says and looks at me with a loving smile.

'What do tha mean?'

'In the long wall shelf in your adoptive parents' living and dining room, I noticed on the bottom two boards thick illustrated books about art history, and towards the top thinner books about geography, culture, cultural travel and language.'

'We are *educated bourgeois*,' says Mom. 'She's really proud of that.'

'Just the stories and the world view of the winners.'

I've never thought of it that way before.

'The books on your shelves show me a Western education in four languages, from *The Never Ending Story* to *Alice in Wonderland*, the *Chronicles of Narnia* and the *Lord of the Rings* to The *Little Prince*. But I have never seen Alexander von Humboldt's voyages of discovery, Konrad Lorenz's geese, Jacques Cousteau's marine research and an illustrated book on the constellations in the winter sky on the bookshelves of such a young woman.'

'Bizarre... for most ... not for me. Just my world. Humboldt was one of the first to understand that everything forms a coherent ecosystem. And his drawings, full of cool infographics, are something many a professor at university can really learn from today. He just didn't make a distinction between science and truth. I think I have the same longing inside me. Only what tha know and understand tha love, and only what tha love tha protect. Isn't that right?'

'Yes, it is... but I see no books with the stories of your blood. No African stories that connect man, earth and sky and see them as one.'

'Mum did not allow such books. She always said: "Be thankful tha're Belgian and no longer one of those poor wretches."'

'But in all the books about the cosmos, earth, stones and animals, your soul is speaking.'

Now I have to smile. How quickly she analyses me, almost like Grandmother Mepi, but she only looked at my body.

'Mum rejects modern technology, Aunt Walikia, and that is my happiness. She has no idea that I buy eBooks with my money and read what I want on my tablet. Of course I read stories from the Congo.' I take the tablet off my desk and hold it up almost like a trophy.

'The metals in it, the tantalum for microchips and semiconductors and the cobalt for the batteries: all this is the curse of the Congo.'

'But why? The Congo has a lot of coltan ore to produce tantalum and the largest cobalt reserves in the world.'

'When Belgium granted us independence in 1960, the freely elected Prime Minister Patrice Lumumba was deprived of power and killed a few months later. He wanted the riches of the Congo for the Congolese. The foreigners, especially the Americans, did not like that. They still abuse the Congo today as a supplier of raw materials at low prices.'

'I did not know that. I only know that Mobutu and then Kabila were corrupt dictators.'

'Now is not the right time for politics in the Congo. It is about your future and your task ... You've always been alone a lot, haven't you?'

I just nod. 'The kids at school were mostly mean to me. My skin colour bothered them. But it bothered their parents even more that the one with the wrong skin colour was the best in school. And because it bothered them, it bothered their kids.' How good it is that

Walikia is here now. I look at my ring, my mother's ring, and I am overcome with the wish to give Aunt Walikia something special as well. 'Please, choose something beautiful from my stone collection. The one tha like best. I'd like to give tha a big present too.'

'Are you sure? You might regret it.'

'No, I'm so happy today, and I know what tha like too, and tha can have it.' Without waiting for her answer, I take my dearest and best piece, the almost 1.3 kilo agate dragon head, and give it into her gentle hands. 'I give him to tha and I am glad that tha love him as I do.'

'You know and feel me.' She smiles gently again. 'This is the most beautiful gift today ... Welcome home, Lucia.'

'Somehow I'm able to do that. Imagine if we all saw the energy of people with all its facets instead of just their bodies!'

HUMANITY LOG

Chronicle time 18.762.019 - 12.13
Project: *Let there be light*
Avidya Moha (aspect of SOLAS) and Dr. Thomas Müller (aspect of THEODAR)
Located 47° 18' 22.867' N 8° 33' 10.606' E

The car with Thomas and Avidya drives into the large, electronically secured garage on the left of the villa at around eleven o'clock. Outside it is broad daylight now. Both men get out of the car. The housekeeper approaches them and takes Avidya's coat and briefcase. Avidya looks around. Thomas and Maya's Porsches stand side by side as if the world were in perfect order. If there is something Avidya dislikes about Thomas, it is his love for expensive cars. For Avidya, these are the toys of the middle class, with which they can be kept busy and submissive.

The two men go through the garage door and up the stairs to the entrance hall of the villa. The grey-white Italian marble at their feet shines. In the middle of the room there is a round smoked-glass table, on top of it a white vase full of lilies which are starting to open. Opposite it on the wall is a huge, gold-framed mirror, which makes the entrance hall appear twice as large. Avidya's gaze wanders further up to the high ceiling, which is made to sparkle by a chandelier of dark red-violet lead crystal. *A reception hall for high society*, he thinks. Only at the bottom right corner of his eye, next to the entrance door, two large cardboard boxes with Chinese characters disturb this immaculate appearance. Avidya looks at Thomas questioningly.

'Just don't look, Pops. Electronics, David wished for his birthday. The boxes are about to disappear into the cellar. He'll be putting the electronics in his SAM over the next few days.'

In the living room, into which they walk straight ahead, Maya Müller's overexcited voice warbles. She is standing on the wall at the opposite end of the room, one hand leaning against the mantelpiece, in the other a glass of gin and tonic. 'Namaste, Father.' Maya, frail and as small as her father, walks purposefully towards him for a hug. Her long black hair is uncombed, her face looks mask-like around her glassy brown eyes and bloodshot cheeks. A sight Thomas has got used to by now, but it is still embarrassing for him. Maya did not wash herself this morning. She is still wearing her silk pyjamas and a dressing gown over them.

'Just look at you! That's no way to greet your father.'

Maya grimaces, turns around and walks towards the sofa, which stands against the back wall of the room to the right of the fireplace. David is sitting in an armchair to the right of it, watching attentively what is happening as he strokes his hunting dog Bea on the head. Avidya's facial expression shows him that he is disgusted as he inspects and absorbs everything. The dark wooden floor radiates more warmth than the entrance hall. The black Steinway grand piano, a shining splendour on a cream Persian carpet. The sofa and three armchairs are made of fine, cognac-coloured leather. Only now does Avidya's gaze linger on his grandson. David is holding a shiny, wood-mottled box in his hand. When he is sure of his grandfather's attention, he stands up, puts the box on the knee-high glass coffee table and walks towards his grandfather. David is almost as tall as Thomas, a spitting image from his younger days. Only his mop-like hairstyle displeases Avidya. He turns up his nose at it, but says nothing.

'Not so hard, you're crushing me,' he jokes, but it's really no joke, David's hug hurts. Bea also sniffs at him, barks briefly and then wags her tail.

'How nice of you to come, Grandpa. I haven't seen you in so long.' Then David whispers in his ear, 'That's the third gin and tonic she has had this morning.'

David turns to his father. They hug each other like best buddies, Bea wags her tail and barks. Avidya's heart is warmed again at the sight of the two young men.

'Shiva be praised, the future of the Vijay Group is assured.'

Maya calls for the housekeeper and orders champagne. 'We have to celebrate.'

Immediately afterwards a deep female voice says: 'May I take your orders?'

When Avidya turns around, a strongly-built Eastern European woman with short hair and strong hands in a black blouse, black skirt and white serving apron is standing behind him. She observes the family from watchful eyes. He wonders what she might think about Maya.

'I'll have Earl Grey tea, white and a cress-and-cucumber sandwich.'

'Yes, sir.'

Thomas asks for a double espresso, David for a hot Ovo, and both want chocolate cake for their second breakfast.

Maya draws a snort. 'What is wrong with you people? Well, I hope my men at least like my gifts from the best jeweller in town.' She gets up, sets her glass down on the coffee table in front of the sofa, takes a package lying there and walks towards Thomas. She hands it to him with one hand, stretches upward and wraps her other hand around his neck as much as possible to kiss him. Avidya gets sick from watching.

'For my golden boy!'

Thomas exhales deeply, pushes her gently away from him and sits down on the left of the two chairs on the wall. 'Please, Pops, sit down, this is the best seat.' He points to the armchair beside him. 'From here you have the best view. You can look out through the high windows over the lower houses onto Lake Zurich as the sun brings it all to life.'

Avidya first goes to the comfortably crackling fireplace, looks into the blazing fire and rubs his hands against the cosy warmth. His eyes wander to the reading corner. A solid wood bookshelf is attached to the fireplace on the left. It is followed, standing freely in the room with a small glass table in between, by two Eames armchairs with ottoman, and all this in front of the room-high windows facing the lake. It has been four years since he was here. Thomas usually comes to London for confidential meetings in private to save him the trouble of the journey. Four years ago the interior was not so elegant, and there were no sports cars in the garage. Avidya turns back to Thomas. He opens, probably for the sake of peace in the family, the gift from his wife. The same box that David held in his hands appears, containing a manly, angular chronometer in pink gold with a chocolate brown composite bracelet. Maya buys such wristwatches for her husband and son several times a year. Thomas presents the new chronometer for all to see. 'Hm.' His face betrays indifference. Maya notices it, but covers it up with artificial cheerfulness in her shrill voice. 'You both have the same, as always. Everyone should see that you are father and son.'

Bea barks irritatedly.

'Do you have to spend so much money?' Avidya intervenes. 'Surely a watch like that costs 30,000 pounds or more. Didn't I teach you to keep possession of your money?'

'Yeah, blame Maya for everything! It's my money. I can do what I want with it.'

David winks at Thomas, Thomas winks back, then David stands up and takes his father's watch, including the box and wrapping paper. David has been bringing Maya's watch gifts to a dealer in Geneva for several years already. In the original packaging, unworn and with papers, they bring in good money which Thomas invests for him.

'What nonsense.'

'Don't you talk nonsense, father, it's a profitable investment,' Maya defends herself.

'As if you know anything about investing money,' David mumbles softly to himself, without his mother hearing it.

The housekeeper comes in and serves Avidya tea and a sandwich. She also places cake plates, forks, napkins, espresso and Ovo on the coffee table. Then she hurries out again and comes back with a chocolate cake decorated with an 18 made of almond slivers. Her movements are tense. As she picks up the empty gin and tonic glass, Maya calls out: 'Another one!'

'Enough, Maya. You've had enough. Go wash yourself, get properly dressed or get some sleep,' Avidya orders.

The housekeeper flinches and disappears in a hurry towards the kitchen.

'I am no longer a child. I do what I want.'

'You act like a spoiled brat.'

'Fee, open the windows; the men need fresh air,' Maya shouts towards the entrance hall, as if the house keeper could hear her at the other end of the house in the kitchen over two corners and through walls. Turning to Avidya, she returns: 'Better start talking like an upscale Englishman. Leave out the Indian chant. We are somebody now. We have a reputation to uphold.'

'SAM, open the two windows in the reading room for fresh air, five minutes.'

There is a whirring sound. Two windows on the opposite side of the room open diagonally as if by magic. David sees Avidya's stunned look.

'Cool, huh, Grandpa? SAM can do so much more.' He puts his father's watch down on the coffee table and drinks his hot Ovo but does not touch the birthday cake. Instead, he goes to the grand piano, sits down on the stool, adjusts it and lifts the cover off the keyboard. Bea lies down beside him on the heated wooden floor. He stretches his fingers to loosen up and then plays *As Time Goes By* with passion. Maya recognises the melody in the first few bars, gets up abruptly, passes everyone on her way to the entrance hall and wants to go up the stairs. But her coordination fails. Thomas jumps up, goes to her and accompanies her upstairs. Bea does not even look after her. Avidya leaves for the guest room to rest.

After lunch, Avidya and David stand at the window in the dining room with a cup of tea in their hands and look out over Lake Zurich. Hardly a boat is visible. Everything is peaceful, civilised, clean, orderly and pure.

'Pops,' Thomas blurts out with shallow breath as he steps to them from the kitchen with his espresso in his hand, 'please give me some advice. She doesn't want to go to a detoxification clinic, claims David and I just want to get rid of her.'

'I'm taking her to London with me the day after tomorrow. I'll call Amal right away. She will certainly lure Maya to London with some exclusive VIP invitation for a fashion or jewellery show. Then we will keep her there. You really don't need such a burden right now ... And cancel her credit cards, the wastefulness must stop for good. We don't earn our money to squander it or to put it fearfully into safes. We are entrepreneurs.'

'I cancelled her credit cards long ago. I didn't give her the money.'

'And who does the shopping?'

'SAM does the shopping, Grandpa, at least everything that belongs in the fridge, the housekeeper handles the rest.'

'And the watches? How did she get them?'

'She must have at least one more credit card from her

mother, maybe even two.'

'Oh, my Amal, that's more than can be fitted into one life. May you have to walk the rest of your life as a rich Hindu in India, surrounded by women who waste your rupees like flowers in the Ganges.'

Thomas exhales with relief. 'I don't know if that curse is necessary, Pops, but I'm heartily grateful.'

Avidya puts a hand on his forearm. 'You run the company and later hand it over to David. Then you'll have done your duty, my boy.'

'I'm doing an internship in the IT department next year at the end of the summer holiday, Grandpa.'

'Proficient as the father, Shiva be praised.'

'But before you drive the head of the IT department crazy, and me as well, paralysing the company with new ideas, I'll need to relax for a week with Adam, fishing salmon in Quebec. Otherwise I won't get through all this. Your ideas are more exhausting than ten dissatisfied customers.'

'Why don't you take me salmon fishing?'

'This has always been a man's holiday for two, and it will remain that way.'

'Sure... Pa, relax; and in your IT department I only do what you and the head of department approve beforehand. You act as if that were dangerous. Here at home, SAM runs smoothly and safely, doesn't he?

'Speaking of safe, Pops, to get back to the subject of safeguarding management. Without Amal's consent ...'

'I don't want to hear about it now.'

Thomas lets his shoulders droop in disappointment and drinks the espresso. He doesn't understand why Avidya is evading this important point. But he pulls himself together, doesn't want to pressure his father-in-law; they still have two days to spend together.

LIER, 13 DECEMBER 2019

'Nobody can live or speak for you in your place,' says Grandmother Mepi with a cheerful face, and this makes the wrinkles at the corners of her eyes and mouth more prominent. Her face radiates love and wisdom over green-blue eyes, narrow lips and shoulder-length, stepped red-blonde-brown mottled hair such as I have never seen in a human before in my life. She rests in herself, is in this world, but not in the drama of the world. I sit with her and her husband Ilanato Campita at the dining table in her house. We have an early dinner together and I report on what happened this morning at our house. I was simply drawn here. With them I don't have to be on my guard, I don't have to bend myself out of shape, I don't have to defend myself all the time.

The freshly baked wholegrain bread is still warm and smells wonderfully of rosemary. We eagerly spoon the pumpkin soup with orange and ginger. While we chat, two Jack Russell terriers race around the rectangular table or around our feet. The wood-burning stove emits cozy background music. Everything belongs here. Even me, in a way. Even a photo of me hangs on the long wall in the living-dining room among the other photos of their five children, deceased dogs and holiday memories. Grandmother Mepi is sitting opposite me, Ilanato Campita at the head end towards the kitchen. This couple does me good. Only my feet are cold, and I pull my legs up from the wooden floorboards into my armchair. As soon as I sit cross-legged, the younger of the two bitches jumps into my lap and demands attention. Of course I stroke her.

'Now you must accept what unique gifts you have been given,' says Grandmother Mepi and takes a sip of her homemade stone water.

'I always wanted to ... but nothing happened.'

'There is a time for everything, Lucia.'

'My energy field has changed, hasn't it? Tha see it?'

'Yeah. Some of the blockages have been removed, but there's one very persistent ... still.'

'Can tha describe it to me?'

'Let's break it up instead of talking about it.'

'Mega ... when?'

'What do you think, honey?'

Her husband laughs all over his face and then grins broadly, as always, and ends in *hihi*. He is tall and strong, has short-cut grey hair and wears rectangular nickel glasses. He is the joker, and his way of taking things lightly has brought laughter to my face many a time. 'I'll put the dishes away, clean up, and you two go to the treatment room. I don't think it'll be long, and then we can always go to the sauna.' He gets up and starts to clear the soup bowls.

'But tha wanted to leave right after dinner.' I feel bad about always coming in here unannounced and getting their help.

'Don't worry about it.' He laughs.

'For real?'

Both nod.

'Cool.'

'I am in this life to empower people to be themselves.' With a wink and a twinkle, she means for me to stand up and follow her. 'We all have to learn to sing again, how our beaks have grown, and shake our feathers vigorously to do so. Then we'll be able to fly.'

In her treatment room on the first floor I always feel in good hands. In the middle is the treatment couch, above it hangs a dream catcher with light brown feathers from the ceiling. On the shelves on the right wall are specialist books on energetic healing, with crystals, Aura-Soma essences, various singing bowls and tuning forks in between. In front of the window straight ahead is a small table with a water carafe containing small, coloured, natural stones to purify the water; I can see rock crystal, rose quartz, violet amethyst, red jasper, green aventurine and orange calcite. Next to it there are two glasses and two chairs to the right and left of the table. On the left wall lean three big drums covered with brown cow skin.

'Let us first pray together the Invocation of the Great Spirit.' She stands in front of me next to the treatment table, and we hold each other's hands. At her nod we close our eyes and speak together:

'Great Spirit, whose voice I hear in the wind and whose breath gives life to all people in the world, hear me. I need your strength and your wisdom. Let me walk in beauty and let my eyes at all times see the red and purple sunsets you have created with me. Let my hands respect the things you have made and my ears hear your words and your voice clearly. Let me learn the lessons you have hidden under every stone and leaf. I seek strength not to be greater than my brother, but to fight my greatest enemy ... myself. Always make me ready to come to you with clean hands and straightforward eyes, so that when my life ends like the setting sun, my spirit can come to you without shame.'

We open our eyes, she smiles at me and lets go of my hands. 'Really nice to speak it together with you.'

'I always have that book *Messages from Great Spirit* on my tablet and I read it almost every day, mostly in the morning.'

She smiles. 'Let's get on with it. Lie down with your back on the treatment table, close your eyes and relax. Did you hear that? Relax, let go. I don't need help doing my job.'

Now she smiles. How well she knows me. Relaxing is mega

difficult for me. I am curious, want to experience everything that happens, want to know and understand everything. She notices my tension, asks me to breathe out deeply a few times and close my eyes. When I manage this, I hear deep, soothing drum beats, sounding rhythmically for a few minutes in the whole room. Then silence: I begin to relax, but internally I scan my whole body for signals. My left leg is hard, my heart is beating wildly, in front of my third eye a violet light is growing. I have to grin at myself. Control freak: probably has something to do with my love of science. Then follows a soft bright sound from a singing bowl next to my right ear and then clockwise around me. Silence again, my body tingles slightly, as if my solar plexus cells were vibrating together with the sound of the singing bowl. The violet light begins to dance, becoming bigger and stronger. Soon afterwards she strikes a tuning fork. I feel a vibrating point on my left ankle, hear the slowly fading hum of the tuning fork. The vibration penetrates me and becomes quieter and quieter. Grandmother Mepi strikes the tuning fork several times, puts it sideways on my knee, then on my hip bone. Suddenly I hear her say: 'A being comes through, its energy is very strong ... it wants to tell you something ... wait, I have to sit down ... I do not know this vibration.'

It is silent for a while; she breathes deeply and heavily, as if carrying an incredible burden.

'You know who I am!'

'Yes,' I answer. I recognise the voice; it is addressed to me. It is the familiar voice that I have been hearing in my head from time to time for years and that made itself known as YESHUA on my 16th birthday. One day earlier I had received my initiation as a Reiki Master and was floating as if on clouds in shimmering colours. Now, here in the treatment room, his voice clearly comes from Grandmother Mepi's mouth. It is his voice, not hers. I open my eyes, sit up, so that I can see too. Grandmother Mepi is sitting on one of the two chairs. Her facial features are even softer, more loving, more gentle. She seems to be enchanted while talking with closed eyes.

'You'll have to get rid of a lot of things now and put them behind you, Lucia. Be without fear. We have always been with you, guiding your every step when you let yourself be guided, and we have protected you when you let your own

will prevail'.

Silence.

'YESHUA?'

'*If your heart is warm and pure, go your way now, even if others want to slow you down or stop you, even if they resent you, call you names or do not want to go with you. Only their fear speaks. They don't know your path; only you will be able to understand it better and walk it with every passing day. Try not to control or force anything, do you hear? Trust your intuition, not your power of thought. The fire of self-knowledge only burns what you are not. Do you understand that?*'

'Yes, I got that.'

'*Then all is said and done for the moment, Lucia. Feel loved and honoured.*'

'Thank tha.' It's getting hot in my heart.

'*My thanks to Grandmother Mepi! And I hope you, Lucia, now know that I have many ways to speak to you.*'

Silence.

I feel dazed. Grandmother Mepi is breathing heavily. She opens her eyes, shakily pours herself a glass of water and drinks hastily. 'I'll be fine, don't worry.' I get off the treatment table, sit down opposite her at the table, take her hands.

'Who was that? The energy was so strong.'

'YESHUA.'

'Who is this?'

'Jesus.'

'You must be joking.'

'For a long time I didn't want to believe it myself ... Yeshua comes from Yah and Shua. Yah is the source from which everything originates and to which everything returns. Shua means *making whole, healing, saving*. Yeshua is an Aramaic first name and the original, the real name of Jesus. Yeshua was only made Jesus at the Council of Nicaea in 325, because Emperor Constantine adapted the name to the language of the Roman Empire in order to make him a god. The YESHUA who has just spoken through tha is none other than Jesus.'

She looks sceptical. 'Anyway, the energy was overwhelming, full of love, pure ... I'm still dazed.'

'I also doubted, but he confirmed it to me himself the last time he appeared in my head as a voice. Next time tha can ask him yourself.'

'I must rest for a while ... go ... please go down to the kitchen and get me a coffee the way I like it ... and peanuts ... and dark chocolate ... I have to recover ... my energy field now also needs earthly food.'

'Yes, of course.' Although I am wobbly on my feet, I set off immediately, while she slowly lies down on the treatment table to cope with it.

I don't know what it means now, but it's awesome and so blatant that I can't tell about it at home. Grandmother Mepi, Ilanato Campita and I are still sitting together at the dining table to have a warm drink. She is completely flat out from his energy and doesn't have the strength for the sauna anymore. I feel bad that I spoiled it for them. But she says that everything is okay.

To calm down before I can look Mum and Dad in the face, I take a long walk on the dike and hum to the rhythm of the grass swaying in the wind. Although it is already pitch dark, I can see and hear better than ever before, even the greys are finer and sharper, the calls of the ravens are even purer, the energy field of a horse in the meadow is even more clearly defined. I want this never to stop again. Grandmother Mepi said that my energy field is now more open and vibrates at a higher frequency. That's true, my whole body is trilling, all the cells are vibrating faster and more harmoniously, I can feel it and my legs are getting heavier with every minute. When I speak now, how my beak has grown ...

'Come in, we have to talk to you,' calls Mum loudly in a scratchy, angry voice from the living room as my key turns in the lock to close the front door from the inside. I take off my jacket and boots, go into the living room and sit opposite them in the middle of the sofa.

Mum's features show me that it will be hard and bitter. She pushes Dad's arm, probably to get him started. Both are sitting tense in their favourite armchairs, and the atmosphere is frosty. 'What happened this morning', he begins quietly and clumsily rubbing his hands, 'cannot be changed. If your blood family invites you to visit them, visit them. We are sure that after the trip to the Congo you will understand better what you have here with us.'

'Is that all?' I reply and draw my eyebrows together.

'Listen to that,' Mum croaks with fire-spraying eyes and stretches her upper body. 'Haven't we taught you to be grateful? Have you still not understood that *we* are your great happiness?'

'Tha have taught me thar truths and wisdoms and I am grateful for that. But my life - that is something only I can recognise and live. My religion is the tree, not the prestige.' I get up and turn around to leave, want to go up to my room. I really don't feel like having this conversation right now.

'Our religion is Catholicism, and that goes for you too, you naughty brat.'

I turn back to them. She looks as if she was about to jump up and slap me. Very well, let her have a verbal fight. 'The word religion is made up of the parts *re* for *back* or *again* and *ligare* for to *bind* or *unite*. It is about connecting, not splitting and thinking you are better than the others. As a language teacher tha should be familiar with the meaning of the words, or do you know only grammar?'

Mum turns bright red and jumps up. 'I'll show you. Sit down,' she commands harshly and points to the sofa with her finger stretched out.

I remain standing demonstratively, just to see.

'This was your last visit to this Maria here in the settlement, do you understand me? We've been watching you go there for a while now, the neighbours keep me informed. We know that you go to this woman who claims to heal people. Mrs. De Smet says she is just an impostor with a dissociative personality disorder. Mrs. Janssens has sent me YouTube videos of this woman pretending to channel some kind of beings. Ridiculous, just ridiculous!'

'Tha and thar gossips are a bunch of self-righteous ignoramuses,' I blurt out angrily. How unjust they are! I feel like I have to defend Grandmother Mepi. I put both hands on my hips demonstratively and bend my elbows in a sharp angle.

'You!' cries Mum. 'You impudent, unruly child. This is your gratitude for all the sacrifices I have made for you. To bed with you - out of my sight, before I forget myself. You'll be dancing to another and stricter tune as of tomorrow. You can bet your life on it.'

I shake my head, put my hands even more firmly on my hips and yell back: 'Tha are not my mother, and tha certainly don't deserve to be called Mum! From now on I'll call tha Elizabeth, just like Daddy.' My blood is boiling, I whirl round and walk towards the stairs.

'You come back immediately and apologise to me,' she yells after me. I let her rant and rave. I just feel sorry for Dad. I climb up the creaking steps to my pad and pack everything I love, including my daisy water. I'm out of here at dawn, for good. Not like that, Elizabeth. I'm a grown woman. Maybe I'll get a plane ticket from Brussels to Kinshasa before Christmas, or maybe I'll just be alone in my dormitory in Aachen. Anything's better than staying here. I can do without tha, Elizabeth, even if tha make sure that Daddy cuts me off. I'll find a way to finance my studies. But I can't live without truthfulness!

AACHEN, 24 DECEMBER 2019

Bloody Christmas ... Aachen is crowded with people. They can't see enough of the World Heritage Site of the imposing octagonal cathedral, which stands for the unification of Western Europe and its spiritual and political revival under Charlemagne. They feast their eyes on the town hall with its Gothic façade and coronation hall and the Prussian-Classical Elisenbrunnen. But seeing is not enough. They eat and drink more than enough, thanks to the countless restaurants and cafés in the cobblestone streets and, of course, the enticing smells of the Christmas-market stalls. But I can't enjoy that, none of it. I feel just lousy.

A red candle is burning on my desk in my dormitory tonight. All around it are photos of my mother Amaike, my grandparents Shaira and Elyas, Aunt Walikia, my beloved Tilly, one of Dad, but none of Elizabeth and Robin. Robin has been playing dead since my birthday: crass, totally crass. I don't know why, I can't think of any reason. That's why I've started to fantasise and can't sleep properly anymore, have heartaches, cry all the time. I text and text messages, have even called - not the slightest sign of life from Robin. Absolute silence. I'm not hungry anymore either. My favourite stones form a circle around the family photos. I hum *Silent Night, Holy Night* from my heart, but I can't sing. Elizabeth used to call me every day and wanted to know exactly where I was and what I was doing. Not once since I left. Nor has Dad, because he's not allowed to. Elizabeth monitors not only the account, but also his mobile phone. In return,

Tilly now transfers money for my studies and sends me parcels with my favourite chocolate, books and secret messages from Dad. I send back parcels with Aachener Printen and other goodies for both of them. It's a good thing that cool Tilly exists.

Outside it is pitch dark, the candle is almost burned down. The bells of a church ring in the background during midnight mass. Now with my belongings from Lier it's even tighter between bed and desk, bookshelf and wardrobe. I printed out the photos from Kolwezi in the drugstore and pinned them on the wall above the bed as a vigil. That is my truth, and I want and need to change something about it. But how?

It is quiet here in the dormitory. That's actually good for thinking. The corridors of the two floors, each with twelve rooms and two kitchens, are empty. Every step I take echoes on the polished tiles in the corridors and stairway. Dimitri went home to the Barents Sea; he took Tasha with him. Dimitri wants to fight against the destruction of his home by Nornickel, and Tasha against that of the South Americas by the Brazilian Vale company. But they are like me: a lot of will, a lot of anger, but no money and no power to make a difference. Dimitri thinks we need to become activists like Greta Thunberg; we are already half-scientists. Tasha texted me today that she doesn't like the long darkness in Northern Russia and the constant boozing of the men there. She'll be back as soon as she can. Everyone is so melancholic in Russia, so dull. She's never seen Dimitri behave in such a way.

I pull out my meditation cushion from under my desk and place it in the middle of my few square feet. I have to let go and relax, otherwise I won't be able to fall asleep ... right away. I sit down on the pillow, cross my legs, wiggle my bottom until I'm sitting properly, and stretch my spine and neck. I breathe out strongly several times and then breathe in calmly. I close the right nostril with the thumb of my right hand, exhale through the left nostril, pause and inhale again. Now I close the left nostril with the ring finger of my right hand and breathe out through the right nostril. I pause, breathe in again and close the right nostril with my thumb. I repeat this nine times and the tangle of thoughts in my head is gone. I close my eyes, check the sitting position, correct again until the spine is completely upright and straight. From now on I only observe my breath. Up and down, up and down, up and down, up and down, letting happen what nature can do without me. A gently cool breeze flows in at the nostrils, a noticeably warmer one flows out. In—out—in—out—in—out. Wide awake, but calm and peaceful. At some point the disturbing thoughts stop. With every moment I feel lighter, freer, more unbound. I float in a boundless space.

Welcome, Lucia, I hear again the soft, loving voice of YESHUA. *How beautiful, you have made your way to us.*

'Did I?'

Who else could have done it?

'Tha?'

No, your free will, not mine. But it has allowed me to lead you, and given up controlling you, for a little moment at least.

'Why did tha not come when I called tha? Why didn't tha answer when I desperately arrived here in Aachen after the fight with my parents? Why didn't tha come when I cried my eyes out at night over Robin?'

I have always replied.

'I really didn't hear thar voice.'

If you are full of fear, anger and negative thoughts, full of these low vibrations, then I cannot reach you even if I were to scream.

'But tha ... tha don't scream ...'

I only reach those who are willing to hear and to see what they have not wanted to hear and see before.

'But, why do I hear tha now? Why do tha come now?'

It is time for you to make acquaintance with those who have been guiding and accompanying you as I have since you arrived on Earth on the 13th of December 1999.

'What?'

Can you see me, Lucia? Can you see where you are?

'No.'

Set your gaze more finely; in the ether the vibrations are higher. Blink a few times; you can do it, you just have to allow it ... not want to force it.

I'm blinking. But I can't see anything except my dorm room.

You doubt. As long as you doubt, you can't. Trust.

'But there must be a trick!'

No! There are no tricks or shortcuts to get into the ethereal Shambala. Only with pure thoughts, pure heart, free from your own desires, can you succeed in being here with us. Even those who try to reach it with drugs only fool themselves. They open their perception, control less, but they do not reach Shambala.

'I want to, but I really can't, YESHUA, please believe me.'

You want it too intently. Go to sleep and let go. You'll see.

'YESHUA?'

Silence.

'YESHUA?'

He's gone, I can't hear him anymore. I've failed, damn it. Angrily I go to the bathroom, turn on the tap, fill my palms with cold water, splash my face and then brush my teeth. I go back to my room, put out the candle and go to sleep. 'I want this to work now, tha hear, YESHUA! I'm ready, really, tha hear!' Nothing happens. To calm me down I say the invocation for the Great Spirit that Grandmother Mepi taught me.

I'll wake up and it's still pitch black. I turn my head to the side, look for the smartphone, want to know what time it is, but it's not there. I turn my gaze back towards the ceiling, but it's not there anymore either. Instead a high shiny golden dome or a vault, I can't see it very well. But I am still lying down. What is that? I put my palms next to my body to verify this and feel warm stone instead of blanket. I sit up, look around me and see a whole circle of blurry beings all looking down at me.

There you are, Lucia.

A being speaking with YESHUA's voice, wrapped in a robe of light, golden yellow and rose-coloured, with a shadowy face, offers his hands so that I can stand up.

Come, I want you to remember your friends and helpers again and be happy together with them.

I rise with his help. Around me are many vague-shaped beings. They are twice my size, all unknown to me, but it feels familiar. I see them only as one sees tiny droplets in the mist through which a rainbow shines.

'Where am I? Who are tha? Sorry, but I am confused.'

That will soon pass. Just let your body get used to our vibrational quality first.

'Where am I?'

In the old office of the Lord of the World; you are in Shambala, where the spiritual hierarchy of the Earth was gathered.

'Lord of the World? Who is the Lord of the World?'

His name is SANAT KUMARA, but people also call him The Old Man of Days or The Youth of Sixteen Summers.

'Never heard of him. I always thought God was the Lord of the World.'

God is all that is and all that is not. In the universe He has representatives, preparers, administrators, messengers, builders, keepers of knowledge, librarians, glyph writers, communicators, networkers, diplomats and many others. SANAT KUMARA is the supreme spiritual authority for the Earth, in the service of the Great Being that forms the Soul of the Earth. You know each other, but you do not remember yet. It was he who made sure that you came to the aid of the Earth.

A being almost twice my size is approaching. I cannot see its face. It has a huge peach-coloured robe of light, like a sphere of energy. I suddenly shiver, my heart beats wildly and warmly. The being says my name and then completely surrounds me. It just goes inside me and then through me. I am in the middle of it, in his huge energy sphere. All around me I see only delicate, peach-coloured mist. We are one. I hear applause. Then the being separates from me again. I do not want that. I feel so good, so safe, so secure, so joyful when I am in it.

'Why are tha letting me go? Who are tha?'

My name is TRUSLAN. I am your soul, and a small aspect of my divine spark is now incarnated with you as Lucia and serves on Earth.

'But ... I don't understand ...'

TRUSLAN has been my name for ages and will remain so until I reunite with the Creator. Lucia is your name in this Earth life, but TRUSLAN is your complete reality.

At that moment someone else approaches me. I blink a few times and the shadowy picture becomes sharper. A radiant young man, with blond hair and a delicate rose-coloured light robe. I keep blinking, and each time I see more distinctly. He has blue eyes.

Do not be deceived, Lucia, says YESHUA. *SANAT KUMARA came here from Venus 18.76 million years ago to establish and guide the spiritual hierarchy of the Earth.*

Welcome, we have been waiting for you, he says to me as if I were an old friend.

I don't know what to answer. I lack the words, overwhelmed by his light, by the peace and love he is sending me and which now permeates every cell of mine.

Look, here. He points to several groups of beings standing a little further away, which I can only dimly recognise. Then I hear a choir of many voices: *Welcome to Shambala, Lucia-TRUSLAN, welcome back.*

A warm shiver runs through my whole body.

We want to show you what is real, and hopefully when you are back on Earth you will remember it in dense matter, in your flesh-, blood- and bone-body. It is extremely important for world affairs.

'Why?'

You took on a major task before you incarnated. It is of utmost importance for the destinies of mankind and the whole Earth that you accept and act upon it.

'And what is this?'

On my right you see the Ascended Masters of all cultures and times, souls in Earth service: YESHUA, LAO TSU, CONFUCIUS, ABRAHAM, MOSES, KRISHNA, BUDDHA, MOHAMMED, MOTHER MARIA, GUAN YIN, DJWAHL KHUL, KUTHUMI, MORYA, SAINT GERMAIN, to name but a few. I don't have time to name them all. He laughs mischievously.

I am at a loss for words.

On my left you can see the light-beings of other planets: our Off Earth Allies, also called ETs on Earth, Extra Terrestrials; and of course the very important DEVAS and some CONREES.

I see shadowy figures of light, I am overwhelmed with who they are and what they do. 'Will I come back here again?'

As soon as your body has become even purer, vibrating even higher. It will be increasingly easier for you to come together with us and to see us clearly. This is desired and necessary in order to fulfil your earthly task. But for this you still have to go through some developmental steps.

'I ... I ...'

But I must warn you too, Lucia.

'Warn me about what?'

When you are back in your student room in a few moments, you will feel more alone than ever before.

'But why?'

Who do you know who has also been here? Who do you know who has experienced what you are experiencing now? Who will you be able to talk to about it?

It flashes through me like lightning, my whole body seems to sink in a few inches. 'Yes,' I reply after a few moments, 'I understand what tha mean. Only Grandmother Mepi and her husband will believe me immediately. Perhaps Tilly, Tasha and Dimitri too, but Robin would have ...'

It is your self-chosen task to follow the path in service to mankind and to Earth. You have selected what gets in your way, who can move with you and who cannot. Some will laugh at you. Some will call you crazy or sick. Some will even fight you. Only those who are already working on Earth as light-workers will applaud you. But soon millions of people, previously unsuspecting, will wake up and follow you. They will intuitively recognise as true what you are experiencing. They will add the new to what the Ascended Masters before you taught in their time, and now they will also provide people with new information. The consciousness of the planet is rising noticeably, because its frequencies have been increased. And as the consciousness of the planet rises, so do all the kingdoms that are connected to the Earth, through an expansion of consciousness. For the expansion of consciousness of all land-dwellers, we must expand our teachings and thus their beliefs.'

'But I ...'

We will be at your side, every step of the way.

'Thank tha ... but ...'

With each day we allow the veil of ignorance and partial knowledge become a little thinner for all people. Their chakras vibrate on a higher level, begin to awaken. Most people are still frightened by this. They cling to individual books of spiritual teachers, church dogmas and even stones. But every day thousands of people on Earth become more conscious and more courageous. You are one of the great lights in my service. From today until the end of this earthly century and far beyond ... if you fulfil your task and people follow you. If we fail, the human family will once again come to an end. Let us do our best to lead them back to the Light and their mission in the Galaxy.

'What do tha mean? Could tha be more specific?'

You learn what you need to know at the time you need to know.

'Do tha think I'm so simple-minded?'

There is so much to know. With your earthly body you can only grasp and remember it in a limited way. You don't even remember that you yourself gave the starting signal for the project with all of us in this Great Hall.

'No ... I don't remember that,' I reply sheepishly.

On the 1st of January 1997 Ascended Masters, Devas, Conrees, Off Earth Allies and wise earth souls, poets and thinkers of all nations and ages gathered in this very Great Hall. Together with me they gave the starting signal for the consciousness expansion project 'Let there be light' for humans and Earth in a ceremony. TRUSLAN, your soul was the centre of attention. We gathered a project team of twelve around you before you went into the Great White Pyramid for your dense-matter training. We also chose earthly parents from indigenous soul families to prepare you for the task on Earth. Others will now support you in the undertaking. Still others, such as GUNAH, are ready to assist you in your greatest need. Still others, such as SAINT GERMAIN, OMSTARA and PHILOHSTAN, will open the channels to divine and cosmic well-being and knowledge.

'I'm sorry, I really don't remember.'

You have the ability, and therefore the task, to set a milestone in human history on Earth, a milestone which far, far exceeds your own expectations. You are and can do more than you are able to understand at this time. But great tasks also cause fear. Fear of responsibility, fear of failure, fear of how others around us will react, fear of loneliness.

'In my life there is already no stone left standing...'

You wouldn't talk like that if you knew TRUSLAN's galactic resume. You wouldn't doubt for a second that you have brought to fruition everything that was necessary.

'Then why is everything in my life upside-down?'

Some of those who had to prepare you for your earthly mission have chosen not to accept their task or have been prevented from doing so. We had to find unexpected interim solutions. But that is not important now. What is important is that you declare yourself ready. It is high time to start; we have already missed too many opportunities due to the weaknesses of some people. Remember your true name TRUSLAN *and its meaning. And then let go of what has passed and proceed forward. We are with you.*

I wake up. I am dazed, my teeth hurt; I can't think clearly, but my heart is warm. I feel the blanket under my hands. I am a student in a dormitory in Aachen, without parents, and I am supposed to move the world in a new direction, to give it light ... crass, totally crass. Am I crazy or just devoid of imagination?

HUMANITY LOG

Chronicle time 18.762.019 - 12.27
Project: *Let there be light*
Avidya Moha (aspect of SOLAS) and Dr. Thomas Müller (aspect of THEODAR)
Located 51° 29' 12.995' N   0° 10' 12.133' W

Amal Ali rises and in a bright red designer dress opens the business meeting of the family members in the dining room of her Chelsea home. The small chubby woman with black shoulder-length hair and shiny red lipstick looks over all the family members gathered around the table. Thomas, sitting directly opposite her, winces. He watches her attentively from top to bottom. He is used to her wearing expensive clothes and jewellery, but today she seems inexplicably threatening to him. Avidya is sitting to the right of his wife in a wheelchair, in the middle of the other long side of the rectangular dining table with twelve chairs, seven of which are occupied. Apart from the three, the two sons of Amal from her first marriage, Ismael and Ibrahim, are present, as well as their common daughters Pritha and Maya. Ismael and Ibrahim are seated at the head ends, Maya on the right and Pritha on the left of Thomas. Behind Amal on the wall are two verses by the prophet Mohammed, framed in gold, so skilfully written in black ink on parchment that it usually takes the breath away from any observer. But Thomas does not perceive their beauty today. Something is different, very different.

Amal's sons have leaned forward. To Thomas they appear ready to attack like tigers, about to jump. Avidya appears haggard. His face is pale as a corpse, his eyes have retreated deep into their sockets. Thomas suddenly doubts whether the plan they forged in Rüschlikon a fortnight ago can still be carried out.

'Avidya and I have asked you here today to discuss the future of our family business. Changes are inevitable.' Amal looks down mercilessly on Avidya. 'The mining industry urgently needs a sustainable concept. Our metal trade, on the other hand, is well-positioned. I ask Thomas to tell us what he thinks should change in mining.' Amal sits down again and looks Thomas piercingly in the eye. Thomas gazes at Avidya, but he is only a sad sight.

'The ingenuity of Avidya's corporate structure,' he begins, stretching his body, 'lies in the fact that we make multiple profits from one-and-the-same product. We mine the metals and minerals ourselves in their countries of origin as cheaply as possible. We push the tax burden down again via the Swiss holding company and letterbox companies in other tax havens. This construct enables us to offer the raw materials to ourselves as traders at the lowest possible conditions and then to resell them with the highest possible profit margin. Depending on the route the raw materials take through our group, we win three to five times over.'

'It's street-kid wisdom. Everyone lives as well as possible at the expense of others. Our competitors don't do it any differently,' Ibrahim replies and looks at Thomas from the side with narrowed eyes and raised shoulders.

Thomas senses that they want to corner him. Ibrahim would never express himself in this manner if Avidya were still healthy and strong. His neck muscles contract, but he continues. 'In any case, I want to make it clear to all the members of the family around the table that our business model is beginning to crumble.'

'That's nonsense, at least for commodities trading,' Ibrahim attacks Thomas once again. 'The World Bank predicts that the demand for raw materials for all tech products will increase forty times over.'

'Forty percent you mean?' Maya asks, wringing her hands restlessly. She looks no better than she did a fortnight ago when Thomas took her to the airport with her father. The only difference now is that she is washed and properly dressed.

'No, Maya, forty-fold, and that's why you can rub your shaky hands, because we'll earn ourselves a golden goose with this boom,' Ibrahim replies. Thomas looks at Avidya, but he just looks powerlessly and apathetically into the void. *Do the Ali brothers know something I don't know yet?* he asks himself.

'We as Vijay,' Thomas resumes after a pause for breath, 'are in a gigantic cut-throat competition. The largest cobalt, manganese, nickel and copper mine operators will use their financial power to push us out of business eventually. Instead of waiting to run out of money and being forced to sell when it is not convenient, we should actively stay ahead of developments.'

'So what do you suggest?' Ismael takes over from the headboard. His expression is opaque. Ismael and Ibrahim, both with heads of full, dark hair styled into an undercut, as well as full beards, differ for Thomas only in their appearance. They could be twins if Ismael didn't always wear a tie and Ibrahim didn't consistently attract attention with impulsive actions and loud, strong expressions.

'We have to think about our grandchildren today and be content with less return for five to ten years.'

'Specific, Thomas: be specific please,' Ismael grasps and gently strokes his thick hair backwards with his fingers on both ears, while his brown eyes sow mistrust.

'We will stay in the industry but move, first to deep-sea mining and then into space. We are voluntarily leaving the fight against the Chinese regarding the industrial mining of metals on land. Let the big players like BHP, Rio Tinto, Vale, Glencore, MMC, Anglo American and Nornickel take them on. We sell our mines step by step as soon as we need financing, but we maintain good contacts with the major players. We are breaking new ground in ways they cannot or do not want to do because they are big and ponderous like oil tankers or do not want to be attacked publicly. We are like a speedboat. We can manoeuvre excellently in the smallest of spaces, approach risks differently. We are always two or three turns ahead of the big ones, but never competitors - rather pioneers.'

Avidya breathes out slowly, nodding his head.

'At some point you no longer need pioneers. This is the beginning of the end,' Ibrahim criticises aggressively.

'What are you actually planning, Thomas?' Ismael adds and strokes the tips of his beard with his hand.

Thomas leans to one side, takes a fist-sized clod from his briefcase and places it in the middle of the dining room table. Ibrahim bends over and grabs it to look at it closely.

'What's with the rock?'

'This is not a rock. This is an accumulation of polymetals into a nodule, as it is called in deep-sea jargon. This nodule in front of you contains 28% manganese, 1.5% nickel, 1.4% copper and 0.25% cobalt. These metals represent the way the global economy works and the way the world's population lives today. Nickel and cobalt are essential to our current technology of energy storage. Between the Hawaiian archipelago and the west coast of Mexico alone, nodule fields in the deep sea contain six times as much cobalt and three times as much nickel as the total land-based reserves of these metals, at least as far as we know today.'

'Pass this nodule or whatever it is around, please, Ibrahim.'

'How deep is this nodule field?'

'At some 14,700 feet below sea level.' Thomas makes a grumpy face. He is displeased that he has to reveal this information to Ibrahim.

'We are selling the cobalt mine in Kolwezi at the end of March 2020 and will first use the money to create a small foothold in the deep-sea mining of cobalt, manganese and copper. At the same time, we are investing heavily in several smaller companies that are developing and already producing the technical equipment for this kind of mining. In this way, we earn money from our competitors during the investment phase, know exactly who is doing what where, and keep possible doors open in many directions. You will find details in the presentation which I will distribute immediately.' Thomas points to the pile of folders lying on the table in front of him.

'Investment-intensive and certainly extremely risky at this water depth,' comments Ismael. Risky is not his style, certainly not extremely risky. That is how Thomas knows him to be.

'China is increasing its influence in Africa and elsewhere in the world every day. Many of our customers are dependent on the red dragon for business. Surely nobody at this table wants to be dancing soon to Beijing's tune - or am I wrong?' Thomas looks around questioningly; the gazes of Ibrahim and Ismael avoid him.

'We explore the moon, even on the side away from the Earth. We will soon be harvesting metals from asteroids. We want to explore what Mars has to offer us. Everyone is in search of these metals and minerals, of which our land masses have only limited supplies. Why shouldn't we be the first to exploit the obvious, namely the deep sea, for our own purposes?'

'And you think we could become a big player in deep sea mining? You've got it backwards,' Ibrahim comments in an even more aggressive tone.

Thomas remains calm, breathes deeply. 'We don't want to become a big shot, we want to become a medium-sized player on the market with excellent long-term earnings: respected, economically successful, trend-setting. To achieve this we have to play our cards wisely. Every country can mine whatever it wants within its two-hundred-nautical-mile zone. In the depths of the world's oceans outside these zones, the UN's International Seabed Authority governs mining. India and China are the driving forces. China is active in the Pacific, India focuses on the southwest of the Indian Ridge. Germany is also involved. France and Russia have set their sights on the Mid-Atlantic Ridge. Great Britain, however, is not even involved in this first phase of exploration concessions.'

'We no longer have an Indian passport. We are British now.'

'No, you're wrong, Maya, I kept my Indian passport. I stand by my roots,' says Pritha. She is a tall woman, with long, dark-brown hair and, for an Indian woman, an almost too white complexion, which is accentuated by her colourful dresses in Indian style. She wears her hair in a ponytail along with large creole-shaped gold earrings. Her arms are littered with thin gold bracelets with ornamentation, and on her forehead she proudly wears a bindi. When she is away on business in London during the winter, she dresses western-style. Her clothes from home in Mumbai, where she has her medical practice, are not warm enough for England. She usually comes to London once a month to help out in the doctor's office of an English friend.

'Your passport combined with mine will be extremely useful, Pritha. I have a German and a Canadian passport and Swiss citizenship.'

'Thomas is quite right,' says Ismael. 'Our passports are the gold of the future. They open the doors at the best conditions in the country concerned. Go on, Thomas.'

'Depending on how the legal and tax situation develops, we will either remain with the Group headquarters in the Swiss municipality of Zug or move again.'

'Is there trouble in Switzerland?'

'Yes, Ismael, the Green Parties are increasingly targeting companies from the extractive industry.'

'Where do you want to move to?' Amal asks and almost shrugs.'

'Surely London is the only place to go?' Ibrahim slaps his flat hand against his forehead, as if that were the only solution, which everyone must recognise immediately.

'London would come into consideration, but there are other

options. Some countries are now putting themselves in place. Luxembourg, for example ...'

'We've been British since my sons were little boys. Here we have prestige and power, and we want it to stay that way,' Amal draws on her authoritarian voice and her power as the female head of the family.

'Exactly,' Maya speaks up. 'I don't want to go back to Switzerland anyway. I want to live here. We're moving back to London, Thomas!'

'Where you live ... determines the business,' Avidya raises his barely audible voice. 'If we want ... that it continues ... so well ... we must be farsighted ... act reasonably ... must ... must stick together.' He rises as high as he can, puts his fist on the table with his last ounce of strength and collapses again. Now he slumps in his wheelchair as if he had been shot.

'Your time, Stepfather, is over. Now we decide what our generation wants and who will be boss in the future,' Ibrahim announces. He stands up and, with a crack of his fist, strikes the table as if to suggest that he is deciding now.

Everyone looks at Avidya, curious to see if he still has the strength to keep a rebellion in check.

'I ... I have appointed Thomas ... as my successor,' he breathes in barely audible tones.

'What?' Ibrahim exclaims loudly and raises his arms with an angry expression. 'That's out of the question!'

Avidya pulls himself to the tabletop with both hands, using all his strength. 'Silence,' he gasps, 'I ... hold the majority of the company's shares ... must ensure ... that the most capable ...'

'I won't take any more orders from you. Our father, Jibrīl bin Mohammed Ali, founded the company. We had the money. You're just a street dog who snuck in here, took everything and sullied it with his Indian name. Do you really think the company will be called Vijay one day longer when you've finally kicked the bucket?' Ibrahim rumbles back.

'Nobody talks to my father like that,' Pritha insists.

'Shut up! Like Maya, you're just holding out your hand for money without contributing.'

Avidya closes his eyes, lets go of the edge of the table and collapses completely. 'I ...' Pritha rises and rushes to him, feels his pulse, looks him in the eyes and mouth and then sits down again in her seat, closely observing him.

'What?' asks Ibrahim, who is still standing.

'Sit down, my son. Avidya is terminally ill. He has pancreatic cancer. Pritha, as his doctor, and Thomas, as CEO of Vijay Group, have known for some time.'

Thomas suspects that Amal wants to discredit him in this way and thus shove him out of the way. Which of her sons will now slam the battle axe into the table against him? Or is this all just for show, and has Amal long since informed her sons so that they can eliminate him right here and now? He doesn't know the answer.

Maya's face betrays surprise and horror. She gets up, rushes around the table and hugs her father convulsively from behind. Without him, she might be a saleswoman in a store or a maid somewhere. She is smart enough to realise that.

Avidya gurgles. Maya remains behind his wheelchair, presses her head against his and cries unrestrainedly. Amal gets up, goes to Maya, hugs her, calms her down and leads her out.

Thomas suspects what is to come. Pritha knows nothing about business, only worries about her father, and before he dies on the spot, she will him back to bed. The two brothers can then make short work of Thomas.

'What can you tell us about this, Pritha?'

'All we can do now is ease the pain, Ishmael. How soon will it end? I do not know. Above all, he needs to rest, to take it easy and stay away from anything that could further weaken his immune system.'

'Then I hereby cancel our family meeting. We must all calm down and reflect.'

'I think that's the most sensible thing to do, Ishmael.' Pritha rises, attends to her father and slowly guides him out of the room in his wheelchair.

Thomas breathes out as imperceptibly as possible. The battle is on. After Pritha and Avidya have left, Ismael stands up and closes the door behind them. *Two against one, consummately contrived*, Thomas thinks.

Ismael takes a seat again and looks at him insistently. 'Now that we know about what a decision needs to be made, we men should think carefully among ourselves about how to proceed.'

'I won't accept him in the boss's chair!' Ibrahim points his index finger at Thomas. If he had a gun in his hand, he'd probably pull the trigger. 'Thomas has no shares. His salary is far too high, with a ridiculously high bonus package on top. If he hadn't married Maya, he wouldn't be sitting at our table. We don't need him. He just said himself that his business is going down the drain.'

Ismael turns to Thomas. 'How do you see your future without Avidya?'

Thomas looks back calmly and remains silent. He doesn't want to lay his cards on the table, not until he knows whether Aviday's will has indeed been made in his favour and is legally valid.

'Ismael, I appreciate your level-headedness,' he finally replies calmly, while his neck muscles are already giving him headaches. 'You heard for the first time today how things are with Avidya; at least I suppose so, maybe I'm wrong.' He observes exactly how Ibrahim reacts. He smiles. Now Thomas knows that Amal has been rehearsing things in the background for quite some time already. So he must doubt whether he will actually get a part of Avidya's shares in the Vijay Group. 'We should try to make the time that Avidya still has left as pleasant as possible for him, while we all think things over thoroughly.'

Ismael smiles and leans forward, eyebrows raised in unmistakable interest. It is now clear to him that Thomas cannot be lured into the trap. 'I will call a new family meeting in due course. May Allah have mercy on us.'

Merciful? Thomas' heart cramps. They will hardly be merciful to him and Avidya.

KOLWEZI, 3 JANUARY 2020

On this patch of red-brown earth, the bullets hit my mother and grandmother in the back and in the back of the head on the 13st of December 1999. I turn 180 degrees and look at a busy factory gate thirty yards away. Heavy lorries rattle in and out amid heavy rain. All under the eyes of guards in military-looking combat uniforms, black berets on their heads and machine guns in their hands. A barbed-wire fence, probably 15 feet high, shields the mine from intruders. Between the mine area and me, poorly but colourfully dressed women, children and also men pass by with plastic bags, buckets and sacks. All are dripping wet. *United Metals and Minerals* is written in blue letters on a white background on a sign at the entrance to the mine. A bitterly cold shiver runs through my whole body, despite the oppressively humid air and almost 86 degrees Fahrenheit. On the paved main road, more trucks rumble past, many with Chinese characters on them. On the other side of the road are wooden sheds, as far as I can see. They are poorly protected against rain by thick plastic tarpaulins, the kind of sturdy shopping bags we use in the supermarkets. Most of the tarpaulins flutter in the wind, because only pieces of self-made rope attach them provisionally to the board sheds. An old woman has been watching us for some time. She has a colourful, flowing robe, a cloth artfully wrapped around her head and a dented umbrella in her hand. She waves us over to her on the other side of the street.

Walikia and I set off from grandfather Elyas' house in Kinshasa for Kolwezi in the morning of the 1st of January in her heavy Toyota SUV, the boot well filled with everything we needed for such a trip to the south of the Congo. 'You are vaccinated but not immune,' said grandfather Elyas as he bid me a tender farewell with a kiss on the forehead. He did not want to let go of me at all. He is like a huge, strong teddy bear, wide face, huge nose, protruding ears and huge, happy eyes. Every day since my arrival on the 27st of December, we had spent hours together talking, making nonsense, laughing and eating. And again and again he lovingly embraced me and kissed me on the forehead. I am one-metre-seventy tall and yet I only reach up to his chin. Again and again he asked Walikia if she had thought of everything. And urged her to protect his Lucia and never let her out of her sight. We were not going to the east of the Democratic Republic of Congo, to Goma, to the border with Rwanda. There, where the coltan mines are, guerrilla troops are still waging daily war for control of this source of wealth. Too dangerous, said Grandfather. I am only allowed to go to Kolwezi, in the south of the country. I clearly felt that he would rather keep me with him. But he also wants me to see the place where my drama began. Walikia and I have brought boiled, clean water and food, small banknotes and cigarettes to pave the way. We were going to bypass areas of unrest. But Grandfather Elyas still has no peace of mind and wants to be called in the morning and evening. We should avoid the Chinese comptoires like the devil. 'The Chinese have Africa in a stranglehold. Everywhere it is swarming with them. They only admit to unpleasant things when there is absolutely no way to cover them up.'

This warm and humid, wet developing country - I already came to understand that much in the first few days in Kinshasa - is mega-hard on the people. The poorest make ends meet with odd jobs. They only own the clothes they wear. They sleep under bridges and on the side of the road. They eat when they have a few francs in their hands. The street food stalls, which are everywhere, generate income for the slightly less poor who run them. If they weren't all walking around with such bright big eyes and in such colourful clothes, the sight of children barefoot or running around in broken plastic sandals would tear my heart out.

We Keitas are among the privileged people in the

Democratic Republic of Congo. Walikia is and Grandfather was a university professor. Both are civil servants with a regular and reliable income and pension. Walikia and her children had been showing me around the city in the last few mornings. How cheerful they were, despite all the things that disgust me. Huge bugs, beetles, spiders and vermin are crawling and creeping everywhere. This is sheer madness in all other respects, too. Few stretches of asphalt, instead muddy roads with holes and puddles. No water and no electricity for hours, sometimes, so they say, not for days. The Internet is so slow that you can forget it. But still, the Keitas are among the twenty percent who have any electricity at all. That's crass.

'Jambo, I can help you?" the old woman asks us when we have finally crossed the road at the mine in Kolwezi and stand in front of her. She watches us from top to bottom. 'You look like her, and that's exactly where it happened.'

'Jambo' we reply, shake her hand and introduce ourselves. Gloria is her name; she looks at me from top to bottom like the body scanner at an airport. I look at her too. She only has one front tooth left, her skin is wrinkled; I can't guess her age, but her light-brown eyes are wide awake and sparkle like the stars. She looks at me piercingly. My appearance should not really be noticeable here. I'm also consciously wearing the same as Walikia: a light, colourful cotton dress and, because of the mud, sturdy, ankle-high hiking boots. Only my behaviour ... I seem insecure and clumsy. Gloria takes me by the hand and leads us into her wooden hut. It has a window to the back, away from the road, or rather an opening into which a dented wire mesh is inserted and a mosquito net is stretched over it. She points to small stools standing directly in the reddish brown mud. We sit down. She pours yellowish water from a plastic canister into a screw-on glass without a lid. Walikia immediately declines politely. No, we would not be thirsty, thank you very much. Gloria takes the glass for herself, drinks and sits down with us. Walikia and I have 100 litres of boiled Kinshasa water in ten canisters with us. Even in Kinshasa, drinking water from the tap is not possible for me. The groundwater in Kolwezi, however, is contaminated with metals due to the mining activities, full of germs and bacteria. Walikia explained this to me when we loaded the water canisters into her car. Now I see what she meant. The water in Gloria's glass would be forbidden in Belgium, even for cattle.

'You saw with your own eyes what happened back then, Gloria?' Walikia speaks French to her, so I can follow too.

'I stood next to Shaira, a bullet whizzed past my ear and I immediately threw myself on the ground. But Shaira and Amaike had no chance. The first bullets already hit them.'

My throat closes up, my hands start to tremble.

'You remember that Amaike was pregnant, don't you?'

'Yes, when the shooting stopped, other women came running, and we both carried them to a car which we stopped, then brought them to the hospital in Kolwezi.'

'Did tha demonstrate with my mother and grandmother?'

'You're the girl who was born alive at the last minute, aren't you?'

'Yes, I'm Lucia.'

'I heard your first cries.' She takes both my hands, turns them up and looks at them devoutly. Then she looks at the birthmark on my left forearm. 'God is good to you, my child. Follow the stars.'

'We put her up for adoption in Belgium so she could grow up without danger.'

'I know, I know. Shaira ordered it herself back at the hospital just before she closed her eyes.'

Gloria looks at me once again with a vengeance.

'Please, tell me about back then. Tell me what happened to my mother and grandmother.'

Gloria lets my hands go, rises and shakes her head. 'No.'

'Why not?'

'You must see it with your own eyes ...'

Together we drive north in Walikia's car for about fifteen minutes. We cross the national road N39, on which loaded trucks, heavy jeeps, mopeds and bicycles are criss-crossing each other. The drivers honk, shout and gesticulate wildly. Over a muddy track between man-high grass that claps against the car, we finally reach the edge of a village surrounded by tall trees. Walikia stops the car on a kind of village square and we get out. It is swarming with mosquitoes. I do not brush them away. I have been sprayed and am taking pills.

'Four hundred thousand people in sub-Saharan Africa die of malaria every year. Because of our tropical climate, it is particularly bad in Congo. So please take your pills and always spray yourself, Lucia,' Grandfather has said to me every day since I arrived here.

'United Metals and Minerals expanded the original mine site and snatched our land away from us. They promised us fertile farmland in exchange, concrete houses, a safe well, a school with two teachers, a hospital with a doctor and nurses; and to the men, work in the mine. When the contract was signed, a small amount of money was paid, to keep us convinced that all would go well and we would remain quiet. Now go, Lucia, see for yourself, talk to the people yourself.' Gloria's voice carries anger and bitterness.

I have a look around. The houses are made of clay, partly eaten up by termites. Two have already collapsed. At a large hand pump, children, who hardly wear anything on their bodies, fill yellowish water into glasses and plastic buckets. I go to them, say 'Jambo' and let water run into my hand. It is interspersed with suspended particles. I ask the children in French about their school. There is no school, a little girl answers. Then everyone runs away, barefoot through the mud. I can't find a hospital either. In front of one of the houses a young woman is stamping green plants, maybe vegetables, in a wooden tub. She carries a baby on her back, wrapped in a cloth. Suddenly I hear wailing sounds from close by. I want to know what is going on and ask her in French. 'They are burying a little girl. Over there among the trees.' She points her hand impassively in the direction of the heartbreaking wailing. 'Very few children grow up long enough to make money. The older children work together with the men as porters, or with hand shovels in the wild mines.'

I'm shocked at how jaded this woman says that while she keeps stomping greens. But I guess one hardens up when constantly confronted with death here. Her husband, she says, brings home on a good day about one euro fifty for fourteen hours of the most dangerous work. That is not enough to survive. If something were to happen to him - be it merely a careless step, a careless blow with a pickaxe or a collapsing shaft - they would lose everything. I feel sick, but I'm afraid that's not all.

The three of us get back in the car and continue our journey. I am angry and shocked. Gloria also wants to show me where the digging men of her tribe work. They have not been given jobs in the mine despite all the promises. Migrant workers from other provinces got those jobs. They are more docile.

We arrive at an area surrounded by bushes, get out and follow a narrow path into a kind of pit. A young man with a haggard face is barefoot and lets himself down on a self-twisted rope into a hole in the ground, perhaps five feet in diameter. Two others are standing at the top, holding the rope. We greet them, and Gloria asks them in French to tell us how they earn their money here. When the man has reached the bottom of the pit and they can let go of the rope, one of them begins to talk. 'The three of us dug the shaft ourselves with hands and shovels. We are looking for a layer of cobalt. If we find one, well, we'll have food for a few weeks or months. If we don't find a vein of cobalt or if our hole collapses, which happens quite often because we have nothing to secure the entrance or the walls, we will go to bed hungry and get up hungry for many days and nights.' The man next to him starts to cry. 'Go, go on,' he then says to us. 'Those over there have better luck.' With his head he points to a hill about three hundred feet away. As we walk in the direction indicated, Gloria says, 'They haven't found any cobalt vein. Only reddish brown earth around the hole. Did you see that?' I hadn't paid attention to that, but I believe her immediately.

We climb up the hill. Below us is another pit with many small holes. Here several equally poor-looking men work together with children in small groups. The children are eight or nine at most.

The men heave plastic sacks of dark-brown earth on ropes out of the holes; the children pull them with all their strength a few yards further, empty them, sort the dirt. In the humidity it is hard work.

Shortly afterwards the children fill the bags with the cobalt-containing earth. Then together with the men they load them onto bicycles or small handcarts and take them away. We follow them. At the river, women and children wash away even more unsaleable dirt with big sieves. Then they take the precious earth to a big road, which leads to the eastern border and to the seaports in Tanzania. There seems to be a huge market for cobalt-containing earth here. Thousands of persons are jumping around each other as in a gold rush. One wooden or brick barrack with weighing- and analysis-equipment follows the next. Mainly Chinese, but also a few Indians seem to be in charge here. Open trucks are loaded with sacks by hand. Right in front of us young men without shirts are filling containers of the Congo Dong Fang Mining with loose cobalt soil. A Chinese comes and wants to scare us away. Gloria attacks him eloquently. He turns around and calls for reinforcements. 'Quickly,' says Walikia, 'look briefly at the dealer's counter and then immediately back to the car.'

While Gloria and Walikia are having a battle of words with five Chinese men, I scurry past the barracks' counter. A board with the daily prices is posted. *Ton of 16% cobalt rock $881 - Ton of 3% cobalt rock $55*. Behind the counter is a Chinese man, calculator, pen and paper in front of him. He is calling out a command to his Congolese packers.

'In the Democratic Republic of Congo, it is illegal for foreigners to engage in this kind of comptoire activities, this kind of intermediary trade,' says Walikia, as the three of us sit back in the car and drive off with dirty spraying tyres and a roaring engine.

'Why doesn't anyone fight back?' I ask quietly, still on guard somehow; but inwardly I would like to get out and face the superior forces in battle.

'We Congolese are easily vulnerable. In the financial crisis of 2008, all Chinese and Indian comptoires disappeared from one day to the next. The price for cobalt-containing earth plummeted.

The diggers did not get rid of their sacks for a long time. When the Chinese and Indians returned, it was even clearer who was in charge here in Kolwezi.'

'But don't the powerful in the Congo do anything about it?'

'The Congolese elites set their armed guards loose onto anyone who resists. You have the choice of being shot or leading a miserable life waiting for disaster or an early death. This is not a place to live, Lucia. This is a fight for survival.'

That's why Belgians prefer to go to Namibia on safari or to Mauritius for surfing, just like Mum and Dad did with me. I need to know more. 'What happens to the cobalt-containing earth?'

'The diggers sell it to the comptoires, the comptoires to Congo Dong Fang Mining, who then transform it into pure cobalt. It is then shipped to cathode producers. The cathodes are sold to battery producers and the batteries to producers of smartphones, tablets, computers, e-bikes, e-cars, wind turbines. All products that need high-performance batteries are eligible. No producer of the end products can say with certainty where the cobalt in the batteries comes from. Too many hands in the supply chain and no effective control. This is deliberate and plays into the hands of corruption and crime.'

'And the cobalt mined at United Metals and Mining?'

'Is refined into powder still here in the country. Then it goes through a dealer in London into the same chain: cathode manufacturers, battery manufacturers, end manufacturers.'

'And who owns United Metals and Mining, Walikia?'

'At first the mine belonged to the Anglo-Belgian Union Minière du Haut Katanga. Then it was owned by the Congolese state-owned company Gécamines, which sold it to a company based in London. From then on, the trail runs through nested corporate structures and letterbox companies. The local manager here is a Frenchman. But he's only been on the job for three months and doesn't know his way around. We are observing all this very closely. We hope that at some point the company will expose itself and we can fight for our rights.'

'I will fight with tha.'

'Lucia has to see something else.' Gloria directs Walikia behind the steering wheel to another remote muddy track, which disappears into high grass from both sides. We make progress only at a walking pace. Sometimes the wheels spin briefly. But Walikia is a skilled driver and always manages to bring the car forward. In the end the track comes to an end in a forest.

'Here you can see those who come to our province alone, without a village community and from far away, and have not found work in the industrial mines. They try to survive on their own as wild diggers. They possess nothing, and they have nothing to hope for except to open their eyes again tomorrow.'

We get out. There are no more shacks with tarpaulins or mud-built huts eaten by termites. Here are scrawny twigs from the surrounding trees stuck into the ground and wrapped and covered with torn-up plastic bags that have been tied together. 'This is how thousands live. They sleep on the wet ground. They carry drinking water in canisters over miles.' Gloria's gaze betrays boundless bitterness.

A man wearing only shorts is sitting with a small trembling boy, who may be seven or eight, in front of a hut made of sticks and plastic bags. Gloria greets them both with 'jambo' and offers them her hand; we do the same. The eyes of the boy protrude wide-open from their sockets. He crouches, moaning to his father. 'His whole body aches from pulling up the sacks filled by his father in the hole in the ground,' Gloria translates. 'The little one empties the sacks, throws them back into the hole for his father. They have no one to help them.'

I want to know where the mother is. 'Died,' the man answers me in French. 'We found no cobalt in this hole,' he points to an opening in the ground about ten yards away from us. Then he says something in his dialect, and Gloria translates. 'They haven't eaten in six days.'

Gloria is silent; so is the man, and I know what I have to do. I go back to the car, get two complete daily food rations of mine and a canister of clean water. I also give the father some money, the equivalent of about fifty euros, so that he and his little son have time to start somewhere new. They both cry when I hand over the presents. My tears are flowing as well. I will never forget that for the rest of my life. I swear to myself that I will fight for them.

Walikia and I take Gloria back to her wooden hut at the mine, leaving her food and a canister of clean drinking water too. She thanks Walikia and blesses me. I am embarrassed. When we both are sitting in the car again, I ask, 'Why did Gloria do this?'

'Take it as a lesson in life, showing how the Congo really is, and as a support on your journey.'

'I will.'

'It requires people who hold up the mirror of conscience to exploiters. Since they do not like what they see in the mirror, they blame the mirror.'

Back in Kinshasa, grandfather Elyas and I have a last evening alone. We stand before each other in his meagre study. A simple wooden table with blank sheets of paper, notebooks, a black fountain pen and black ink. In front of the table, a chair with a cushion. From there he looks directly at an avocado tree behind his house. All the walls of his study are filled with wooden shelves brimming with books, from the bare concrete floor to the bare ceiling. Every inch is used. The books are arranged in two rows, in some places even three rows. And in front of the long bookcase there are two armchairs with a little table in-between. It looks like a place to ponder and discuss the essentials.

'I want to give you something, my heart. To take with you wherever you go, my dearest Lucia,' he says with a wistful undertone in his voice. He hands me a booklet with a hard cover, on which is the present national flag of the Democratic Republic of Congo: a light blue rectangle, a five-pointed yellow star at the top left and a thick red ribbon running from bottom left to top right, bordered by two narrower yellow ones. The hand-written title of the booklet on a sticker makes me smile. I accept it with thanks and turn the pages. Poems in the French language, neatly handwritten with a fountain pen ... since 1999 ... every year on 13 December ... about me ... for me ... as he carries me in his heart. At my birth he wrote:

Oh heavenly joy,

drenched in unspeakable suffering -

It tears my heart apart.

I have to swallow, my eyes become moist. Touched, I close the booklet, look up at him, my tears flow unrestrainedly. His too. He takes me in his big strong arms, presses my head gently against his broad chest with one hand. 'Heaven is with you, Lucia, and God is watching over you.'

The next day, on the way to the airport, I and all the members of my family dive into this seething metropolis of twelve million people for the last time, where everything is louder, more colourful, fragrant, damp, smelly, honking and painful than I have ever experienced before. To say goodbye in the departure terminal, all my nieces and nephews kiss me on the cheeks. Grandfather tenderly presses me for minutes, cries, wipes tears from his otherwise happy eyes with his big hands. I do not want to let go of him. Never has a grandfather given me so much love as he has. Walikia hugs and kisses me on the forehead too. She whispers in my ear: 'Use what you have learned.' Then she hands me an envelope with my birth and parentage papers.

'Won't I see tha again?' Walikia doesn't answer.

Dazed by endless love and boundless rage, I sit on the plane back to Brussels. It is the privilege of the white man and all the powerful to do what they want and to impose their will on the world. It is the privilege of the black man and his family in Congo not to die on this very day. I am both white and black, but above all I am a woman who will change that.

HUMANITY LOG

Chronicle time 18.762.020 - 02.22
Project: *Let there be light*
Dr. Thomas Müller (aspect of THEODAR)
Located 51° 29' 12.995' N   0° 10' 12.133' W

'Are you even listening to me?' Ismael drums at the head of the meeting table with two fingers on the table top. Thomas has to give himself a shake; he hasn't mentally arrived at the meeting in the dining room of Amal's and Avidya's residence in the London borough of Chelsea. He finds it difficult to concentrate on the questions. His thoughts are with Avidya, who is wrestling with death in St. Thomas' Hospital on the other side of the Thames. This morning, right after his plane from Zurich had landed at Heathrow, Thomas was first drawn to his sickbed. Avidya no longer recognised him.

'What? Sorry, I can't get Avidya out of my mind.' *Why are we still pretending to be civilised with each other in this dining room?* he asks himself. Ibrahim's and Ismael's knives are sharpened and already shine out from under the edge of the table! Amal, Pritha and Maya have not even appeared. It's the two Ali brothers against him, so it seems.

'Deep-sea mining requires considerably more investment than the industrial mining that we now operate in Congo, Australia and South America,' says Ibrahim, who is sitting opposite Thomas in Amal's chair, opening the actual battle.

'It is, many times over. But if you look at the development of business over the last two years, we are facing difficult times in Congo. If the big players, especially the Chinese, keep their foot firmly on the accelerator ... two more years and we have to sell, taking what they graciously offer us.'

'How do you see the future of our Group then?' Ismael asks calmly and thoughtfully.

'There will also be significant changes in the retail business. End customers will want to know exactly where the raw materials come from that are processed in their mobile phones, tablets, laptops, e-bikes, cars and whatever else they use. We will have to reveal where and how we mine and trade, and provide a reliable and unbroken chain of raw materials.'

'Bollocks! It's enough to have a supply chain certificate and file it away.'

'No, Ibrahim, complete transparency will soon be an imposed reality. You know as well as I do that supply chain certificates were invented to avoid raw materials being used to finance wars. At some point people no longer wanted diamonds on their fingers that are soaked in blood. And you know only too well how many supply chain certificates are fake or bought. Reputable companies have employees who cross check the supply chains of their suppliers. Others hire companies like SGS to do the checking. We don't do that; we close our eyes. It has always worked out well. But it will not go well for long. In deep sea mining, on the other hand, we are on uncharted territory, like Columbus, and are also more invisible underwater. For the curious guys from Global Witness, investigative journalists, local activists and politicians, it is harder to see what we do and how we do it in the deep sea. Moreover, the ocean currents quickly carry away the traces of mining.'

'Columbus, Columbus - didn't he want to go to India but ended up coming out at the other end?'

Thomas has had enough. He no longer wants to play Ibrahim's game. 'Cut the pretence, shall we?' he replies only seemingly calmly, with a lowered tone of voice.

Ibrahim smirks.

'As you wish, Thomas, as you wish.' Ishmael tilts his head towards the door and then looks at his brother. The smirking becomes even wider. Ibrahim packs up his documents, gets up and leaves the dining room without another word.

'I don't want you to have any illusions about your position here, Thomas,' Ismael replies.

'What is that supposed to mean?'

'Avidya will not live to see the next morning. What might be new for you is that he has agreed with our mother that *I* will take over the management of the Group.'

'I don't think so. Not after what Avidya has told me all these years.'

'Well, then he just changed his mind.' Ismael opens the briefcase in front of him, takes out a sheet of paper and hands it to Thomas. His dismissal as CEO and the appointment of Ismael as the new CEO of the Vijay Group, signed the day before yesterday by all shareholders, including Avidya, and effective as of today. Thomas has to swallow. Was he really so naive? Did Avidya just lie to him and use him? He does not know what to say.

'As you can see, all we have to do is talk about the conditions of your departure. If we leave it to the lawyers, we'll both just pay extra.'

'Knowing you, you've already prepared an agreement.'

Ismael smiles smugly, opens his briefcase again and hands Thomas a two-page document. He skims it. A severance agreement, dated today. *They have done a good job*, it shoots through his head.

'We're fair, provided you sign the agreement today.'

'And my bonus for 2019?'

'Out of the question.'

'What if I don't sign the agreement?'

'You know, Maya's whining is nagging at us more and more every day. So our tendency to let you go like an employee with whom we were extremely satisfied is diminishing.'

The Ali family always treated him subliminally like an employee, not like a son- and brother-in-law. Such an undertone was always present in Amal's voice over the years. Thomas thinks back for a moment. He and Maya had agreed on the separation of property when they married. The villa in Rüschlikon is in his name and is free of debts. His personal reserves in Swiss banks, his investments in start-ups, the value of the art on the walls, Maya doesn't even know about that. He is thinking about whether he has a chance for more. This chance depends solely on Avidya's will. Maybe Ismael is just bluffing.

'Thank you, Ismael. Give me a few hours. I'll take my time to consider your offer favourably. I'd like to speak to David and Maya first.'

'Agreed, call me or leave the signed document with Amal.' He gets up, shakes Thomas' hand, walks out and closes the door behind him.

Thomas reads the agreement again carefully. One year's salary severance pay. Separation by mutual agreement, silence on both sides. The Ali brothers, he is sure, have no idea what it takes to run this company. But he must not worry about that now. However, it is gnawing at him how they managed to disempower Avidya before he dies. Thomas decides to go to St. Thomas' Hospital to see Avidya again, maybe somehow talk to him after all. He wants to know, not speculate about what he is up to.

At this moment the dining room door opens. Amal enters, closes the door behind her and almost walks up to his chair. Thomas gets up, not wanting to let this little chubby person look down on him.

'Avidya has just died.' Her face shows no sign of emotion or grief.

Thomas shudders at the coldness of feeling presented. Tears immediately trickle from his eyes, his head sinks down. Dazed by the pain, he sits down on the chair again.

Suddenly he feels her hand on his shoulder. Amal says more than she asks: 'You loved him very much, didn't you?'

He raises his head and looks into her eyes. 'Yes, he was a better father to me than my own.'

'You must go, Thomas. You are too great a burden to our family.'

He can't believe what she's saying.

'Don't look that way ... one day you will understand my words. You don't fit in here. I beg you, take what we're offering you and leave.'

'And what does Maya say?'

'Maya stays here. She filed for divorce this morning.'

'What?'

'You weren't right for each other for a single moment. If you're honest with yourself, then you know that ... just like Avidya and I were never right for each other.'

Thomas takes the glasses off his nose, dries the tears with one of the two clean white handkerchiefs from his trouser pockets and puts the glasses back on.

'I hope you see more clearly now. Maya doesn't want to talk to you anymore. The lawyers will do the rest.'

'Who does she think she is?'

'Whatever it suits her to be.'

'Has she thought even once about David or me?'

'Maya is neither a wife nor a mother! You'll have to take care of David by yourself.'

'Where other women have a heart, she has a Pound Sterling sign.'

Smack - Amal slaps him for it. *Serves me right*, he thinks. *Why did I ever get involved with this woman in the first place?*

'Have the housekeeper pack up Maya's jewellery and clothes and have them flown here by courier.'

Thomas is appalled. *In which Hollywood movie did I live as a fool?* he asks himself. He stands up and looks down threateningly at Amal. She instinctively takes two steps back.

'I was always just your money-making donkey. But rest assured Amal, Ibrahim and Ismael are not capable of running this Group. You will see your fortune melt away like the ice cubes in your gin and tonics. If you want my advice, get help from your sister's husband in Dubai. Even if he is not of the same Muslim faith as your sons, he understands what has to be done and what skills are needed to do it.'

Amal shows no emotion, gives no reply, steps aside to clear the way out for him. Thomas turns back to the table, pulls a pen out of the breast pocket of his jacket, signs both copies of the severance agreement and puts one in his briefcase. He stands up, stretches as high as he can, clamps the briefcase under his arm and walks past Amal to the room door. In an impulse he stops, turns around, pulls his wedding ring off his finger with disdain on his face and throws it at Amal Ali's feet. 'My parting gift for Maya. This should be enough for the next Botox injection.'

'You'll be sorry for that.'

'Will I? I don't think so. Your daughter is a burden for any man who still has his wits about him. And the way she looks today, she's unlikely to find anyone with money to put up with her airs and caprices.'

'You'll pay for those words.'

'Tell her that if she dares to play badly with David or me, we will expose her ugly face to the world. Also tell her we don't want her money. Tell her to keep it. I guess that's all we have to say to each other. Goodbye.'

A minute later, Thomas is standing on the pavement in front of Amal's house in Chelsea, as if hit on the head with a hammer. He turns around and looks up at the tall red brick building with white arched windows. A safe and happy world, but only from the outside. Two boxwood spheres in terracotta pots to the right and left of the dark blue front door feign manners. In front of them, for protection against intruders, the man-high iron grid with sharp points. *Don't dare to touch us*, it says, *you there, outside the door.* Yes, he is outside the door of upper class life again. In silence he quotes his Goethe to admonish himself: *You are ultimately - what you are. Pile wigs with countless curls upon your head, wear shoes that lift you up an ell, and still you will remain just what you are ... Let every wise man hasten away! The place is dreadful.*

Thomas walks away with his head down towards King's Road. *Maya was supposed to be my remedy, the antidote, but I got it wrong. Nothing works, nothing.*

He beckons a black London taxi. His return flight is only booked for the evening. Now he longs for a place of retreat and wants to call David. 'Claridge's Hotel,' he says to the taxi driver. He needs a quiet corner, a little something to eat, wants to drink coffee, think and make phone calls.

'So they just put us both out in the cold on the street? Crass, crass, Pa.'

'I don't know ... When has Avidya ever told me the truth? I feel like I'm in a bad movie.'

'We have Pritha. All the others are just berks.'

'Honestly, I don't know what to believe anymore.'

'Do we have enough money?'

'Don't worry about money, David.'

'Do we have to leave, I mean, away from Lake Zurich?'

'I will have a new top position in the raw materials industry in no time at all, and with Zug in Switzerland has a tax haven for this. Everyone understands that, even the dumbest investor.'

'What makes you so sure, Pa?'

'My experience in the industry. Almost all of them are in this business for only one reason. They want to make money.'

AACHEN, 7 MARCH 2020

It's five o'clock in the morning and a call on my mobile phone wakes me from a restless sleep. *Daddy!* He hasn't called since I left home. Dazed, I accept the call. 'Daddy, is that tha?'

'Yes, my dear child.' His voice is far away, somehow muffled, powerless.

'Is something wrong with tha, Daddy?'

'Elizabeth is dead.'

'What?' I sit up in bed as straight as a candle, rubbing my eyes with my hand and then all over my face.

'Mum is dead, Lucia.'

'It can't be.'

'We were on a skiing holiday in Ischgl. We came back three days ago. She was already feeling terribly sick on the drive home. She couldn't breathe properly, at some point getting almost no more air. I took her to the Sacred Heart Hospital immediately. She was in intensive care for two days. She died half an hour ago.'

'I'm coming, Daddy, right away.'

'No, it's too dangerous. The doctors suspect a virus. I could have it too - or transmit it.'

'But who takes care of tha?'

'Don't worry, Tilly will come and fetch me.'

'Daddy?'

'Yes?'

'I love tha, tha know that, right?'

'Yes, and I know that Mum loved you too, in her own way. Call me whenever you can. But stay in Aachen, please, stay safe.'

'But couldn't Tilly be infected? Tha two could ...'

'Tilly said *there are higher forces at work and for me they are just a breakthrough to self-liberation*. I don't know what she means exactly, but I trust her.'

When we hang up, my heart is sad for Dad, but it doesn't hurt for Elizabeth. My head only formulates questions. Why did she have to die? What did she die of? I get up, take a shower and drink daisy water to wake up properly.

I can help you. A friendly voice resounds in my head, but I am not familiar with it. 'Are tha YESHUA?'

No. My name is HONGYETSEE. YESHUA and I work closely together.

'But how did tha ... I mean ...'

As soon as your thoughts are formed, we can hear them. We master telepathy at the highest cosmic level. You are just beginning to learn telepathy in a land-dweller's body.

'Elizabeth just died.'

I am aware of that.

'I have some urgent questions.'

Urgent for you.

'Tha already know my questions?'

You want to know why and what Elizabeth Peeters died of, right?

'Since tha know everything ...' I'm angry, this is not how I imagined it. It's quiet, I can't hear him anymore. 'Are tha still there?'

Have you calmed down again?

'Tha feel that too?'

Let's put it this way: It has not escaped YESHUA and me that you have firm ideas about how things should be. If they are different or occur differently, you get angry, mad or even freak out. You should rid yourself of that tendency. It does not help you and it does not help your cause.

That hits me and hurts for a moment. 'Who are tha? I do not know tha.'

I am a close confidant of YESHUA. We work as a team when it comes to you.

'Can tha be a little more specific? Who are tha? Have tha been on Earth like YESHUA, and if so, when?'

You bloody well want to know for sure. Very well. I am HONGYETSEE, but I already told you that. I know the people on Earth, their way of living and making it difficult for themselves and others, from my own experience in dense matter. In my most famous incarnation, I was a Russian painter, philosopher, writer, archaeologist and spiritual seeker who intervened in world affairs. Together with my wife Helena and our two sons, I endeavoured on our famous five-year Asian expedition, under the guidance of MASTER MORYA, to explore impulses from cosmic evolution. We then made the results available to people all over the world for their own development. The Tertjakov Gallery in Moscow and a museum in New York, which bears the name I had at the time, testify to this. My name was on the Nobel Peace Prize shortlist several times. A pact between nations bears my name, the Roerich Pact. For this task I was born on 9 October 1874 in Saint Petersburg and died on 13

December 1947 in Kullu, India. Already on 22 March 1941 I incarnated again in Shawano, Wisconsin, United States of America, under the name Wayne S. Peterson. After studying political science, I worked for the Peace Corps for several years and built up a private charity for the poor in Brazil which still exists today. Afterwards I worked in the Diplomatic Service of the United States of America until my retirement. Since childhood I was in contact with MOTHER MARY and over the years I became a close confidant and also a channel for messages from LORD MAITREYA and other Ascended Masters like YESHUA. I report about my cooperation with them in the book 'Extraordinary Times, Extraordinary Beings.' On YouTube you can also watch videos from the year 2013 in which I, together with a highly esteemed and gifted friend, have lent our voice for messages from LORD MAITREYA to humanity. I died on April 20, 2017 in Henderson, Nevada. However, my home is not the Earth. I came long ago to serve. I hope that is enough for you right now.

I am overwhelmed, I don't know what to answer. My heart has weighed a ton since Dad's call, and now all this on top of it. I'll have to go on the Internet and check it out.

Would you like me to continue with your questions now?

'I...' Actually I don't feel like it, but I don't want to let this opportunity pass me by either. 'Yes, please. HONGYETSEE.'

Elizabeth Peeters died of lung failure caused by the coronavirus. The virus has been spreading across the world from Wuhan since early December and will cost hundreds of thousands, possibly millions of people their lives. The Chinese do not want to bring themselves into disrepute, and Western companies, tour operators and restaurants want to continue doing business. Everything depends on how quickly the human family engages in reflection and its members stand up for each other.

'I don't understand. Please explain in more detail.'

A cosmic law demands that accumulated causes be compensated by effects. In the cosmic plan for the development of the Earth there are and were no wars, no abuse, no exploitation, no oppression, no degradation of others or the Earth, let alone pollution. Nor were any destructive acts of nature envisaged such as earthquakes, storms, floods or pandemics.

'That means that in the history of mankind we have set all this in motion ourselves? Is that what tha're saying?'

Yes! And you will have to face the whole mess as a human family, I'm sorry to say. We'll stand by you as best we can, but you have to let us.

'Help us?'

We cannot intervene directly. Your free will must always be respected by us. We can listen to you, offer guidance, but you must act. There is nothing to delegate. Dear God, please do this and that ... No, you must act yourselves; we only help.

'Then there is little hope.'

You are here to make a significant contribution by ensuring that the human family returns to the plan for Earth, recognises itself as one family and lives accordingly.

'Isn't that a bit much to ask? I don't even know the plan, and I'm alone against billions of bullheads, ego-trippers, greedy and power-hungry people. Not to mention being a simple student with little money.

You know the part of the plan you need to know. You just have to remember. You are not alone either. You never have been. Bodies are alone; souls never are.

'I don't want to discuss that now. I want to know what needs to be done about the virus.'

I want, I want, I want. How about what WE should do together?

That remark hurts just as much as the one before.

If you keep your living space clean and tidy, you won't have a load of vermin, fleas and viruses that make your life difficult, right? But the living quarters of many members of the human family are untidy and unclean because other members of the human family dump their rubbish, their sewage, their toxic chemicals, their wrecked ships and much more onto the poorer people because they exploit people, water, air and soil. The wealthy members of the human family only take care of their own room and are then surprised when the vermin and viruses from the rest of the house get into their room as well. The house of the human family must be tidy and clean for everyone. There is only one house for one human family. But some land-dwellers have institutionalised disrespectful domination, and they are constantly competing for power. These are destructive energies that must be balanced, harmonised. And until that happens, the whole planet and all life within it will be going through hard times.

'What can I do?'

The house of the human family must be cleaned. Everyone must work together with respect and good will to keep the house clean and tidy. What is the right thing to do must be decided by all together.

'I saw what is going on in the Congo. A handful decide what is good for them and the masses live in misery.'

First Europeans exploited other countries and people; then Americans, Russians, Chinese and a few more copied them and perfected their methods.

'I will do something about the exploitation of the Congo, tha can believe me.'

What are you planning to do?

'My smartphone, my tablet, my laptop - I've researched that - most certainly have cobalt in their batteries which was dug up by men with their bare hands and sold to Dong Fang, perhaps even by the man and little boy I left my food with.'

No one must be a stranger to you on your way. And you just proved that you understand this in the Congo.

'That was just a nano-drop on a hot mountain. I need the laptop and stuff for my work. But the devices would have to last longer and also become more expensive. And companies don't want that. They want us to always buy the latest model and they offer it for little money.'

Every smallest act of respect, goodwill, kindness and humanity balances the old ego karma and prevents further pandemics, conflicts and injustice.

'That's a heavy package tha're putting on my shoulders.'

No, others carry the heavy package. People who live in places where there are no hospitals, where there is no income, where there is no food, where governments send the military to the streets and death by bullet is even more likely than death by the virus.

'What do I need to do?'

Live the example that there is only one human family in one house, across all languages, cultures and regions! Let your light shine! Everyone is part of the balance of karma that underlies the terrible events which dominate the news.

I let my head hang down, dejected at this view. Then I think of Elizabeth in intensive care, imagine her gasping for breath, losing the fight for her life. I feel bad that I've always bickered with her. 'Why did Elizabeth have to die?'

Many are leaving who cannot follow the path of the new energy now streaming from the cosmos to Earth, or who are blocking the changes it is bringing about.

'What kind of energies are tha talking about?'

From the seventh beam, the violet flame. They are increasingly transmuting everything that does not express the unity of the human family. The time of unlived ideals and lip service is over.

Then suddenly his voice is gone. Is that it? Probably. His message was clear enough. I stay wide awake, excited, can't think clearly, partly because I have an appointment with Robin at ten thirty. Last night he called me, spoke in a short, choppy, halting voice, for the first time since he was summoned back to Singapore by his father in mid-December. Since my birthday congratulations, no phone call, no Facetime, no chat, no text message, nothing at all - Robin disappeared from the face of the Earth. I am pissed off, angry, have an aching heart. What does he still want from me? To stab my heart with a knife again? For us too officially break up? To tell me his parents won't let a coloured woman be his girlfriend? Han Chinese - I've understood that by now - think they're better than us.

At half past ten, Robin and I are sitting awkwardly in front of each other in the Café Dom. Two cups of green tea on the table in front of us. We have always had tea here. They have two kinds of green tea, Sencha and Chinese Love Dream. That dream has now burst. Robin does not dare to look me in the eye. His thick black hair is now cut short. It sticks out like on a hedgehog. I've never seen him like that before. Until now he wore it longer; it fell as gently as his character and the words he formed into poems with ink and brush on rice paper. His gentleness was the first thing I noticed about him when we met in the lecture hall on the first day of study and we exchanged our first few words in English. Like today, he was wearing trainers, jeans, a white shirt and a dark blue blazer. Just as I came into Café Dom from Schmiedstraße at the appointed time, he was already sitting with his back to the wall on the disused church pew at the far right, at the last table by the huge glass window with an exit onto the cobbled Münsterplatz and the tables there. He didn't even look at me, just stared at the table, muttered 'Sit down please' and ordered me a Chinese Love Dream.

'What is this? Will tha explain it to me, please?' I ask quietly and restrain the anger in my voice, although the café is empty and no one is listening. I've never seen myself like this. I'd like to explode.

'Be merciful.' His head almost touches the tabletop. 'You have no idea what I've been through.'

'All right, first thar story. But don't think I've been doing well in the meantime.'

Our tea is brought. Still he doesn't dare to look at me. The waitress looks at us in amazement, but leaves immediately because she gets what is going on.

'When I flew home on the eleventh of December,' he begins stammering, 'I thought something was wrong with my father, my mother, my two sisters or my grandparents.'

I feel the urge to talk in-between, but I somehow keep my mouth shut at the last moment.

'For a Chinese, family and ancestors are something very important, do you understand? For every Chinese family ... whether they're called Ong or Wong or Wang like me.'

Why is he engaging in this miles-long run-up?

'The Ong family once came from China. We have been very successful commodity traders in Singapore for four generations ... I'm supposed to continue this tradition someday ... To prepare for this, my father sent me to study economics at the London School of Economics for three years ... I did an internship at the London Metal Exchange, the exchange for base and other metals in London. Before that I spent a year with the National Wealth Fund of Singapore.'

'Cut to the chase, Robin,' I say in a chill voice. I can hardly hold myself back and claw my hands into my thighs to somehow control the stress. The glass with the tea is still too hot to hold on to.

For the first time he looks at me. His eyes are tearing up. I have to swallow; it breaks my heart to see him like that. But I have to protect myself. I don't want him to hurt me again.

Suddenly there is a clanging at the bar, a glass has been slammed onto the black-grey stone tiles and shattered into a thousand pieces. It couldn't be more fitting - that's how I feel.

'When I was at university in London,' continues Robin, 'I had a girlfriend ... who was from Hong Kong ... Conny Wong. Her father is a bigwig on the stock exchange there. The Hong Kong Stock Exchange bought the London Metal Exchange. It was through him that I got the internship. Conny and I have stayed in touch; we are friends, you understand?'

'Must I?'

'To expand our metal trading business, my father was in Hong Kong last autumn. He also met Conny's father there, several times.'

'So what?'

'They have agreed to do business together ... He's also met

Conny ... she ... he ... He thinks our families belong together.'

'Please speak up, Robin.'

Robin swallows, wipes away the now unrestrained tears with his hand and then clings to his hot glass of Chinese Love Dream with both hands. His head is still hanging down. He continues: 'During the Tang Dynasty ... a great poet and statesman lived in China ... Wang Wei ... I have read you some of his poems.'

I just say 'Right - definitely.' I can't remember the name and I really don't understand why he's making this loop instead of getting down to what really matters.

'Remember the book *300 Tang Poems - Bilingual Edition*? It is on the shelf in my flat next to the statue of Guan Yin. The best poems we Chinese know; Wang Wei is also in it. Do you understand?'

'Sod it! What am I supposed to understand?'

'Father and Mr. Wong have found out that ...'

'What, Robin, what? Spit it out!'

'Wang Wei is our common ancestor ... they therefore want to make the bond between the Wong and Ong families as strong as they can.'

'And?'

'Dad wants me to go to Hong Kong this summer after I receive my bachelor's degree ... open a commodities trading office there...'

'And what the hell does that have to do with us?'

He remains silent. More tears run. Then he looks me straight in the face and breathes: 'And marry Conny ...'

Angrily I jump up. I gotta get out of here. I can't stand it another minute. My heart cries out as if someone had stuck a switchblade in it and now is turning the knife with pleasure in the wound to make it even bigger. 'I don't want to marry her. But ... I must obey Father.'

'You're twenty-five and you're an adult - or am I mistaken?'

'There is a Hokkien saying in Singapore 家己人 (kā-kī-lâng). *One of us.* You are not one of us!'

'No, I am not!'

'My mother consulted the I Ching. It says: *The creative achieves sublime success, fostered by perseverance.*

'Business marriage from the oracle book. I can't believe it.'

'*Fate cannot be fooled*, says the I Ching.' 'Have tha told your parents about us?'

'No.'

'You coward!'

'I owe obedience to my father. To a Chinese, family means everything, and the I Ching says my father is right.' Robin slowly rises, looks me in the eye, but stands there frozen.

'To me, family means love, tha hear? Love!'

'I prayed for mercy every day at Guan Yin Temple in Jalan Toa Payoh ... it did not help ... My father ...'

'How long have tha been back in Aachen?'

'Six... '

'Six days'?

'Yes.'

'What? And only now tha deign to give a sign of life? Let me tell tha something, tha self-righteous coward. My biological mother and with her my grandmother were shot in the Congo on the day of my birth. Only by a miracle did I survive. My Congolese family gave me up for adoption in Belgium so that the killers would not murder me too. My grandfather lost three women he loved in one day ...'

Robin turns deathly pale. My face is probably turning bright red right now and I start crying, too. Then I get myself together again.

'And just so you know, Elizabeth died this morning, and I ... I can't stand to see tha here at the university for another second. So ... now you know. I'm about to get on a train to Switzerland, to my projec which the professor got me there, and so I'm off! I have nothing more to say to tha, except goodbye and be happy with one of your kind and thar business oracle.'

Before he can reply, I turn around and run out of the back of the Café Dom onto Münsterplatz, crying, and turn right between the tables, then left onto the yard of the Cathedral and from there into Aachen Cathedral. Those are only fifty big steps. I want to be alone now. I want to cry, be sad, be angry, without anyone talking silly to me. My heart is about to burst. I put my right hand on it. It hurts so much.

The dome empties at this very moment. I slip into the entrance, down the three steps and then through the main door made of glass and black iron bars. Inside, the air is sweet and suffused with the scent of incense. I instinctively turn left, walk the few steps to the entrance of the gothic St. Nicholas Chapel, up the four steps, enter through the heavy glass and iron lattice door and leave the world of cruel people behind me. There is nobody in here. Thanks be to Spirit. I let myself fall into the first bench, right in front of the picture of the Sorrowful Mother of God. With folded hands and lowered gaze she endures her suffering. I must do the same now. A bouquet of white and red roses stands in front of the wooden frame of the picture. Pilgrim candles are burning on the walls to the right and left on artistically forged frames. What am I actually doing here? I usually do not go into the cathedral. I was only here for a guided tour, like every student at university probably did in their first days in Aachen. I marvelled at the splendour and artistry of the

Barbarossa chandelier, the dome mosaic, the Pala d'Oro at the main altar, the golden shrine, the brightly coloured leaded glass windows in the choir hall and the Throne of Charlemagne. But since then, and that was two and a half years ago, I have not been back here. As if by a miracle, however, the world is letting me cry here in peace. I ask myself: *What do I have to hold onto now?* I dry my eyes with the tissue handkerchief from my shoulder bag. Elizabeth dead, Daddy and Tilly perhaps in danger, mother dead, father unknown and those who love me adoringly, like grandfather Elyas, thousands of miles away on another continent.

My heart suddenly gets hot and it stops hurting.

I promised you I would always be with you.

It is his voice, clearly, but I want certainty; maybe I am going crazy. 'YESHUA, is that tha?' My head is dazed, but his answer comes through my heart.

Yes, I am, and I am with you.

'What are tha doing here?'

I am always here in the cathedral and talk to everyone who comes to me and genuinely seeks counsel.

'Are tha serious?'

I am a teacher for anyone who truly searches within.

I breathe deeply, blow my nose with the already-moist tissue; I am quite agitated ... angry ... confused ... mega sad.

'Do tha know what was going on at Café Dom next door? I mean, do tha know what Robin said?'

Of course - I was with you and calmed you down as best I could and for as long as I could.

'Why, YESHUA, why must all this sweep over me now? Why are they all abandoning me?'

There would be many answers to that question. Robin has yet to learn that true family is something other than ancestors, names and selected bloodlines. Those who create or maintain separation choose the path of suffering.

'But can't tha help?'

The free will of man is always to be respected by me and all others here in Shambala.

'So what do I do now?'

Take care of the things you can take care of.

'Great - now what does that mean?'

HUMANITY LOG

Chronicle time 18.762.020 - 03.11
Project: *Let there be light*
Dr. Thomas Müller (aspect of THEODAR)
Located 47° 9' 58.201' N   8° 30' 55.782' E

Avidya was cremated. The funeral service, which wasn't really one, took place in the inner family circle. That was twenty-four hours ago. Now Ismael is standing in Thomas' Zug office on the top floor of headquarters to officially take over the position of CEO. A formal and distant 'good morning' between the two is the only greeting. Thomas took his photos of David and Maya off his desk only last night so that no employee would notice anything. The signature folder for the CEO contains a pile of documents. As he could not sign anything anymore when he returned from London, he had no choice but to inform his secretary. Ismael looks around in the dignified Swiss elegance. Fine wooden table and shelves, cognac-coloured leather, discreet carpeting that swallows the words which no one is allowed to hear. Ismael passes the inside of his hand over one of the four armchairs in the meeting corner, then stops in front of the Himalayan painting in bright salmon and blue tones and looks at it with obvious pleasure.

'Stunningly beautiful, isn't it?'

'You said it, Thomas. Nicholas Roerich?'

'Yes. It's mine. I will ask my secretary to have it delivered to my home.'

'I will ask *my* secretary to send it to you.' With that, Ismael sets the tone for their hand-over.

'Why didn't you come to the funeral service?'

'I carry my grief for Avidya in my heart, and a picture of him is in my home office. I didn't have to come for his sake; and for you it would have been annoying to be confronted with someone who doesn't fit into the family.'

'I guess so.'

'Let's not pretend that this is more than just an employer-employee relationship. Let's finish this professionally and I am out of here.'

Ismael wrinkles his nose. 'I guess that's what you Germans are like, huh?'

'What does it matter?' Bitterness rises in Thomas.

'I'm just observing.'

'Let's leave your prejudices out of this. German-Canadian-Chinese blood flows in my veins. German-Canadian-Chinese-Indian-Lebanese blood in my son's veins.'

'Well, let's not go into that now.' Ismael sits down at the desk in the boss's leather armchair, enjoys a brief glimpse of Lake Zug and then opens the document folder.

'Since you called me off a few days ago, you have to sign all of this. As you can see, a lot has accumulated. You also have a lot of appointments: Meetings with the representatives of major customers, some festivities for the next few months. Oh yes, and next week a very important funeral in Johannesburg, where you should definitely show your face for business purposes. By the way, did you know that Robert Wong's daughter got engaged in the commodities industry?'

'No.'

'I congratulated Robert by telephone this morning, right after the news was officially announced in Hong Kong. He was flattered that congratulations came from Europe too, and within minutes of the announcement.'

'In these things you are incredibly fast. Do you have some kind of sixth sense?'

'One does what one can, Ismael. Such things always pay off in business.' Thomas keeps to himself the fact that he uses David's SAM three times a day to have all his contacts scanned for news and announcements in the global press and industry news, as well as on online platforms and in the social media. He wants to be always up to date with events. 'I suggest we go through the folder together, and in the process I will introduce you to all the day-to-day business and issues such as personnel and so on. I assume that you bring different ideas to some projects, so we should also stop what does not suit your future plans.'

'First of all, I would like to speak to all employees, but only those who are staying. First you have to dismiss all those involved in your deep sea mining project and have them leave the building immediately. Meanwhile, I'll read through the folder, and then you can hand over the day-to-day business, about which I have some questions.'

'You are the boss now.' Thomas is appalled about the depth of Ismael's aversion to his deep sea project. He turns on his heels and leaves the CEO's office. His breath stops, his heart races as he makes his way to the deep sea team leader. *How am I supposed to convey this to the team leader and the employees? Get up, get out right now - you're no longer wanted, go home?* His steps become slower as he opens the glass entrance door into the corridor to the opposite wing. He is desperate to strike the right note, mumbling new sentence variations to himself. Or should he go to the personnel manager first? No ... he'll do it himself ... or maybe not? He is but five steps away from the team leader's office when his door opens. A young, beautiful woman with Afro curls and milk chocolate brown skin in a green wool dress with military style lace-up boots approaches him. Thomas is once again breathless.

'Grüzi,' she says awkwardly and wants to walk past him.

'Know ... hm ... do we know each other?' Thomas asks in a trembling voice.

'No, I don't think so. My name is Lucia Peeters, I'm on an internship here ... I make calculations, analyse the effects of deep sea mining on the ecosystem. The team leader recruited me through my professor in Aachen. I am a student of Geo-Resource-Management at the RWTH, working on my Bachelor thesis on the Anthropocene as well.'

'Thomas Müller ... enchanted,' he replies. 'I will not shake your hand, Corona caution, you understand.'

'Something wrong with tha? Are tha not feeling well? Tha're chalk-white around the nose, and thar voice is hardly audible.' Lucia looks at him worried.

'Me? No! What gives you that idea? I just have to talk to the team leader about something very delicate. Even at my age, there are still things you do for the first time, if you know what I mean.'

'I see.' She moves to the side and then walks past at a distance. Thomas needs a moment to collect himself. He straightens his tie, clears his throat and pats his cheeks with the inside of his hand to get some colour back in his face. Abandoning his favourite project, saying 'pack up and get out' makes him feel like an asshole. There are situations that burn themselves irrevocably into the dark corners of the mind. For Thomas this is another one of those painful moments.

'This is the most unusual way to get laid off I've ever experienced.' The team leader is still irritated and overwhelmed at the same time as Thomas sits with him, the other dismissed employees and Lucia Peeters in the early afternoon in the best restaurant in Zug and apologises with a terrific meal for what happened in the morning.

'I want to continue this project. I want to shape the path of deep sea mining. Your severance pay should be plenty for the time being and I would be pleased to have you back in my team soon, at another company that is able the discern the signs of the times ... well, you know what I mean ... And you, Ms. Peeters,' he turns sideways to her, 'I will look after you separately right after this.'

'You should, Dr. Müller, you really should. This woman is brilliant, and I don't usually say that after just a few days of working together.'

'Anyway, it's not my style to let someone down.' Thomas croaks and drinks quickly from his water glass.

The team leader orders two bottles of Prosecco on his account, and everyone toasts to the future together. Only Lucia stays with water. 'No thanks, I don't drink alcohol. It gives me an immediate headache,' she says with a smile and raises her glass of water with everyone. A gush of joy and horror rushes through Thomas' whole body. He excuses himself, goes to the men's room to calm down and think, and then briefly walks outside the restaurant to phone David.

After a short conversation his son is informed and agrees. Thomas is determined to keep Lucia Peeters in Switzerland. He reckons with a lockdown in the country because of the corona virus, which has spread to Western Europe via a bar in Ischgl, Chinese companies in northern Italy and the airports. He wants to bring Ms. Peeters home with him. She is to continue working with him on the deep sea project, either until she has to return to university after the end of the semester break or until he gets a job with another company and can integrate her there right away.

An hour later, he has already accommodated Lucia in the guest room, given her access to the Internet and, in his view, provided her with everything she needs to get back to work in home office. He was amazed at the scanty luggage and the two crystal jugs with quartz stone she travels with. When he comes into the living room late in the evening, Lucia is sitting in the armchair with a booklet. She looks into the fireplace, Bea lies at her legs for a cuddle.

'Oh, look, you can light a fire and Bea is already at your feet. Does it always go that fast?'

'I like dogs, and dogs like me. I always wanted one myself, but my Mum wouldn't allow it. So I always petted the neighbours' dogs and went for walks with them when the owners were too busy.'

She strokes Bea's head lovingly and Bea comes even closer. Thomas is fascinated.

'And what are you reading, may I ask?'

'Poems—my grandfather Elyas wrote them for me. I read them every night. *My Asteroid B612* is the title of his booklet. Funny, if it wasn't so sad.'

'Sad? What is sad about that? No one has ever written poems or rhymes for me. Except Goethe in his *Faust*, but they are addressed to everyone.'

'On each of my birthdays, Grandfather Elyas wrote a poem, waiting to see me, waiting to give them all to me. He waited and hoped for twenty years, wasn't it crass? Anyway, they should be a signpost through my life and remind me of him. Tha know, I've only had this booklet for a few weeks. It touches me so deeply ... spurs me on. Shall I read tha one of his poems?

'Of course, if that isn't too personal.' Thomas rubs his itchy nose and sits down on the sofa opposite her.

'Bea, now you'll have to do without my hand for a little while.'

She pulls back her hand and opens the booklet again. Bea looks up at her almost sadly. Thomas can't understand why his son's dog reacts so strongly to this young woman.

'On my fourth birthday, 13 December 2003, Grandfather wrote:

What head and hand compel
Creates a living hell!

What do tha think?'

'Wisely and very succinctly expressed. I guess you don't understand something like that until you've fallen flat on your face.'

'Have tha ever done that?'

'Just now, but don't tell anyone.'

Both have to laugh.

'For me, this poem has a painful truth to it right now.'

'May I ask why without offending you?'

'Because,' she has to swallow, 'because ... well, because my boyfriend broke up with me to bow to his father's financial and family interests. He is marrying for reasons of business and ancestry.'

'Excuse me?' Thomas needs to cough.

'Exactly, what an idiot! Thank tha for agreeing with me. I thought I was the only one.' Her eyes moisten. 'I know I shouldn't cry over him, but ... it hurts. I can't bear to see him at the university. But after the summer semester, thanks to Spirit, he's gone forever.'

Thomas gets up, pulls out a freshly starched white handkerchief from his pocket and hands it to her. 'Is there anything I can do to cheer you up?' With the second handkerchief, which he then pulls out of his trouser pocket, he dabs his own face extensively.

Lucia shakes her head and blows her nose. 'Tell me about tharself.'

'So, well, look around ... I've made it to the top. My father didn't have anything like this to show for himself at that age.' Thomas lets his eyes wander through the living and reading room. He is relieved that there is no empty or half-empty gin and tonic glass anywhere. But he keeps that to himself and changes the subject. 'You said this morning that you are concerned with the age of mankind as the dominant influence on the Earth. Some people call the Anthropocene the 'Age of the Earth Destroyers'. Do you think we are still going to save the planet? Or have we already gone too far, in the way we destroy our environment with plastics, chemicals, slash-and-burn agriculture and monocultures?'

'Hm.' Lucia puts the handkerchief in her trouser pocket. 'Tha should know that better than I do. As an exploiter of natural resources in mining, tha are involved in it every day. Tha see with thar own eyes every day what we do there as well. Do tha regularly clean up all thar mine sites and the surrounding area to stop or even reverse the contamination of the groundwater?'

'I'd like to, but it doesn't pay off. The prices of metals are set by the market, and the Chinese are pushing them down wherever they can. I need my profit margin in order to do business, which means financing the activities and standing up to the Chinese. There is no budget for something like soil and groundwater remediation, at least if you want to prevent China from taking away our future and making us look stupid without raw materials.'

Lucia stares at him in horror and wants to reply, but Thomas' smartphone rings in his pocket. He pulls it out, looks at the display, raises his free hand towards Lucia and says: 'One moment, Ms. Peeters.'

'Good morning, Giacomo, to what do I owe the honour?'

'How are you, old friend?'

'Thanks for asking. I'm sitting at home in front of the fire and answering the phone as often as it rings.'

'Has it rung a lot?'

'You're not calling to ask me that, are you?'

'Heard a rumour and wanted to ask if I could tempt you. People of your caliber don't come around too often.'

'Make me an offer in deep sea mining I can't refuse, and I promise you a quick decision.'

'Well, that's all I need to know now. You'll hear from me again, Thomas, very soon indeed.'

'I am glad, Giacomo.' Thomas presses the off button and wonders what that means now. Is he really happy that Giacomo is interested in him? Maybe it was just a test to find out if he has really left the Vijay Group. Thomas puts the smartphone back in his pocket.

'Looks like cool-headed calculators like tha are in demand in the raw materials world. As a student I had never imagined it to be so cold-blooded.' Lucia is annoyed, with him and with herself, that she accepted his offer.

'You almost pretend that I clap my hands enthusiastically in the morning and say: "Let's exploit man and nature once again." No, no, we live in a world of constraints. These include that the strongest get more and the best leaders quickly get a new job. I think it will take another week or two, then I will have enough offers to choose from, so that David and I can decide.'

'Is he thar life partner?' Lucia is curious. While she was sitting in front of the fireplace with Bea and wasn't sure if it was smart to accept his offer, she also thought about using this chance to collect information she wouldn't otherwise have access to. Now, at this very moment, she realises in a flash that she has made the right decision. If she desires with her heart and soul to change the world of cobalt mining in the Congo, she needs to know the internals of the extractive industry as a whole.

'No, how did you get ... Oh, no, no—David is my son, eighteen, studying computer science at ETH Zurich. He should actually be here already. We will decide together where we go next. I don't make a decision he doesn't agree with, you know? We are very close to each other. I adore my son.'

'My adoptive father is an intellectual henpecked husband, criminal judge. He seldom stood up to protect me when there was trouble between his wife and me.'

'Was there lots of arguing?'

'Daily, actually several times a day.'

'I see. Where do you actually come from? Please don't misunderstand, I don't mean that in a racist way. I have blood in my veins from three continents and cultures.'

'I grew up with adoptive parents in Belgium. My German-born adoptive mother died last week.'

'My condolences.'

'Thank tha. Horrible as this may sound, I am not sad. She couldn't manage to show love to me.'

'I see. And your adoptive father?'

'There is a bond of the heart between us. My godmother is taking care of him now.'

'You're not there for him?'

'He feels guilty. He doesn't want to keep me any longer from going my own way. He says: "Don't put yourself in danger too, it could be a contagious virus."'

An amazingly calm young woman, or is she just playing it cool? Thomas is not sure. 'Interesting, Ms. Peeters—do you already know where you're headed next?'

'Ever since I met my blood family in the Congo a few weeks ago, travelling around, seeing where my mother was shot, seeing the misery of people living near a cobalt mine, yeah, I think so, yeah. I'm completing my Bachelor's, will be starting my Master's in the winter semester, and at the same time I'm becoming an activist. I always thought that I would only become a scientist, but that alone is not enough. I will not be used to exploit people and nature.'

Thomas shrugs briefly.

'I could not live in a house like thars until I have relieved the suffering of the people. I'd rather give away part of what I earn.'

'But you don't earn much as an activist. And scientists who take to the streets or seek controversy in the social media don't get good jobs in a company; and if they do, it is only for PR purposes.'

'Money is not important as long as I make the world a better place.'

'But only with the raw materials we mine is it possible to have a smartphone in your pocket, and an inexpensive one at that.'

'People will have to learn to live with less so that everybody can have a decent life.'

'Do you really think you can do this? People are selfish. They only uphold values as long as it costs them nothing.'

'Not all of them: very few in my generation, actually.'

'Well, I guess guys like me are in for a rough time, huh?'

'Tha can bet on that.' She smiles tactically, thinks maybe she's told him too much already.

'Aren't you a bit hypocritical yourself? You're sitting here in my house, not in the youth hostel.'

'I would have gone back to Aachen today if you hadn't invited me to stay and continue working on the project with tha.'

'Why did you take up the invitation?'

'In order to at least understand the projec, I will probably need the knowledge if at some point I take a stand against exploitation in the deep sea.'

'So that's what you are!' Thomas must laugh. He thinks this is youthful chatter that lacks any reference to reality. She is only twenty; he has to be indulgent, he is with David as well.

'Why did tha invite me? What do tha hope to achieve? Tha could have asked the team leader to continue working for tha. Or is he too expensive?'

'Touché! I admit it, I too act selfishly, even extremely selfishly. I like you with your sincere manner. In short: you are excellent and still available at a reasonable price. The team leader has assured me that neither he nor anyone else on the team can do what you are supposed to do on the project'.

'Tha want the calculations, don't tha?'

'Of course, and I want you because the team leader told me your professor considers you to be a once-in-a-century genius. And as CEO I am convinced that the one with the best team always wins.'

'At least tha are honest.'

'On this point, at least.' He laughs. 'You are a rare phenomenon, Ms. Peeters, in every way. You'll have more fun finding out for yourself what makes me tick. But I'm not going to make it easy for you.'

'I accept the challenge, and I'm going to give tha a run for thar money.' She laughs to take the edge off her answer.

'Okay, it's a deal, but now it's time to go to sleep. Has the maid shown you around?'

'Up the stairs to the right, huge room with a grandiose bed, fire in the fireplace, large desk with high speed internet connection and printer, separate dressing room and a bathroom for the gods. Who usually lives in this divine guest room?'

Thomas has to laugh again. 'My late father-in-law always stayed there when he came to us on business. That was seldom enough the case. Otherwise it remains empty. When you wake up tomorrow, just come down to the kitchen, take whatever you want, or ask the housekeeper to make you whatever you want. Okay?'

'It'll take some getting used to ... Okay, let's call it a day. Good night.' She gets up and Bea follows her straight away.

'Good night.' Thomas looks after her and has to smile. He is curious what will happen when David comes home. What will Bea do then? His neck muscles are tense. His head is buzzing and his heart is pounding. Lucia Peeters triggers unexpected states of stress in his body.

HUMANITY LOG

Chronicle time 18.762.020 - 03.12
Project: *Let there be light*
Dr. Thomas Müller (aspect of THEODAR)
Located 47° 9' 58.201' N   8° 30' 55.782' E

'Did you fall out of bed?' When Thomas steps into the kitchen, Lucia is sitting at the kitchen island, her laptop in front of her, and apparently concentrating on her work. Her glass of green tea is half-full, and Bea is lying at her feet, as if it were the most beautiful place in the world. Thomas was brooding all night and hardly slept a wink. Doubts were gnawing at him. He wanted to make a decision but, when he looked in the bathroom mirror, found he was not brave enough.

'Good morning, Ms. Peeters. How was your night in the Divine Guest Bed?'

'Pleasant and brief.' She smiles at him and then looks down at Bea as if seeking confirmation for that. 'Tha know the dog snores?'

'No. Didn't David come home? Whatever. Bea never stays in my room ... SAM, double espresso. Would you like one too? Have you eaten anything?'

'I don't want coffee, thanks, but I'd like something to eat.'

'Anything in particular? Our fridge has everything, and the housekeeper can also make anything: scrambled eggs, fried eggs, omelette, pancakes, waffles, whatever you like.'

'A slice of whole wheat bread with vegan spread, hummus or something, and a piece of fruit would be cool.'

SAM brings the coffee machine to life, the grinder whirrs, steam hisses, and then Thomas' brown lifeblood runs fragrantly into the pre-warmed cup. In the meantime, Thomas has opened the fridge door and looks at a mountain of soft drinks in bottles and cans, fruit and vegetables packed in plastic, about twenty eggs, a cheese- and a ham-keeper, shrink-wrapped steaks, the butter dish and a whole shelf of different types of beer.

'Well, vegan spread, I think that might be difficult. But we have plenty of fruit, already pre-cut, in abundance. How about pineapple?'

At this moment the housekeeper comes into the kitchen and Thomas withdraws to giving instructions. 'Good morning, Fee. For the young lady, a slice of whole wheat bread with vegan spread, hummus, if we have any, and fresh fruit please. For me a large portion of scrambled eggs with ham, followed by French toast and a small fresh fruit salad. Oh yes, and another fresh carrot-apple juice, please. Yes, I think that's about it.' The housekeeper replies to the morning greeting, nods and gets to work. Thomas takes a seat next to Lucia on one of the bar stools on the kitchen island to enjoy his espresso and look over her shoulder.

'Tell me, what are you doing so early in the morning?'

'I'm researching the facts I need for thar calculations.'

'Why, you got all the numbers from the team leader, didn't you?'

'They are not enough. So far I have no reliable, i.e. verified, figures on the impact on the ecosystem at all. Geo-Resource Management requires care. Or do tha want to display the same ruthless, destructive frenzy in the deep sea as in thar mines in South America?'

'Uh, no, of course not.' Thomas thinks she's a bit too brash for an intern, but he's holding back with a comment. He's determined to find out what she can really do and use it to his advantage.

'Did you find anything exciting?'

'Yeah, through a personal contact I have received a preprint of an article by Stefan Krause in the journal *Scientific Report*, which will be published in June. He is a biochemist at the Helmholtz Centre for Ocean Research in Kiel.'

'I'm really curious ...'

'A twenty-year-old curd cheese package and a rubbish bag containing a Coca-Cola can, special edition Davis Cup 1989. Most likely dumped into the sea by German researchers five hundred miles off the coast of Peru between 1989 and 1996, when they were exploring potential areas for the mining of manganese nodules. The three pieces were found at a depth of over 13,000 feet.'

'And?'

'Not only have curd cheese pack, rubbish bag and cola can not disintegrated, but microbes from the sea floor which are not dominant on the sea floor have settled on them.'

'And?'

'Don't tha get it? This leads to a shift in the predominant species. Just by dumping this stuff, we are already endangering the functioning of the ecosystem. Marine mammals don't even have to swallow our plastic waste to die from it.'

'I see.'

'I hope so. Because I don't intend to work for someone who just wants to make a lot of money and doesn't care about people, animals and nature.'

'You know what scares me about you?'

Lucia takes her fingers off the keyboard and turns to him on her bar stool. 'Do I look like a monster?'

'No, it's not your looks. You are beautiful, if I may say so. What frightens me, what really frightens me is the inner straightforwardness and speed with which you march towards the facts, and you are only twenty ... Plus you are also a bit too cheeky.' He can't help it, but the experienced businessman in him needed to make this last remark.

'Only those who go too far can look around properly.'

'Oh, you're that kind of girl.' Thomas smiles. Lucia exhales with relief.

'I was always like this. What's more, I was alone a lot. Either I spent time in the meadows watching the wild animals, or I read. There wasn't a day when I didn't read a lot about animals, about stones and the earth. Humboldt is my hero, not Harry Potter. At some point you can bring this knowledge together and make another leap in knowledge and understanding. Since I've been studying Geo-Resource-Management, fewer and fewer people have understood what I'm all about.'

'Okay then, I am reassured. I thought you came from another star,' jokes Thomas, still overwhelmed by her. He wonders how even more impactful and assertive she will be when she is thirty or forty. And he wonders if she will ever be able to really use her abilities. *She is too disruptive. She sticks her finger too clearly into the wound.* 'Let's have breakfast in peace, shall we, and then I'll show you something that will make even you speechless, Ms. Peeters - guaranteed.'

'That's really cool,' exclaims Lucia ecstatically as Thomas shows her his pictures from a dive with a research submarine in the trench off the coast of Vancouver Island.

'Look!' His voice also gets enthusiastic. 'Doesn't that jellyfish look like an English dandy? And here, these are tubeworms, over six feet long. And over there crabs, octopuses, squids, alien-like creatures, transparent and fluorescent. Hundreds, probably tens of thousands of species that we have never seen before, that we know nothing about. At least that's what the scientist from the university who took me on this dive said. She alone has described and catalogued more than a hundred new species.'

'And tha're seriously thinking of interfering in an ecosystem like this?'

'Each country will claim its 200-mile zone to get the raw materials it needs for its economy. Not to mention mining in the trenches of the Pacific and Atlantic. We have to mine raw materials there; there is no way around it. It will still be easier and cheaper than in space, and that too is only a matter of time'.

'Tha sound determined to destroy ecosystems just because our consumption demands it.'

'I am Canadian, Ms. Peeters, born and raised in Vancouver. It would be only natural for me to return home and work there.'

'I see,' says Lucia in disappointment. 'I thought tha were German.'

'No. My father came to Canada as a German engineer to build bridges and then stayed. I do have a German passport, but only to make my life in Europe easier. I feel and think like a Canadian, and I am one.'

'I see.'

She looks sad; a cold gush runs through her body and she has to shake.

'Have you ever dealt with deep sea mining before?'

'Only superficially.'

'Well, I am curious to know what that means when you say *superficially*. Tell me what the student knows so far.'

'There are three types of ecosystems that are suitable for deep sea mining: seamounts, on which corals or sponges grow, and the crust on which they grow consists of minerals such as iron-manganese. Then there are hydrothermal vents that look like huge chimneys. From them, metal- and mineral-rich water with a temperature of up to 660 degrees Fahrenheit gushes out of the earth's interior. It evaporates in the ice-cold ocean water and forms a kind of chimney. Some are up to 200 feet high and consist of manganese, copper, nickel, cobalt, gold, silver, zinc and lead. The chimneys attract microbes, which then form the food and source of life for countless animal species. And thirdly, deep-sea plains, where polymetallic nodules the size of tennis balls or even a grapefruit lie around ... that's all I know so far.'

'Hat off - crisp and to the point.' Thomas nods contentedly and incredulously at the same time.

'Just because I am really interested in what I study? Didn't tha get excited about thar studies?'

'Believe it or not, I wanted to be a Mountie. One of the famous Canadian mounted police officers with black trousers, a scarlet tunic and a wide-brimmed hat. I wanted to be part of the unit that patrols the forests with its helicopters and hunts down those who cut wood illegally and smuggles it out with boats and jeeps.' Before Thomas can start chatting away about it, his smartphone rings. It is David. 'One moment, Ms. Peeters.' He goes out into the entrance hall to speak in peace and quiet, and comes back shortly afterwards.

'My son. The university will probably close next week. Switzerland will order a corona lockdown starting Monday, and Germany will close its borders.'

'Then I guess it's time for me to head back to Aachen. Who knows if I'll even be allowed into Germany as a Belgian.'

'But you don't want to go back, do you?'

'I will lock myself in my student room and can do a lot of work online. I think I better go upstairs and pack up, I'll be right back. Come on, Bea, one more time up the stairs together.'

She stands up and the dog follows her as a matter of course. She has just left the kitchen when Giacomo Aringhe-Rosse calls again. Thomas is pleased when he sees the name on the display.

'Good night, Giacomo, I didn't know you would stay up through the night on my account.'

'That's how important you are to me. Listen, I want you to come to New York tonight. Meet me at my hotel at Central Park. I've reserved a small suite with a park view for you.'

'But …'

'Get on the plane and come. It's about things we can't discuss over the phone.'

'But Switzerland goes into the coronavirus lockdown on Monday.'

'You'll be back Sunday morning. It's the only way. I need a face-to-face with no witnesses or listeners now.'

'My son … I must … wait a moment … maybe it can be arranged. Just give me half an hour, okay?'

'But not a moment longer.'

'I'm ready then,' says Lucia, when she returns to the kitchen shortly afterwards, travel bag in one hand, water bottle in the other, the small rucksack on her back and her handbag over her shoulder.

'How about you staying here after all?'

'Here with tha, during the lockdown? We don't even know how long it'll last.'

'Three weeks.' Thomas is lying.

'So ... '

'Come on! You could continue to work on the project with full pay, on your Bachelor thesis as well, and you don't even have to avoid your former boyfriend. You have Bea around, my son will be here soon. I have to go to New York and won't be getting on your nerves.'

She puts the index finger of her right hand to her lips, remains silent, thinks for a moment and then asks: 'Does Bea also follow your son around all the time?'

'Constantly.'

'Honestly?'

'Honestly.'

'Fine, I'll take my chances.'

'Great. Well, get your stuff back to the Divine Guest Room right away, and I'll pack for a night in New York.' As Thomas walks towards his dressing room, he is not sure if this was really the right decision.

RÜSCHLIKON, 13 MARCH 2020

David and I are chilling in the living room. First he played for me on the grand piano: *Perfect* by Ed Sheeran and *Claire de Lune* by Debussy. Now we are lying together with Bea on the thick carpet in front of the fireplace and I read him poems from *My Asteroid B612*.

I wait, alone,
By the river, it flows by.
My heart breaks in two,
My eye yearns for her.

'Mega beautiful.' He has a tear in his eye. 'Tell me, what does that strange title, *My Asteroid B612*, actually mean? What does your grandfather really want to tell you?'

'I didn't ask him, but at school I read *The Little Prince*.'

'I did, too. The Little Prince says: "You only see well with your heart. The essential is invisible to the eyes."'

'That's right, and his beloved home is Asteroid B612.'

'Is your grandpa trying to say you're his home?'

'He could also mean that I should love my home, the Congo; after all, I was born there and that's where Grandpa and

Walikia and their whole family still live today. They really love me, and they show it too.'

'I'd like a home like that too.'

'Tha won't say that again when I show tha the pictures from my trip to Congo.'

David holds his Phablet, his TabletPhone, in front of my nose. 'Say something.'

'What do tha want me to say?'

'Anything, go ahead.'

'I'm Lucia.'

He looks at the display, lets the sentence play over the loudspeakers and laughs.

'What for?'

'You'll see.' Then he grins mischievously and takes another picture of me. 'You've no mother?'

'Shot, and my adoptive mother is dead now as well.'

'My Ma never looked at me, but she looked in the mirror ... in the shop window ... on the scales ... spent hours in the bitchburner. Pimping herself up is her only concern: spending money on clothes, jewellery, making other women look at her jealously. But as a mother, she is just a noob.' Now several tears roll down his face.

I comfortingly lay my hand on his. 'Who was watching over you?'

'As long as I wore the nappies, nannies, then housekeepers, since I was ten, Bea, then the guys at boarding school, now SAM and Nur, but only secretly. Pa knows nothing about my new girlfriend.'

'But thar father says tha two get along great.'

'He doesn't know much about me. Too busy butting in.'

'I see.'

'Since I was fourteen, I've had at least two girlfriends a year.'

'How do you do that?'

'Play piano and look sweet.'

'And did you sleep with all of them?'

'Sure.'

'So this is who you are.'

'Only now with Nur, it's different. Her real name is Nurochma. She is a Muslim and is also studying at ETH Zurich. The coolest woman I have ever met. If I don't come home at night, I'm with her. Thank God Pa doesn't ask, and her parents and siblings don't live in Switzerland.'

He shows me a photo of her on the Phablet. She is radiantly beautiful, smooth light brown skin, black straight hair, crass red lipstick.

'Can I see a picture of your lover?'

'It's off, all photos deleted.'

'Sad?'

'Mega ... I cried for weeks ... couldn't sleep... heartaches ... just can't understand it. Would you break up with Nur and obey if thar father said: "Son, marry this one, she's good for my business?"'

'I'd kick his ass and tell him to fuck off.'

'But tha're rich too, like Robin's father, aren't tha?'

'Pa's working his ass off to make himself rich. He knows which side his bread is buttered and he want's jam on it too. But the big money's in Ma's family. I'm a kid of folks who'll do anything for business, go anywhere and get all bent out of shape. What you get in return are the best schools, luxury houses, expensive clothes, jewellery, cool holidays, *valuable* contacts to other rich people, invitations to fancy events and lots of human dummies who have no feeling for what kids really need. They don't know what an Asteroid B612 is.'

'Crass.'

'Yeah, that's pretty crass.'

'And thar Pa?'

'Kind, generous, but a faker. Don't talk about it, but my Ma finally realised that he didn't marry her, but her money. Since we moved from London to Switzerland in 2008, she's been drinking, and for four years now she's actually always pissed. Pissed is normal.'

'Is that why tha went to boarding school?'

'Sure. But Pa says, because of the international contacts. His pretext: nobody is supposed to check what's really going on.'

'I guess tha've been alone as much as me.'

'Since I was twelve, the computer has been my best friend. Back then, I knew what is going on at home. At first I didn't trust adults any more. I was addicted to games for a year, then I started programming myself. Pa bought me all the hardware and software I wanted. I took maximum advantage of his guilty conscience, I admit. But I don't use drugs anymore for that.'

'Did tha do drugs long?'

'Everybody at boarding school did coke or smoked pot. Because it was cool or because they too were frustrated with their cold-blooded parents.'

'And thar Pa didn't notice?'

'Nope, he has no clue what I'm up to with my life and with SAM. To him, SAM is a cool smart home toy that brews espresso, collects and presents information about his worldwide contacts, has the floor cleaned, and does the shopping. But he does not know that SAM is artificially intelligent. But he could know it. I constantly send him the latest information on artificial intelligence from the great gurus like Ray Kurzweil from Google. He doesn't read it, or at least not attentively.'

'I guess money can buy everything, huh? Tha live in a high-end neighbourhood.'

'Part of the game. Pa says he has to show that he and the company are doing well. Many foreigners live here in Rüschlikon; they make big money in Switzerland through tax constructions. Many from the commodities business. The municipality is now and then embarrassed to be getting so much "dirty money" from taxes. If it is noticeably large, they argue about whether to make a charitable donation of part of it back to the countries that are being exploited, or whether they prefer to put marble floors in the schools.'

'Crass. And thar Pa?'

'A small fish, pretends to be an important man, can be bought and used.'

'Do tha think that's okay?'

'Nope, but he does really good things too. Bringing you along, for example. You don't let yourself get lulled, you can trigger people, you know what you're doing it all for. He has real respect for you; he told me that on the phone when his plane rolled to the runway for New York. You're a destroyer, a Woman of Honour, and Bea loves you as much as me. Can you program?'

'No, I do maths; I'm good at research and explaining.' I'm kind of embarrassed to praise myself, and his eyes tell me he noticed.

'Explain the Earth to me so that I never forget it. Go ahead.'

'Let's see. Let's take ... Earth history.'

'Sure.'

'If the history of the Earth were a day of twenty-four hours, man would only appear in the last five minutes, and the industrial age, that is, the last two hundred years, would only be two thousandths of a second, and in that time we would destroy everything we and the Earth need to survive.'

'Wow, Pa is right. He says you're absolutely great at getting to the heart of things. And in maths. Show me something!'

'I don't like to brag.'

'Okay, let's go and have a bite then.' David gets up and gives me his hand so I can get up off the floor. My whole body hurts, and I can't figure out why. Bea yawns, rolls herself once and trots along behind us.

'Can you cook?' David asks on the way to the kitchen.

'Can't tha?'

'We've never been without a housekeeper before, and SAM can only make coffee so far. It's fucked up that Fee's out right now.'

'If tha take Bea for a walk, I'll cook us some dinner.'

'Deal ... Bea, get the leash ... and then we'll go out into the bio-noise.'

Humming, I get to work. The giant fridge is full of everything many people would desire, most of it packed in plastic. First I go through all the food and check where the use-by date expires today or tomorrow. I take it out and make a rice pan and a mixed salad. For dessert there is mousse au chocolat ready in a plastic cup. It's crazy; only the housekeeper knows how to cook here, and she's back in her home country. Her mother died. When David comes back, he looks critically at the plates I prepared for us on the kitchen island next to each other with cutlery and glasses.

'I thought you could cook. There must be steaks in the refrigerator.'

'I'm vegan, and I don't throw food away. This is made of everything that needs to be eaten today or tomorrow.'

'Excuse me?'

'I have seen starving eyes, David. Have tha ever seen starving eyes? Have tha ever been hungry? I was only hungry for two days in the Congo recently, but that's enough to last a lifetime.'

'Okay, okay ... it's okay.' He raises both arms like someone who is surrendering. 'But I want to add tacos and salsa. And I don't like water either. I want a ginger beer.' David walks purposefully towards a wall cupboard full of tacos, chips and other snacks, and then towards the fridge.

'Spoiled to the bone, ain't tha?'

'Come on, a little food ...'

'What we have on our plates here - others would have to make it last for three days.'

'Come on ... don't tell me stories.'

'I'll show tha after we've eaten.'

When I have cleaned up and gotten everything in its proper place again, I show David all my photos from the Congo, which actually are only a few. I only took pictures with the smartphone when I was sure I wouldn't embarrass anyone. David gets very quiet with those from Kolwezi of the diggers, the village of those who have been cheated out of land, jobs, schools and hospital, who only have contaminated water. I swallow. I show him the pictures of the digger with his house made of four sticks stuck into the earth and plastic bags wrapped around them. I tell him about the starving father with his son crying in pain, about the reddish brown, ankle-deep mud, the mosquitoes, Ebola deaths, vermin, about dying children, about the struggle for survival and how it made me feel. David's face turns green and yellow.

'I don't want to argue with that, David. I have seen people in Kolwezi who must live in hell. Also because of us. I want that to stop, do tha understand? I don't want anyone on Earth to have to live like that!'

David slides off the bar stool and goes outside.

'Me neither.'

'Why are tha leaving?'

'Because tree ...'

After a quarter of an hour - I'm feeding Bea - David comes back; his head is bright red.

'We're exploiters in your eyes too, huh?'

'At least tha don't have to worry about who's going to *pay for* the fact that tha're having a great time here and nobody can knock on the door and say with teary eyes: "hungry, thirsty, I am frightened to death, malaria ... help me." The team leader told me that Vijay has most of its mines in South America. I'm sure it's not much different from the Congo.'

David sits down on his bar stool again. Something is wrong with him. His eyes have become glassy, his head is glowing. 'Do tha have a fever?'

He puts his hand to his forehead. 'I don't believe so.'

'Tha don't believe fever, tha measure it. Where do tha keep a thermometer?'

'I don't know.'

'Do tha have a medicine cabinet?'

'I don't know.'

'Tha have to help me look.'

'Don't order me around ... SAM, where are thermometers?' He lets his upper body sink to the kitchen island, lying there like a wet sack. Bea howls. SAM's male voice answers: 'In the parents' bathroom, small cupboard on the right, first drawer, and in David's bathroom in the mirror cabinet.'

No idea how SAM does it. David just stays lying there and doesn't move. So I set out on my own to find it. In his parents' bathroom, which has big mirrors on all the walls - I've never seen anything like it - I even find two. A modern thermometer, battery dead, and an old-fashioned one. I put David on the upholstered bench by the kitchen window and place the thermometer under his tongue. He looks at me like a frightened five-year-old who has been told by his mother that the doctor will come and cut open his stomach if he won't behave right away. When the five minutes are up, the thermometer shows 39.4°C. Damn it.

'What is the name of thar family doctor?'

'Doc.'

'By name?'

'I don't know.'

'Call the housekeeper and ask her name and number. I'm gonna go make cold calf compresses.'

'Excuse me?'

'Bollocks. Call the housekeeper and ask for the doctor.'

'SAM, call Doc.'

I hear a dialling tone over the loudspeaker system, then it rings somewhere and a woman's voice announces: 'Praxis Dr. Künzle'. So that's how it works here. When David doesn't say anything, I explain what's going on and she promises that the doctor will come by later in the day, with a corona test. Until then I'm supposed to take his temperature every hour and write it down and give him plenty to drink. First I'll put David to bed and make him cold calf compresses. Bea lies down in front of the bed and howls heartbreakingly. I alternately stroke David and her head. The fever rises and I am glad when the doctor with protective mask, suit and gloves finally comes after four hours. The family doctor listens to me. David is glowing, there are beads of sweat around his nose. The doctor sits down with him on the bed, feels his pulse, listens to his breathing in the lungs, measures his fever and takes a sample of mucus from David's nostril with a kind of long cotton swab.

'Sore throat?'

'Nope.'

'Cough?'

'Nope.'

'Shortness of breath?'

'Nope, just a long download.'

'A what?'

'Shit, in the toilet.'

The family doctor smiles, I can see it in the corners of his eyes despite the mask. 'You youngster use expressions these days.'

He pushes up David's left pyjama sleeve and makes a tight loop on his upper arm to draw blood. I can't breathe with what I'm seeing. I look away at first, can't believe it, look again. My heart begins to race. Damn it, I can't believe it. It can't be. I have to breathe deeply, turn around, hope he hasn't noticed anything.

'It's going to be all right, David, it's going to be all right,' says the doctor with a calm undertone as he drains the blood samples into various plastic tubes, removes the noose and applies a patch to the puncture mark to prevent secondary bleeding.

'Thanks, Doc.'

The doctor gets up, packs his bag and turns to me. 'Are you the new housekeeper?'

'Nope,' replies David, 'a friend, and she's looking out for me.'

'You must be scared shitless I'm gonna send you to the hospital, huh?'

David pulls the blanket over his head. The Doc and I have to laugh.

'If the fever rises to forty degrees, take him to hospital immediately and call me. If not, I will come back tomorrow, hopefully with the test results of blood and saliva. David has had fever attacks like this since he was younger, whenever something didn't suit him at all. I don't think he has the virus.'

After I have brought the doctor to the front door, I sit down alone in the kitchen for a moment, drink a glass of daisy water, try to become quiet and listen inside myself. Who is David? He has a birthmark on his forearm, and it looks exactly like mine. A star cluster of 11 stars, only my skin and the dots are darker. Could it be that he is my brother and Thomas Müller my father? When I have calmed down, I go back to David. His left arm is hanging out of the bed and Bea is licking it.

'I'm scared, Lucia.'

'Everything's gonna be all right, I know it, David.' I put my right hand on my heart, it's still calm and warm. It's a sign that everything is all right as it is. Walikia taught me that. I take his left hand away from Bea, hold it with my two and sit down with him at the edge of the bed.

'I'll take care of tha. Tha're not alone.'

'Promise?'

'I promise.' Then I stroke his hand with my right hand, feel his head with my left. 'I'll get you another cold cloth for your forehead.'

'But you come right back here, right?'

As the cloth cools his forehead, he grabs my left hand with both hands and presses it firmly. The fever soon rises to 39.8°C, and I now change the cold compresses every quarter of an hour, giving him daisy water to drink again and again. I give David the impression that his temperature is starting to go down.

'Should we call my Pa? But he's always immediately scared shitless about me. He's not as calm as you are when things are chaotic.'

'It's tha decision.'

'I'll wait, but you stay here with me, okay?'

'I promise.'

At some point Bea runs out and comes back with the leash in her muzzle. I guess I am responsible for that as well now. David looks at me with the same faithful eyes as Bea. 'All right, Bea, tha'll get what tha need, too.'

'Don't stay too long, okay?'

'And how do I get back in? Where do I find a key?'

'Ring the doorbell, and when the voice asks "Who is there?" you say, "I am Lucia."'

'I'm Lucia?'

'Yeah, you'll see.'

I get my jacket and also grab my shoulder bag with a small bottle of daisy water. As I walk down the stairs from the front door to the street with Bea, she pulls the leash like a madman. She apparently wants to go to the meadow on the other side of the street, which leads even further up the hill. There is nobody around. I let her off the leash. She dashes off, high to the left, across a path to the next meadow and further left up towards a detached house surrounded by a large hedge and trees. I call out after her, but she is gone. Damn it, I run after her quickly, shouting: 'Bea ... Bea.' When I am just outside the house, I hear an older man's voice from the other side of the hedge. 'Bea is here, with Dante. Come around to the right, through the trees,' he says in a Swiss German accent. I follow the hedge, have to go through a cluster of tall trees and come to the paved forecourt of a large house. In front of it, Bea and another hunting dog romp around, much to the delight of a gentleman in his sixties. I walk towards him, keeping my distance from him and say: 'Hello, I'm sorry, Bea ran away from me and I don't know my way around.'

'Look how that pleases my Dante. They are lovers, you know.' He is of medium height, tanned, with striking masculine features and full, frizzy hair, greying at the temple. The kind of man who becomes more attractive with age.

'Are you new here, Ms. ... ?'

'Lucia Peeters, just visiting, and I let Bea out because David's in bed with a fever.'

'What, our David is sick? That's not what I like to hear. Has the doctor checked on him yet?'

'Yeah, and he thinks he'll be all right. I'll take good care of him.'

'Then come back for a cup of tea with David. Bea and Dante are always happy and so is my wife.'

'I'd like to,' I say instead of 'I promise, because I don't know what's coming. I want to go back to Aachen. I don't feel comfortable here. I feel like I'm becoming part of those who think more about themselves than about others.

'I'll take Dante in the house now; otherwise Bea won't go with you.'

His Swiss German sounds somehow reassuring. 'Tell David that we hope he gets well soon. Uf Wiederluege.'

'Goodbye.'

When Dante is in the house with his master, Bea slowly begins to react to me again. I look for a stick under the trees, call her to stop sniffing at the front door and toss the stick noisily onto the stones. Finally she comes. I throw the stick a few times for her in the direction of home. On the way I empty the daisy water in three places, and so we return to the villa with two stops for Bea to pee. I ring the bell at the front door. 'Good afternoon, who is there, please?' a man's voice asks.

'I'm Lucia.'

There is a whirring noise, and I can push the front door open effortlessly. How did David do that?

Around 11p.m. I have the fever down to 37.8°C and proudly show David the thermometer. I am relieved.

'Cool! But you stay here tonight, okay?'

'I'll leave the guest bedroom door open.'

'No, here in my room.'

'If Bea makes room. Tell me, who is this man with Dante that Bea ran to, as if her life depended on it?'

His face brightens up. 'Bea and Dante belong together, and his master and I have a project together in his cellar. I'm helping him with the software for his artificially intelligent house and business model.'

Well, I'm less interested in that now. I'm tired and prepare myself a bed next to his, brush my teeth, wash my face, put on pyjamas. Then I change the calf compresses again, set my timer on the smartphone to wake me up every hour in order to cool David down repeatedly. I cuddle up next to Bea, who is also getting closer. We both have the same birthmark. Damn, there must be a connection and I'll find out.

When it is already light outside, I wake up, dazed. David is still sleeping, Bea is snoring. I wake up David, give him some daisy water, put the thermometer in his mouth and get new cold compresses. The thermometer shows 37.0°C. 'Done,' I call out, beaming with joy and show him the result of the measurement.

'You are my guardian angel.' A tear rolls down his cheek. 'I'd like you to stay a little longer.'

I hesitate for a moment. I don't want to sneak in here ... no matter ... I dare it. 'Look here.' I pull up the left sleeve of my pyjama, and he sees my birthmark. His eyes grow wide open and his upper body rises up. He feels the mark with the tips of his fingers, looks at me and then back at my skin.

'Blimey ...'

'It can only be the father.'

'Excuse me?'

'Is it possible we have the same father?'

'Impossible.' He slowly lets his upper body sink back into bed.

'Logical and possible. Does that Pa have a middle name?'

'Yes ... Bernhard, like his German grandpa.'

'Are tha sure? Not Adam?'

'No, his best friend's name is Adam. He is also my godfather. But Pa's given names are Thomas Bernhard.'

'Can we ... I mean, would tha check it for me?'

'Pa has several passports. His German one is always in the safe.'

'Look in the safe, please!'

'Why?'

'My father is a German engineer who wrote his doctoral thesis in the Congo in 1999. My mother Amaike was pregnant by him. He knew it. At some point at the end of July 1999, he was simply gone. His name is Adam.'

'Pa must have recognised you ... but Adam did his doctorate with him in Aachen. Whether he was with him in the Congo, I don't know.'

'I look like my mother and I'm wearing her ring.'

'Then Pa would have recognised you! He's not blind.'

'Who tells tha that he hasn't?'

David warps his mouth and wrinkles his brow.

'Do tha think it's normal that he brings an intern home so easily?'

'Nope ... but maybe it's because you're so incredibly smart. Pa called me beforehand and asked if it was okay with me, and said the team leader had said you were an exceptional talent in this century. Dad likes great employees, always says they are harder to find than diamonds. But I want to know now ... the safe with the papers is in his home office.'

In the home office David takes two Japanese woodblock prints hanging side by side under glass from the wall. Behind one is a safe, behind the other a kind of scanner.

'SAM, open the safe.'

'Security check,' SAM answers.

David steps in front of the scanner, a beam of light checks his face. Then it clicks and the safe opens. I step beside him; all I see are documents and jewellery boxes. David looks among the papers underneath.

'There, I told you, his German passport.' He opens it and we look inside, heads pressed against each other. 'Dr. Thomas Bernhard Müller, born 1970 in Vancouver.' I read quietly and am deeply disappointed. Then David pulls out his father's doctoral certificate, December 1999 at the RWTH in Aachen. We look at each other questioningly.

'Is it possible that many people have birthmarks like ours, Lucia?'

'How many have tha seen exactly like thars and mine?'

He remains silent.

I push my sleeve up again, he does the same, and we hold our forearms next to each other. Both birthmarks are shaped like a small star cluster, all points arranged in the same way.

'We'll figure it out!' He stands in front of the screen again. 'SAM, scan my skin this time and look for similar birthmarks on other people on the Internet.'

The light beam moves over the birthmark, it takes a moment, then SAM answers: 'Negative.'

'SAM, scan this one too and compare them.' He pushes me in front of the scanner, positions my forearm, and the light beam also captures my mark.

'Identical, except for the pigmentation of the skin.'

We both breathe out deeply and look at each other.

'And now? Another idea?'

'Grandma Jin Jin. She knows what nobody else knows. But in Vancouver, it's still nighttime.'

As we sit down to breakfast around noon, the family doctor comes back in full gear. No Corona ... any more. The nasal swab shows no infection, the blood tests say David already had the corona virus. Antibodies are clearly detectable in his blood! Crass. The doctor takes his temperature again and listens to his breathing and lungs. 'Everything is fine,' he finally says to David. 'Just a stress reaction. I've known you like this since you were little. Keep checking your temperature, drink lots of water and have some fresh air; dress warmly and rest for a few more days.'

'Sure, Doc.'

Then he turns to me. 'You did great, young lady. Now let's just take your smear and blood sample. Who knows?'

As I accompany the doctor to the front door, I stop him briefly. 'Can I ask tha something else, please?' I push up my sleeve and show him the birthmark. 'Do tha think it's possible that two people have the same birthmark and they're not related?'

He looks at the mark from close up, feels it through his gloves. 'Unusual ... extremely unusual! Well, I'm no specialist in the field, but I'd say there's a connection.'

'Thanks, then I'll find it, come what may.'

HUMANITY LOG

Chronicle time 18.762.020 - 03.14
Project: *Let there be light*
Dr Thomas Müller (aspect of THEODAR) and Giacomo Aringhe-Rosse (aspect of ALANOS)
Located 40° 45' 55.177' N   73° 58' 33.935' W

Giacomo has not promised Thomas too much. A suite with a four-window view of Central Park. Bedroom and living room in beige and dark brown tones, discreet fine wood furniture, fluffy carpet, expensive fabrics, bathroom in marble, spacious - and that means expensive in New York. Only the modern art on the walls does not please Thomas, too abstract and cold for his taste. This princely reception leads him to believe that Giacomo is really serious and not just sounding him out.

Thomas unpacks his clothes, gives the suit to be ironed, takes an extensive shower and then lets himself fall onto the bed in his bathrobe. He has prepared everything to please and convince the Italian. But he is also on his guard, not wanting to rely on any more promises like those of Avidya. Clear-cut contract, specific responsibilities and participation in the share capital. He also wants to turn his team into cash and stay in Switzerland with David. David ... he forgot to send him an SMS to say that he arrived safely. Thomas grabs his smartphone and texts to David: *In New York, cool hotel, everything roger. What are you doing?* And almost immediately receives back: *Chilling, with Lucia and Bea, everything is roger here too. I love you.* I love you, Thomas forgot to write that. Quickly he types: *I love you too, your Pa.*

He looks at the clock and then he says out loud to himself: 'Showtime!' Thomas is experienced in showing himself from his best side, today from his Italian. In the bathroom he shaves perfectly, brushes his teeth again, puts on Acqua di Parma and then a fresh white shirt from Finamore. This is followed by his Reverso wristwatch, of which he knows that Giacomo always wears one, albeit a more expensive version. With the brand new Ferragamo tie and the Brioni suit, now ironed and returned by the hotel service, he is already looking splendid. Finally, he reverently puts on a pair of fresh socks and takes the second pair of shoes out of the shoe bag. He removes the cedar shoe trees and polishes his Ferraris for the feet, as he calls them, with the shoe cloth he also brought along. Custom-made shoes by Gabriele Gmeiner in Venice. Giacomo should recognise at first glance that here comes a man of the world, with an affinity for Italy, and that he can only be hired for big money.

As Thomas looks at himself in the mirror, well-pleased and ready for the conversation concerning his new life, a text message on his smartphone reaches him. *Waiting for you on the 21st floor.* He leaves his suite and takes the lift to the very top. As the lift door opens, his eyes fall on a brass sign: 'President Suite'. In front of the double door made of heavy wood there is a butler on the left. On the right, a muscle-bound, bald bodyguard with bulging lips is positioned on his broad legs. He is dressed in black from top to bottom, with a speech link in his ear and a black Richard Mille watch on his wrist. Thomas pauses. The wristwatch costs more than his two Porsche cars. And he has seen the bald man's face before, but it doesn't occur to him right away where. The bodyguard knocks and opens the door to Giacomo's empire, then steps aside to make room for Thomas. Giacomo is on the phone and says to the bodyguard: 'It's okay, Vito, take a break.' His voice is stronger than Thomas remembered, clear and full as the sound of a heavy bell. The bodyguard locks the entrance door from the inside after the butler has also entered. He passes Thomas, then turns right into another room and wordlessly pulls this door shut behind him as well.

Giacomo is sitting in a cream-coloured armchair, his back to the window, behind him the skyscrapers of New York. The sun falls on the left half of his head; the right half is in the dark. In front of him stands a knee-high oval table with a vase of white porcelain containing a bright, intensely fragrant spring bouquet of red ranunculus and white orchids. Thomas waits until Giacomo has finished his conversation and put the smartphone aside, then immediately walks towards him with a friendly smile and an outstretched hand across the thick, fluffy carpet. Giacomo rises laboriously. On his right is another armchair, also upholstered in cream-colour, with armrests of polished precious wood. On the left, a couch in the same style, all highly elegant and yet discreet. Giacomo smiles, takes a step towards Thomas, shakes his hand and then hugs him, as Italians customarily do. The harsh masculine scent of his aftershave causes Thomas to recoil.

'Welcome to my kingdom, Thomas. Just look around and take a seat.' He puts on a fine face, like inherited arrogance, and gestures to the chair to his right. Thomas sits down, feels the polished wood under his palms and enjoys the unobstructed view of Central Park. He feels like he is in paradise. If only the air-conditioning were not blowing so cold from above. A shiver runs over him and he turns to Giacomo. Meanwhile, the butler waits for instructions and, when Giacomo asks him, gives him an overview of what he has to offer in light snacks and cakes until cocktail hour.

'Espresso, water – still - and cheese cake with extra blueberries for me, please.'

'And you, sir?' He takes a step to the left so Giacomo can see him better.

'A bottle of Krug Clos Du Mensil, '98.'

The butler nods and leaves.

'You are on the gravy train, aren't you?'

'Don't ask me about my business, Thomas!'

'Wouldn't dare.' Thomas raises both hands like a disarmed man and leans back in his armchair, smiling.

'The Bible says that the meek shall inherit the earth. But not the one here. I prefer to see things as did my compatriot Mussolini: *An empire is built with weapons, but you keep it alive with prestige, with the awareness of superiority.* But what am I saying, sentimental Roman that I am? I want you to know how much I value you and,' he grins, 'I cannot risk being seen with you. Not now.'

'It's all right with me if nobody knows with whom I am having discussions about my professional future.'

'You look good, really good. The usual gentlemanly manner. Chapeau, my dear, even an Italian likes your looks at first sight.' He inspects Thomas from top to bottom, and with the gaze of a connoisseur, lingers on his shoes.

Thomas looks at Giacomo in the same scrutinising manner. The top two shirt buttons open, on his hairy chest the fine gold chain with a cross. It earned him the nickname 'The Catholic' in the raw materials industry. The oval face has become fuller and paler. The hair is now grey and sparse, combed and pressed back. And he has become heavier, Thomas believes, especially around the belly. The crocodile leather belt is in its last hole, which is already torn, and his shirt is so tight that a few buttons could pop off at any time.

'How are your wife and kids?'

'Where was the last time we saw each other?'

Thomas understands immediately: nothing private. 'Kinshasa, 2016,' he answers like a shot out of a gun.

'Yes ... and now you're available? I never thought it would be possible.'

'Yeah, but I must warn you, others are already tugging at my sleeve and I want my slice of the pie.'

The door opens gently. The butler is bringing drinks and cakes. The setting down of each glass, the cheese cake, everything is celebrated, especially the opening and pouring of the champagne. 'Anything else, gentlemen?' Giacomo shakes his head and immediately reaches for his glass to toast.

'To the old friendship.'

Thomas shrugs inwardly. Friends - he would not say that. But he toasts him with a friendly smile. The champagne glows brightly golden in the glass. Thomas takes a sip ... in the bouquet as well as in the taste he notes white truffles, chocolates and candied fruits. Citrus fruits and vanilla as well as a hint of herbs resonate with it: pure, velvety soft and persistently lingering. Enraptured by the pleasure, he puts the glass down again and is surprised to find that Giacomo drinks his in one go and then helps himself again from the ice bucket.

'And you're free to do what you want and go wherever you want?'

'No competition clause, if that's what you mean. The Ali family is too stingy, or should I say too naïve. But of course that's not a suitable description of the qualities of Arab business men. Anyway, yes, I can do what I want.'

Giacomo grins, as if he were laughing at the person who drew up the separation agreement for the Vijay Group, 'Deep sea, did I understand you correctly?'

'That is the new battlefield between the Western world, India and China for raw materials. I have built up a team over the last two years, excellent people. I'm bringing them with me, including an exceptionally gifted scientist.'

'Mobile?'

'With Canadian and German passports and citizenship in Switzerland. Plus an Indian passport in the family.'

'This could be worth extra gold.'

'I got other aces up my sleeve.'

'Tell me! You can trust me!'

Thomas just doesn't know yet. But he knows that Giacomo is on intimate terms with many rich and powerful people. Thomas remains on guard and says: 'If we don't get together, do you owe me something for what comes next?'

'Done.' Giacomo empties his champagne glass a second time.

'My concept and the business model behind it requires less capital than the other players need and generates excellent returns faster.'

Giacomo leans forward. 'Don't worry about financing. Money is not the problem. I need excellent people who can do it.'

'Two strategic pillars. Acquisitions that bring immediate return on investment and country advantages through my and other nationalities in the team.'

'I see, you already make money, if the others … clever, Thomas, clever. But that's the way I know you.'

Thomas wants to continue talking, but a second bodyguard, slimmer, comes in from the next room where the first one disappeared. He apologises for the disturbance and asks if Mr. Aringhe-Rosse is ready to accept a call from the Cardinal.

'Forward the conversation into the master bedroom.' Giacomo gets up, walks past Thomas to the left into the next room and mumbles: 'Give me ten minutes, Thomas.'

Thomas concludes that a lot of money and great power are involved and that Giacomo is pulling several strings at once. He rises and walks past the couch opposite him and the paper-laden desk behind it on the right, straight towards the large brass telescope standing there on ebony feet in front of the window. He adjusts it to his height and view and then gazes out over Central Park with relish. The people beneath him are tiny and far away. Just figures in a game. When he has had enough, he turns to the left and sees a dining-room table with chairs in dark wood, behind it a sideboard with bar function. The walls in cream-coloured fabric wallpaper, the carpet light beige, as throughout the suite.

'Back already,' Giacomo calls from behind. Thomas turns around and observes how he is returning from a kind of intermediate living room. Thomas sits down, grabs his glass again and takes another sip with pleasure. He does not touch the cheese cake or espresso. He does not want to spoil this extraordinary gustatory experience. Giacomo pours himself another glass of champagne and sits down again. 'Aren't ya drinking at all ...?'

'To continue, Giacomo. I am in almost-completed negotiations for majority shareholdings with three companies which manufacture equipment for the mining of metals and minerals in the deep sea.'

'You've always been faster and more resourceful than the others.'

'Tell me, Giacomo. Tell me, who is behind you?'

'The big boys. The ones who are nowhere visible, certainly not in the press. Those who pull the strings in the highest political and social circles around the world. Those who rule everything through intermediaries and holding companies. Those who pay no taxes here, but manage their money through tax havens and can even command the secret services.'

Thomas flinches inside, his stomach is cramped, his mouth becomes dry. Then he collects himself and says: 'You'll have to offer me a little more. I am not a Catholic. Let the cat out of the bag.' He smiles and Giacomo slaps his thigh with a hand.

'All right, all right, because it's you. Levi H. Summers from Boston and Jacob Donald Schild from New York are the big cheese.'

Thomas opens his eyes wide. He has heard the names before, but there are no pictures of them. For years, he has been delving into the networks of the rich and powerful, combing through participant lists from Davos and the Bilderbergers, as well as alumni lists of Ivy League and Oxbridge graduates, seeking a direct line to them himself wherever an opportunity presents itself. He suspects that Giacomo's family, old Italian nobility, opened the doors to these circles.

'Discretion is everything. Every business is based on this. Together they cover the business areas that will be important in the future: technology, media, raw materials and food.'

'What are their expectations of the CEO, of me?'

'None. I will be your Chairman of the Supervisory Board, and I expect excellent returns in the long term. The demand for commodities will go through the roof, even the dumbest fool understands that. But where and how exactly ... who can think and lead such a business ... that's what they need me and men like you for.' Then he laughs out loud.

'Tell me what's in it for me and I'll tell you how I'd do it.'

'More than ever, Thomas, more than ever, look around you, this is how a powerful man of the world lives today.'

'Shares?'

'No.'

'Why not?'

'Billionaires only play with billionaires.'

'Then my salary expectation will be much higher.'

'We shall see.'

'There are not even ten people in the industry, Giacomo, who can give you a brilliant answer to all the questions and deliver the desired return. There are not even three who are immediately available and could start tomorrow, without contractual obstacles and shackles from the past.'

He smiles. 'What do ya want?'

'Fixed salary four million a year, Swiss francs, no dollars, and a five-year contract. Bonus to negotiate, company car with chauffeur, the usual ...'

'Really?'

'I will be CEO of the holding company structure, headquartered in Zug, Switzerland.'

'Why move when you're already in paradise, huh?'

'You said it. Tax-wise, things are hardly better in the raw materials business. Companies are settling in Zug, the top managers live in Rüschlikon. I assume your investors are solvent in Switzerland.'

'Money knows no borders.'

'What can you give me in writing today?'

'Are you trying to ruin my day? Am I supposed to sit down here at my desk and write down what we already agree on? Look how many documents are waiting for me there.'

'What you've got in black and white you can take home and then be sure of it.'

Giacomo twists his eyes.

Thomas reaches into his right suit pocket and pulls out one of the two data sticks. He has prepared two different datasets, depending on how far they advance and agree and how certain he is that he will be employed. Both data sticks look the same, but the one with all the data has an eyelet to attach it somewhere. He holds the data stick up. 'I will leave this one, Giacomo, for your investors when we agree on the broad strokes today.'

'God damn!'

'It's all there, financial plans, holding structure, subsidiaries to be set up, partners, concessions needed, initial team, obstacles, International Seabed Authority contacts. You didn't think I'd just come to New York for a chat?' Then he drops the stick back into his jacket pocket. 'I'm not naive!'

'That's why I was on the phone so quickly. Tell me about your plan.'

'Next to the gems you would find on the data-stick ... well, the Swiss holding company shares concessions with partners in Canada, Germany and India - I've already set that in motion. Only the subsidiaries still need to be founded. We are expanding our holdings every year, all partners are eligible, except the Chinese.'

'My investors couldn't agree more.'

'We'll even take it one step further.'

'Spill the beans!'

'Space mining.'

'Space mining? That's dreams of the future, Thomas. Elon Musk is constantly correcting his conquest plans for Mars and in the process is squandering billions.'

'I'm not a big mouth like Musk, I'm frugal. I also don't blow the whistle first and then I can't deliver. I act prudently, with circumspection and for the long term. It will work via Luxembourg.

The country has already enacted legislation tailor-made for space mining and has the research facilities to go with it. About fifty start-ups have settled there, and Astra has been launching satellites into space for decades. I can achieve a lot with a manageable investment, have a foot in every door and a seat at almost every decision-making table, legally secured, but flying under the radar. I want to walk both business avenues in parallel, deep sea in the fast lane, space in small steps. It doesn't matter where the raw materials come from. The main thing, as in the gold rush, is to be among the first to stake the profitable claims.'

'I haven't talked to the investors about space mining yet. But if your data stick has everything I need ...'

'For sharp, fast-moving guys, there are now huge opportunities.'

'You're my man! Cheers, Thomas!' And again he tips the champagne down like a thirsty man.

A little later they are sitting in the dining room with finest lobster, Chateaubriand, Bordeaux, followed by a single malt whisky.

'Still want a hot woman? Very young chicks are not so easy to get since Epstein, well, you know, but otherwise you can have everything.'

'Not my cup of tea, Giacomo.'

'You always say that. Your wife must be a real bombshell in bed.'

'I'm getting a divorce.'

'We're not covering you there.'

'Is my name Jack Welch?'

Giacomo has to laugh out loud, chokes and snorts: 'My investors will love the distinguished and charming Canadian.'

'I hope so,' replies Thomas and hands Giacomo the data stick without the eyelet.

FAMILY COUNCIL SAN

Chronicle time 18.762.020 - 03.15

We are delighted to have you back with us, Elizabeth, aspect of SANCHA. Please tell us how your life on Earth as Elizabeth Peeters, née Schmidt, went from your perspective.

Gladly, SANTHRON. But first of all I would like to bow to the elders of our family and to all those present. I too am overjoyed to be back. I must say that living in a body on Earth was far more exhausting than I could have imagined. This dense matter body is such a limitation for one's own abilities ... Where shall I start? Best with the tasks and learning expectations that I and all of us here had planned for me. In my previous incarnations in the ether, I hadn't succeeded in treating all people equally, to consider them all as equal to me. Well, I am afraid I didn't manage to do so in the incarnation in dense matter either. I divided people into my own kind, others I looked up to, and most others I looked down on and scornfully talked about. I treated those I considered inferior in a way that, looking back, makes me very sad.

We agree with you, Elizabeth-SANCHA.

My guest role in Armand's family was only partially successful. We both had the task of learning to lead an equal and balanced marriage ... but I was clearly wearing the pants in the family. I always tried to show everyone that I could hold my own as a German in Belgium and in the Peeters family. My profession as a teacher certainly also contributed to my being a know-it-all.

As Elizabeth, were you aware that balance was at stake?

No, only a very few times did I have such a thought, and then I feared I would perish with my needs if I treated Armand as an equal.

Please give us an example.

Armand and I took turns deciding where we were going on holiday.

You could not agree on a common holiday destination?

No, never. One year he decided; the next year I did. And if he was allowed to choose, I complained every day throughout the trip about things that didn't suit me.

Do you realise how much you have hindered Armand's development?

Now, yes; during incarnation, no. I always thought that I had to give him a sense of direction; otherwise he would be lost. He's just a henpecked husband, not strong-willed at all; he lets himself be pushed around and undermined by others ...

And you didn't like that?

I wanted a strong and courageous man, one who would conquer the world and protect me.

Armand's incarnation plan was to lead the life of a frugal and good-natured intellectual who fulfilled a function at a middle level of society. In this incarnation, this was exactly the challenge you were tasked with and desired to master in dealing with him.

At the University of Lyon, when we met during our year abroad, he was so different: full of adventure, funny, a real do-gooder. But when I moved from Germany to Belgium to live with him after finishing my teacher training, I was drawn into the comfortable routine of his family. They are all bon vivants who do not drive themselves crazy. As a judge, he resigned himself more and more every year, no longer believed in his power to change anything, and at some point he just hung on the red wine glass ... The real break came when he began to suspect that I was having an affair with Raymond, the headmaster of Lucia's school. But that was his own fault. Why didn't he accompany me to the parent-teacher meetings?

Adultery is adultery, and you are not a Francesca of Rimini who was cheated into marriage.

I am painfully aware of this. I am probably still trying to blame others for my misconduct.

Please let us now move on to the tasks you had taken on to contribute to the plan for Earth.

Frankly, I am still a little confused. It was intended that Armand and I would grow old together. How is it that I had to die so young? I mean, I was only 49 years old.

The karma for the whole Earth must be balanced as the consciousness of all expands. The human family is moving from the emphasis on individual growth and individual power to the Aquarian emphasis on group growth and group power. This alone causes much confusion and tension.

But what did that have to do with my life?

It is necessary to focus on respect and good will for the great and beautiful diversity that exists within the human family. Both you and Armand had a common task to fulfil in the plan for the Earth.

Yes, I know we had agreed to adopt a child from the Congo to help compensate for the cruel Belgian karma there. I hadn't imagined that it would be so difficult to raise a child. Not that Lucia was stupid or unwilling. On the contrary, she was simply beyond me in everything. She absorbed everything so quickly, wanted to do so much and learn so much that it was too much for me.

It was not Lucia-TRUSLAN who was originally intended for you. We had to change our plan. SANAT KUMARA needed parents at short notice who could keep in touch with the Congo and who could also make the German culture and language accessible to her. You were the most tangible option at that time. SANCHA and ADLON, Armand's soul, as well as we ourselves, agreed to dare the undertaking.

I was always jealous of Lucia, of the love she receives from Armand and also from Tilly. And then the admiration she receives from the whole teaching staff, especially from Raymond. The speed with which she learns, understands things, is able to relate them to each other. This child can do everything better than me, except grammar.

And you pulled yourself up through that so as not to sink down alongside her?

I had no idea what was slumbering inside that child. I had no idea what she is meant to do and who her soul is.

Very few parents have that. All souls incarnating on Earth since the turn of the millennium have taken on more conscious abilities and more difficult tasks than the previous generation. The transition to the 21st century heralds a new epoch for the human family. The older must learn from the younger, not the other way around.

But thanks to me, Lucia speaks fluent Flemish, French, German and English. We showed her the world: Egypt, Mexico, Nepal, Tibet, India ... She is well prepared for her global task.

Partly, Elizabeth-SANCHA, partly. Tilly has awakened in her an enthusiasm for mathematics, introducing her to the teachings of Pythagoras, which are necessary for understanding the larger picture. The actual preparation for her mission is now being conducted by the Ascended Masters such as YESHUA and HONGYETSEE as well as by Off Earth Allies. Lucia has to accept her soul tasks and actively implement them. This is of paramount importance for the future of the Earth and the human family.

I really didn't know that. This body is, as I said, a huge burden and restriction.

Please tell us how you evaluate your incarnation as Elizabeth as a whole and what you would balance how.

It would probably help me if I could slip into the role of a man in dense matter. One who, with a high intellect, still clings to childish patterns of action and has to free himself from them. Alternatively, I could imagine overcoming my dominance and arrogance towards others by going through life bitterly poor and barefoot myself, and always being the underdog.

SANCHA and we were in agreement to end your incarnation early, because your contribution to the plan of Earth had been fulfilled and you were now becoming too much of a burden for Lucia. We had to separate you so that Lucia could have a spiritually experienced mother. Moreover, as you say yourself, you had already failed in your personal learning tasks. From our point of view it was not to be expected that you would make it in this life. You will help the development of our soul family more if you dedicate yourself to a new task and make an effort to establish and maintain the connection to SANCHA this time.

But will I succeed this time? I have been rather stubborn, a know-it-all and bossy for ages. Why are you more confident now?

The energies on Earth are in a state of great change. The veil keeping the soul separate is becoming thinner. The disasters on Earth will lead more and more people onto the spiritual path. Religious leaders and preachers have mostly failed, and people are realising this. If Dante's portrayal of hell 700 years ago drove them into the arms of the Catholic Church, the new energies are now ushering them back onto the path of self-responsibility. Thousands of years of knowledge about the connection, the recipient for soul messages and other dimensions within each individual will come to the fore again. Religious leaders will no longer be able to keep this knowledge a secret.

You mean the small gland in the brain, which looks like an eye in cross section and is represented as a cone in spiritual and religious traditions?

That's the one, Elizabeth-SANCHA. But back to you. Your next personal learning steps should take place where you can experience for yourself what it means to be considered inferior and to maintain contact with your soul. You should also finally be able to share a marriage at eye level. As a contribution to the plan for the development of the Earth, we would like you to participate in building a community that supports each other unreservedly and stands by those who are still weaker.

I would like that. What country or place would you have in mind?

We still lack the PERGAMENT of FILATERATES for knowing all your behaviour during the incarnation and all the effects you have set in motion. Once it is available and we have all studied it, we should meet in the planning room for the next incarnation.

Very well. In the time of rest until then, I want to think about whether I would like to be reborn in one of the former German colonies in Africa to experience the consequences of exploitation and genocide first hand. I also want to experience what it means to have dark skin colour and thick black-brown curls.

By the time you incarnate again, the #blacklivesmatter movement, which will begin in the USA at the end of May 2020, will have already brought about many changes. The reign of the white man is coming to an end.

Then I would like to return quickly to the dense matter of Earth. I want to experience the upheaval.

IN CONVERSATION WITH SANAT KUMARA

Chronicle time 18.762.020 - 03.15

My strength is gone. Mothering David was really exhausting, but also wonderful. If only he were my brother ... why not? It's only 9 p.m. and we are both totally flat out and in bed, me in the guest room, him in his around the corner. The doors stay open so that Bea can walk back and forth between us. I struggle with the tiredness ... *Great Spirit, whose voice I hear in the wind and whose breath gives life to all people in the world, hear me. I need your strength and your wisdom. Let me ...*

A thick rope hangs from the pitch dark ceiling above my bed, just like in gymnasiums. Curiously, I grab it with both hands and pull myself up on it, piece by piece. The higher I get, the more the rope gives way to a white-red-blue vortex that pulls me up into the dark.

Then I see a small light. With every second it gets sunnier and bigger. My heart beats faster and faster. Where am I? Through an opening I climb out onto a kind of plateau. When I stand upright, I have a mountain in my back; a light spring wind wafts around my nose and sunbeams dance upon it. Below me in the valley is a beautiful city made of ivory-white stone, filigree-built, embedded in mountain peaks with snow covered heights. The largest building in the middle has a golden dome. The backs of the buildings seem to merge into the mountains. But I am not sure. I see all this only dimly; I blink, and it gets a little sharper. In the middle of the buildings a grass-green area shines. The buildings remind me of Petra in Jordan and monasteries in Ladakh, which I visited with Elizabeth and Dad. Behind the portals were entrances to caves. As I think about it and compare the memory with what I see now, I discover a dome-shaped, grey energy over the whole valley, partly denser, partly thinner. Above it I clearly see planes leaving condensation trails in the bright blue sky. Suddenly there is a strong wind. With a jerk I am grabbed by something and fluffily set down. I blink to be able to see and find myself held between big, brown, black, mottled feathers. A huge bird. After another blink I recognise the sharp eye of a large eagle in front of me at the bottom right. I float with this majestic bird towards the mountain tops and make some circles there. Another giant eagle flies to the right and a third to the left. Cool - what a feeling, free and yet so safe. Then we circle to the ground in a long spiral. My eagle touches down on the green meadow, and I get off my feathered taxi. All around me everything is peaceful; birds are singing, and the eagle takes off again with wide flaps of its wings. The breeze blows even my tight curls into a mess. 'Thank you, my friend,' I call out.

I walk towards an area of the city façade that resembles a pantheon and climb the huge steps made of shiny white stone. A dazzling bright light shines towards me, clearly delineated in the core, becoming finer towards the outside until it extends out into millions of filaments. My eyes cannot stand the sight. I have to hold my hand in front of them in order not to go blind. Tears run out from under my hand. I am deeply moved, but I do not understand why.

Don't start with the hardest part, Lucia.

The voice is behind me. 'Who's speaking?'

Turn around. Then slowly take your hand away from your eyes and wait a moment until your heart calms down and your eyes get used to the subtlety of the ether ...

It takes a moment, indeed. A figure, blurred, much taller than me, about ten feet tall, stands before me. It's like a pair of binoculars that you first have to turn into focus ... a young man ...

that much I already recognise, shoulder-length, full, bright blond hair ... wrapped in a flowing, soft pink shimmering robe with discreet embroidery and ... I blink once more ... blue eyes. 'We have already seen each other ...'

Remember?

'Yes, tha are ... SANAT KUMARA ...aren't tha? Where am I?'

In my old official residence, in Shambala.

'Thar official residence? What official residence?'

I am responsible for the spiritual development of the Earth and everything that belongs to its multidimensional nature and vitality. Not that I initiate this development; no, I assist the Great Being who enlivens this planet for the purpose of spiritual evolution and who just dazzled you so.

'Tha mean God.'

No, I am talking about ZONCRIET, the Soul of the Earth.

'The Earth has a soul, and it's called Zoncriet?'

So it is.

'Crass, totally crass.'

You are in good company with your astonishment, Lucia. Hardly anyone today knows her name and the division of functions that exists between the two of us.

'I know God and Mother Earth.'

Mother Earth is the living physical embodiment of the Great Being, the Earth Soul called ZONCRIET. Just as you as Lucia are the living physical embodiment of your personal soul TRUSLAN. Only that Mother Earth has a special place in the star order. She is a DEVA Soul, to be precise, and she is the most powerful being when it comes to Earth.

'That's a tough one. I'll have to check that out first. What do tha do for her?'

I am her embodiment on the etheric plane.

'Crass, totally crass.'

I thought you'd think that was cool, as young people on Earth say today.

'Surely ... but crass means almost the same. What am I doing here?'

You are here to learn what you need to fulfil your tasks on Earth. Unfortunately, your incarnation plan has been seriously disrupted.

'Haven't tha said that before?'

Sure. He raises an eyebrow. *Your biological parents and grandmothers could not teach you what you need. You made a lot accessible to yourself, in the meadows, watching the animals, the trees, grasses and flowers. You taught yourself a lot when you observed how the grasses gave each other tender signs in the wind and soon after that you spoke to the apple tree in the language of flowers. It was so important that you were alone, open to our guidance and your own unbiased perceptions. We taught you to follow your inner voice more and more and not to accept what the adults around you were trying to teach you.*

'Tha were always with me?'

Others were always with you. But I was and am always informed about your fate. The 'Let there be light' project is one of the most important in my area of responsibility.

'And how did I get here right now?'

In sleep, the body is a compass needle seeking its north. Your north is Shambala, the spiritual hierarchy of the Earth.

'And that's how one gets here? By climbing up a gymnastics rope and being sucked in by a vortex?'

There are many ways to Shambala. You will get to know them all over the years, so you can come here any time you want. Today I want to show you where my office used to be and what it looked like. You will need the knowledge when you talk to those who think they already know everything about Shambala from ancient myths and traditions.

'But are the myths and lore wrong?'

No, they were all right, in their time, for the people who lived in that time. But consciousness is always expanding, teachings are evolving. That too is part of the plan of the Earth.

'I have seen no one here except tha and the blinding light ZONCRIET.'

We had to relocate the seat of office. Do you see the protective layer above us?

'Yes. It's transparent in places. I saw a Lufthansa passenger plane and one from Garuda, I think.'

The passing planes are less our problem than the surveillance planes and spy drones of the military.

'They're after tha?'

Of course. The world's leaders know much more than they tell people. At your next visit we'll meet at the new seat of government. There's a lot going on there, I can promise you that.

'But how did I get here?'

We have brought your consciousness with your consent from deep sleep into the ether.

'Part of me is in a parallel world and the other part is in bed?'

Your etheric body with its consciousness is here.

'Why am I really here?'

I want to remind you of your life's work and need your consent.

'I am a scientist and soon an activist, I know that already. I won't let the powerful men buy me either. But what do tha want my approval for?'

You're wrong.

'Wrong about what?'

As the Lord of the World, I am a kind of Chief Operating Officer for the Earth. I know God's plan for the universe, for the Milky Way, for our solar system, for the Earth and all the sub-plans, all the processes, all the people and their soul tasks, and I constantly receive reports of all that is going well and all that is going wrong.

'Really? Tha can't process that much data.'

You can't; I can.

Touché - that hit home.

You are incarnated on Earth in order, by the end of the 21st century together with your team and together with the Ascended Masters, Devas, Conrees and Off Earth Allies, to realise the unity of all human souls.

'This can't be. I'm just a student. It's the others who have the power.'

... Says someone who is not yet aware of her task or who has not yet found the courage to accept her power and assume the burden of responsibility for this difficult path.

'I am ... '

Just, disciplined, intuitive, sensitive, highly intelligent, hard-working, humble towards nature; but also stubborn, impulsive, cheeky and insolent ... yes, you have come a long way in your development. But you won't get far and fast enough on your own now. We are lagging far behind the plan for the evolution of the human family and the Earth. Therefore we need your active participation NOW.

'Tha said consent a moment ago.'

You've been paying attention. Your soul TRUSIAN has already given her consent and the ministry responsible for you approved the change of your incarnation plan. But you must also participate, Lucia.

'In what?'

First of all we have to refine and improve your perception.

'And how will tha do that? Put ether glasses on me?'

We want the OBLAN to work on your chakras. Your material body must vibrate higher and more harmoniously. You must be able to move freely between dense matter and ether. You must be able to come to us whenever you want, and be able to travel with the DEVAS to learn.

'Stop, stop, stop. This is going too fast for me. I know what my chakras are, that they are sometimes blocked or some are too active. Grandmother Mepi always balances this out and the pain is gone too. But tha're telling me there's some kind of healing heavenly interventionist force?'

Have you ever heard of the Chintamani Stones?

'I collect stones.'

I know.

'Chintamani stones: there are, I believe, twelve. People argue about who has one and where they are now.'

Do not bother with the physical aspect. The important thing is the energy that was in them, where it came from and where it went.

'What do tha mean?'

The Chintamani stones were once material anchor points for the OBLAN on Earth. The OBLAN as beings are further along in their path of spiritual development than are the Ascended Masters. They train members of the Kingdom of Servers on the OBLAN from all over the cosmos.

'Never heard of 'em.'

A small planet at the elbow of the Great Hunter. Astronomers have not yet discovered it. The planet OBLAN is home to a highly appreciated Leadership Academy of our galaxy.

'I'll have to check it out first.'

Understandable. Just ask.

'Well, tell me more about the OBLAN.'

Some OBLAN have recently returned to Earth. On the one hand, they help individual people with daunting tasks like you and cause their chakras to vibrate higher and more harmoniously. On the other hand, they supply the Earth itself with new, harmonising energies. They exert their global influence through energy lines and fields. At the moment a few people here on Earth are helping them with this. ZONCRIET alone no longer has enough power to withstand the iniquities of mankind on the planet. With your consent the OBLAN will now begin work on your chakras. All you have to do is to say: I am ready.

'I am ... at first I'm overwhelmed, to be honest. I need to check everything out first.' My gaze wanders confusedly, seeking support, familiar things ... but I don't dare to turn to the glaring light of ZONCRIET. I feel like Alice, who jumped into the rabbit hole and is now in free fall. I really seem to be floating in a parallel world, flooded with light. And now SANAT KUMARA is asking me, like Morpheus of Neo, to choose between the blue and red pill. I feel small and stupid, a smart aleck, biased ... What can I say? Do I even have the courage to get involved in something like this? Have I perhaps gone crazy? What can I say?

I am ready. It would be the best thing for you and for everyone else.

'Tha can read my mind?'

Of course. Nothing happens on Earth without my knowledge. I told you already.

'But ...'

We are still on Earth, only in the ether, one of its dimensions, and here it is much easier for me to survey everything.

'What happens when I say "I am ready"?'

Then we can guide, teach and train you more easily. The work on your chakras will make your whole perception even more subtle and sensitive. Sometimes you will be inexplicably tired, sometimes you will feel a tingling sensation: sometimes in the roots of your teeth, sometimes pain in other parts of your body you cannot explain. Sometimes all of this together and much more. Give us a sign if it overwhelms you on a particular day. You will feel your body vibrating higher and then need periods of rest.

'I have had this impression many times before. Whenever Grandmother Mepi treated me.'

She has long supported your development, as you yourself have done through the way you live.

'How so?'

You eat vegan food, stay away from alcohol and drugs. You drink good water and tea. The blockages that Grandmother Mepi has already released are a real blessing for the free flow of energy.

'Okay ... okay ... Tha has almost convinced me. But please give me a few more examples of what I need to learn.'

You must remember the path of divine self-responsibility, the logic of love, the cosmic laws, the journey of return, the concept of enough, Amente, the structure of our galaxy ... You must also get used to being surrounded by your guides and trusting the insights of your soul and its indications. You must stop dissecting, analysing and doubting your intuitive perceptions with your head. If you are only in your head, you get lost.

'Can tha somehow prove what tha are saying? I prefer to stick to facts.'

That is the scientist speaking, who until just a few minutes ago was on the verge of going blind amid the glow of ZONCRIET. You will allow me to laugh.

And he laughs, heartily yet somehow politely. I do not feel offended. I am insecure; therefore I'm protecting myself inwardly against what is happening here right now. It does not fit in with what I have learned about life so far. I'll probably wake up in my bed, bathed in sweat from what I'm dreaming right now.

The answer that we hoped you would give us in Shambala frightens you, doesn't it?

'Yes - why me? Why not someone else? I mean, there are certainly enough powerful people who could already unite half of humanity behind them today.'

They are too cowardly, too entangled in outdated systems of money and power. The powerful have failed, almost all of them. Besides, it's your task. You agreed to it before the incarnation. You agreed to everything that was waiting for you. Everyone has their role in this giant puzzle, and if just a few more people see that and do it, the world will soon look very different.

'But what about the big boys? I mean, the powerful ones in the economy who control the big money ... What about the billionaires, presidents, chancellors, prime ministers, kings, rulers at the head of nations? Don't tha talk to them?'

They prefer to believe the alienated nonsense that one of us - an Ascended Master like LORD MAITREYA, YESHUA, BUDDHA, MOHAMMED, KRISHNA and many more - will save the world instead of them ... or a new technology will do so.

'So no go as far as a saviour or high-tech solution?'

We do not relieve anyone of their responsibility. Nor will we change the cosmic laws for human beings. Everyone reaps what he sows and has to live with it. We are now only accelerating the rise to power of a new generation, young men and women who are not yet completely blinded by matter or frozen in fear for themselves or their possessions.

'Why don't tha come to Earth tharself and make a speech in front of the world's running cameras? At the UN, for example.'

My place in the divine order is here. But soon you will see the Ascended Masters of all religions, led by LORD MAITREYA, walking and teaching side by side on Earth among the people. They will proclaim and exemplify, on talk shows on all channels and through the social media, that the human family is one. Do you have to wait until you shake hands with YESHUA in Aachen Cathedral? Do you need that as proof of his existence, my existence, ZONCRIET's existence? When will you stop making your limited logic the measure of truth?

I have to breathe out deeply. That hit home. I guess I'm not ready yet. Too brainwashed ... too full of myself and what I know. Or what I think I know ... but damn it, I have no clue.

I will now let you return to dense matter. I'll give you a few more days to courageously accept your life task. Do you agree that from now on the OBLAN will work on your chakras, that we will send you signs and show you what it means to be guided by us?

'That seems like a fair deal to me, Sanat Kumara.'

The deal is not fair. It's just a means to bring you to a higher understanding.

'I'll just have to wait and see.'

There is no such thing. You are one with God and a creator yourself, with every word, with every thought, with every feeling. Your soul is God, God is your soul. God is more than your soul, but He is also your soul. Connect with Him in your meditation, in your prayer and in your work, in every moment and in every activity, however small it may seem. Since God is all that is, you are also part of ZONCRIET. Understand this harmony and live it. We will now open your eyes so wide that you dare to say: I am ready.

'All right. We'll see.'

You will see, I can already see.

'Tha're not making it easy.'

Your life task is not easy at all. The most capable serve by taking on the most difficult and selfless tasks. This is true power, and only it means spiritual ascent and, with the soul family, the return to the Creator.

'Thank tha for this lesson. I feel stupid and ignorant.'

Creation is not as simple as the human mind would like it to be!

In the morning I wake up exhausted, I am woozy; my limbs are as heavy as lead. I cannot get up and call for David. My whole body tingles: my teeth, my lips, even every ankle of my two hands. What's going on? His Pa will be back soon, and I could still cross the border and return to Aachen.

RÜSCHLIKON, 16 MARCH 2020

'I don't want to help thar Pa to make money and a career out of deep-sea resources. Have tha googled this Giacomo? Did tha see what kind of guy he is?'

'I know.'

David and I are sitting next to each other in the kitchen on the bar stools and having a cuppa tea. His Pa is on his way to Geneva in his Porsche to meet with some investment bankers.

'I showed tha the photos of the unique animals and their environment. They have no light to grow. They follow their own patterns and laws of life, which we do not know today. It is freezing cold down there. There is almost no food down there either. What can renew itself on the surface of the water in a few years, takes centuries or millennia down there. The nodule thar Pa has on his desk ... the laboratory analysis says that it took ten million years for each half of an inch of growth to form. But that doesn't interest him. He didn't tell us either. I found the information because I read the entire analysis to the end.'

'That's him - missed the boat more than once.'

'I have to find a way to shock idiots like him. The scientists are not ready yet. We do not have enough data today to be able to mine deep sea responsibly. But we don't have enough to stop the crime against nature before it really starts either.'

'I know.'

'Sod it, I need a solution.'

'I know.'

'Stop saying *I know.*'

'But I do know a solution.'

My body stretches jerkily straight as a die. I turn to him on the bar stool. 'Get off the fence then ...'

'I'll show you something,' he says, slips off his stool and waves his hand that I should come along.

In the basement of the villa is a disaster shelter. I can't believe David says there's one in every house in Switzerland. But that wouldn't be the most exciting thing. We go on to the end of the basement and end up in a room full of electronic cabinets, shiny black from floor to ceiling, with white and blue lights flashing in between.

'What's this?'

'May I make an introduction: SAM and the solution to your problem.'

'Really?'

'SAM stands for ... Go on SAM, tell her what your name means.'

'*Someone Awfully Mindful.*'

'Thanks, SAM. SAM can give you the proof you still need, and can even translate it into pictures if you need them too.'

'Tha're kidding.'

'SAM is an artificial intelligence. I gave him a seed algorithm and he learns independently, just like a giant tree grows from a tiny seed. His limitations are the rules and values I have set and his hardware capacity. Yesterday I refined his specifications for ordering supplies for the refrigerator. SAM has to scan the expiry date of all food when it is put in and warn us two days before the expiry date. Now if something ends up rotting in the fridge, he won't reorder it.'

'Cool.'

'Learned it from you and fed it to SAM.'

'Now I get it. Tha want to feed him with my data to simulate future developments, right? How quickly does a biotope recover from interventions at a depth of 6,500, 13,000 or 19,500 feet, when there is no light there, the water is freezing cold and when we take our previous findings on lifestyle and growth as a basis, right?'

'Yeah, but SAM alone doesn't have enough capacity. That's why we are now going to visit the Freis with Bea: I'll ask Reto if I may link SAM with his ILSA. Pack up your notes and pictures. SAM, call Reto and Miéko and say, "The three of us are on our way."'

He doesn't have to tell me twice. I dash up the stairs to the Divine Guest Room and pack my laptop, notebook and pens into my shoulder bag. I also fill my bottle with daisy water. In the entrance hall David waits with Bea, who is jumping up and down in a frenzy. David looks at the water bottle in my hand, but says nothing. I put on my jacket and boots and off we go.

Reto and Miéko Frei welcome us together at the front door; Bea and Dante are unstoppable despite their advanced age, romping and running into the house together. The house is certainly twice as big as the Müllers', but much simpler. In the entrance hall there is a floor of light sandstone tiles. From above, daylight streams in through a large glass hatch. Straight ahead, through an arch-shaped opening, you enter the actual house, and this passageway is part of a huge blue-painted vase, certainly fifteen feet high, which fills almost the entire wall. Somehow this fascinates me. The right wall of the entrance hall is decorated with a sideboard, on which a huge amethyst druse sparkles. I feel its energy emanating all the way to me. Opposite, on the left wall, the wardrobe is behind a cupboard-construction of light wood. We hang up the jackets, go through the archway of the vase, then right into a small corridor and then immediately right into a kind of visiting room. My eyes wander around. Here too is the same sandstone floor, the walls painted terracotta. In the middle of the room a round wooden table, again of light wood, above it a futuristic lamp, a free-floating construction. On each of the three walls without windows hangs an ink drawing that shows a cherry blossom branch, a bamboo and a fish. On the table, with exactly four chairs around it, there is already a teapot with four cups. Bea and Dante have vanished.

'I'm used to so many surprises from David, you know,' Mr. Frei says to me. 'Without him, I would never have been able to realise my dream of my own tailor-made artificial intelligence.'

'Does your Pa know what you're up to?' his wife Miéko asks David. She is Japanese, a small, delicate person, about sixty, black thick, short hair in pixie-cut, black round horn-rimmed glasses over almond brown eyes. The contrast of light skin and red lipstick makes her shine even more. She wears a dark blue Japanese house suit made of thick cotton and thong sandals.

'No, we have to bring him to his senses first. The facts Lucia has gathered from deep sea exploration projects are not yet sufficient for dickheads like him.'

'We have to keep our hands off the natural resources of the oceans until we know what we are triggering there,' I add.

Reto Frei looks even more likeable and gets dimples when he laughs mischievously like this and infects us all with it. He pours us tea.

'I'll probably need several days to link SAM and ILSA, and several weeks with Lucia to fine-tune the specifications for the calculator again and again and to complete the programming. What we need as a result is a clearer view of what will actually happen in the oceans, for example, if we mine cobalt, manganese and copper in these nodules at deep sea levels. What will happen to the ecosystem as a whole? What happens to microbes and animals? What else is triggered by stirred-up dirt, dissolved sediments and corals?'

'Can you explain to me, Lucia, where and how they intend to mine metals and minerals in the oceans?'

Before I can answer, the dogs come running in and Dante wants me to pet him. The Freis both acknowledge this with a smile. At some point Dante goes to his mistress and I can answer the question in peace.

'There are three types of ecosystems that are suitable for deep sea mining. The first is seamounts. They are covered with corals or sponges, for example, and the crust on which they grow consists of minerals such as iron-manganese. If you mine there, you destroy the corals and the whole habitat. Then there are hydrothermal vents. They look like huge chimneys from which hot water containing metals and minerals gushes out of the earth's interior at temperatures of up to 660 degrees Fahrenheit. It evaporates in the ice-cold water, forming a chimney. Microbes settle on the outer wall, which then themselves form the food and source of life for countless animal species ... Crabs, tube worms and the most bizarre creatures. We know very few of them and do not understand their way of life in darkness and cold down there. Through these chimneys large quantities of manganese, copper, nickel, cobalt, gold, silver, zinc and lead are flushed up from the earth's crust and interior. This would be the most lucrative mining area, but also the most difficult. The chimneys are located in the ocean trenches along the fissures with a lot of volcanic activity. The UN's International Seabed Authority is trying to regulate by July 2020 under what conditions and who can mine there. The third type is deep sea plains, where poly-metallic nodules ranging from marble-small to grapefruit-sized lie around.' I show them a photo. 'If there were light down there, it would look like this.'

'For the time being, mining in the deep sea plains appears to be the most attractive option, both technically and financially. This is what we should concentrate on with the simulation for the moment. To do this, I can find most of the data and feed it into the computers. Provided that David programs and tha allow ILSA and SAM to work together.'

'Great! What do you think, honey?'

Miéko smiles like a Buddha statue. The whole house of the Freis is somehow Zen. It gives me peace. First she looks lovingly at Reto, then her eyes flash, and finally she says: 'What are you waiting for? Or do I have to send you a Kami first?'

I don't know what a Kami is, but I guess that's what tha call a successful kick-off.

When David and I walk with Bea down the meadow towards the Müllers' villa, we are both pumped up. Dancing in exuberant movements upon the grass, I distribute the daisy water. David just watches, but doesn't ask.

'Let's not say a word about this to Pa.'

'I'm not going to add fuel to the fire.'

'Once a day there is a meeting at the Freis. He will not ask. Reto and Miéko don't worry about Corona. We'll keep our distance and wear masks.'

'Mieko finds mouth-nose-masks important. It seems to be normal in Japan, at least in big cities, I heard.'

'Lucia, this is the coolest project I've ever been on.'

'If we're successful, we can show all the boomers what's really hip.'

'Pa will have to come up with a new job, I'm afraid!'

'We won't know until we have the results. So far I only have a hunch that deep sea mining, as they plan it, is a stupid idea for mankind and the Earth. Those money vultures will repeat all the mistakes they made on land for the last two hundred years.'

'The Freis like you. Did you notice how they always smiled at you?'

'I like them too. What do they do?'

'Reto is a spiritual entrepreneur.'

'What does that mean?'

'When I programmed his ILSA I had to feed the online news and videos of some websites into his daily personal news feed. Everything that is business of course: NZZ, Handelsblatt, Financial Times, Washington Post, Forbes, Japan Times, Times of India, The China Times and so on. But also sites with spiritual news and videos like ThoughtsFromAMaster and WeSeekToServe.'

'And what's on these pages, have tha looked at them?'

'Sure. Both are American .com-pages with news from Ascended Masters.'

'Who?'

'Well, beings who used to live on Earth themselves and now, as a kind of elder brother or sister, you could also say master teachers, help those who have to learn more in order to develop themselves further.'

'Any example?'

'When I visited the websites and the videos, I recognised some names, others I did not know. Mother Mary, sure, everybody knows; but Lord Maitreya, Master Yeshua, Master Saint Germain ... no idea ...'

'Hm ... interesting, really interesting. Is it because the Freis have no children or grandchildren that they have so much time to spend with tha?'

'Yeah, they kind of adopted me; they're my surrogate family. If I don't come for a few days, they're missing something. I miss them too. Grandma Jin Jin is too far away. Today she lives on Vancouver Island and is the coolest grandma a guy can have. Everything I know about nature, she taught me. First she sewed me Indian clothes. Then we made campfires, caught fish, gutted and fried them. We slept in tents together, she sang songs and told me stories.'

'What kind of stories?'

'About the Okanagan people and Lake Okanagan. I like the ones best about the monster in the lake, Ogopogo. Ogopogo is a kind of Nessi like in Loch Ness.'

'And how often do tha see thar grandma?'

'Once a year, during the summer holidays. She lives on the edge of a small town. Don't tell anyone, but I still play with the otters and look up at the eagles when I'm with her.'

'I know how wonderful animals and nature are. But it's even more wonderful to have someone who understands that too.'

David puts his arm around my shoulders and presses me against him. We look at each other briefly and understand each other without words.

'Reto and Miéko understand that too.'

'Are the Freis rich people?'

'Everyone who lives on the hill here in Rüschlikon is rich. Only Miéko and Reto don't behave like that. Reto used to have his own business in Japan; now he has a different one, he says. Miéko is a famous Shinto ink painter, and her colour woodblock prints are spectacular. With this technique she makes really cool mountains, trees, people, bizarre ghosts and gods. They came to Switzerland from Japan at exactly the same time as we did from London. Miéko is now even more famous than she already was in Japan. Pa bought the two paintings in his home office from her. A few years ago, he tried haggling about the price for a unique woodblock print. You should have seen her then. Took the picture right out of his hands and then served tea while repeatedly flashing a friendly smile.'

'I thought he only drank espresso.'

'Her lesson stuck, polite but clear. He waited two years until he dared to ask her again for a picture. At one of her exhibitions in Zurich he chose the two now in his home office and then went on a charm offensive, first loudly showering Miéko with praise and then whispering in her ear that he would buy the two. And what do you think she did?'

'Refused?'

'Nope - cooler, much cooler. She stuck a red dot next to the two pictures, crossed out the price, wrote double the amount on the little sign and announced loudly how much she enjoys selling these pictures to him. You should have seen his face.'

'And he didn't chicken out?'

'Nope. A bigwig from the world of raw materials, with whom we were at the opening day and who knows something about art and collects it, was standing next to us. Pa doesn't know a thing about art.'

We both burst into laughter.

'I think I can learn a thing or two from her.'

When we arrive at the front door, the postman appears with a small parcel for David. His eyes light up as he looks at the sender.

'I have a surprise for you and me.' He shakes the package.

'What is it?'

In a whisper he continues: 'A sibling DNA test from a laboratory in Switzerland. I really want to know, don't you?'

'I think I was just imagining things. David, it would be great to have tha for a brother, but thar dad's not Adam.'

'But he can lie if it's to his advantage.'

'Anyone can do it.'

'The DNA test is very simple. Swab the cheek mucous membrane with a cotton swab and then we send it back to the laboratory. We will have the results in a fortnight. And until then, not a word to anyone. I'll put your test kit in the guest bathroom and collect it inconspicuously in the morning.'

'DNA test—I could've come up with that.'

'The Doc gave me the idea when he took the mucous membrane sample in my nose. Google knew the rest.'

'But wouldn't tha have to tell thar father? Tha're so thick together.'

'When he came back from New York, I questioned him. He said he only invited you because it was good for his future business intentions. He swore to me that he hadn't fathered any children apart from me. But...'

'But what?'

'Everything inside me says you're my sister. If I'm wrong, then nothing happened. Besides, he doesn't always tell me everything. But if I'm right, then I'll have to ask some completely different questions.'

'Wouldn't he agree if tha told him?'

'If he really wanted to clarify it, he would have suggested himself that he take a paternity test. Don't you get it? I love my Pa, but I can't say I know everything about him.'

'But I honestly don't know which result I'd prefer.'

'What do you mean?'

'What do we do if we're siblings and we find out that he's been lying to tha and me, and abandoning my mum really badly?'

David raises his shoulders.

'That's what I'm afraid of, David.'

RÜSCHLIKON, 31 MARCH 2020

Thomas Müller is getting on my nerves. The man has bumblebees in his pants. He's always running around with plugs for his smartphone in his ears, offering himself and his ideas. He's looking for a job, but it has to be a career move up the ladder. The Catholic, as he calls him, has offered him the CEO job he hoped for. But only a three-year contract, less salary than asked for, payable in US dollars, 40 percent fixed, the rest bonus depending on performance. The holding company is said to be in the US state of Delaware. That pisses him off enormously. A medium-sized company from Canada has offered him a managing director's position. But he does not want that job either. Not prestigious enough: career crunch, he told David. Are all men in the business world like that? Are they actually interested in *what* they should do? What significance their work has for the world and others? I don't check that ...

David is with Bea at Reto's, and I have peace of mind to do my research undisturbed. Miéko and Reto want to understand better what I intend to find out and document. David has to rack his brains over how to link SAM and ILSA. He imagined it to be easier than it is. I've been sitting at my laptop since seven this morning, humming softly to myself, collecting research results from universities and research institutes from the Barents Sea to Okinawa, the Indian Sea to Hawaii and the Outer Hebrides, breaking them down and sending them to SAM. My eyes are probably square rather than round by now and are almost falling shut. Rubbing them doesn't help any more. I'll take a break and eat something. But before I do that, I'd like to give Reto and Miéko a short overview. They want to know more about the deep sea, so they can get a more informed picture without having to google themselves to death for hours.

The total surface of the earth measures 510,000,000 square kilometres, 70.7% of which is covered with water - oceans, rivers and lakes. The largest water area is the Pacific Ocean, followed by the Atlantic and Indian Oceans. The average depth of these three oceans is between 12,700 and 11,000 feet. Large parts of the oceans have up to now remained inaccessible and completely unknown to us. We know more about the back of the moon than about our deep sea. Twelve men have set foot on the moon so far, but only four men have reached the bottom of the Mariana Trench in a submarine. This is a deep sea trench in the western Pacific Ocean, at its deepest point 36,000 feet below sea level.

There is no single definition of where the deep sea begins. Some people speak of deep sea from a depth of 660 feet. This is where the transition zone between the continental margin and the continental slope begins. Other definitions of deep sea are based on water temperature or the penetration depth of light.

In any case, the deep sea is the lowest layer of all oceans, from a depth of 3,300 feet or more. There, the deep sea is an extremely hostile environment with temperatures that rarely exceed 37.4° F and can fall as low as 28.76° F. The exception known so far is hydrothermal venting ecosystems (the chimneys I mentioned, which can exceed 662° F). Low oxygen levels and extremely high pressure prevail. At a depth of 6,500 feet, the pressure is 200 times higher than atmospheric pressure at sea level.

The seabed can be extremely diverse. Besides deep-sea trenches, there are wide plains and impressive mountain ranges, so-called mid-ocean ridges. Although seemingly unreal, the deep sea, as a desert-like habitat, is home to a high biodiversity. In this respect it is similar to the rainforest. But what is perhaps even more remarkable: the deep sea is the largest ecosystem on earth. What we know is that deep sea animals have had to develop through unusual and unique adaptations in order to live, reproduce and thrive under these conditions. The lack of sunlight has led to unique visual and chemical adaptations. So far we know ...

My eyes ... I'm tired ... are closing ... I'm dreaming of the blue vase ...

I feel how I'm swimming in deep, cold water. Next to me is another young woman who looks just like me, Afro hair, milk chocolate brown skin, almond brown eyes. We are wearing a kind of seagreen cape that swirls in the current together with our hair as we swim along the bottom of the sea between plants and seaweed. We come to the edge of a smooth rock face and I see a huge hole. A strong current draws us closer. We are sucked in and pulled into a cave on the other side without being able to do anything about it. The water in the cave is shallow. We get up and walk up steps. It is dim, but there is enough light to see. I ask who she is and what her name is.

I am NÃO, your chaperone in the Deva world.

She smiles and I smile back. It feels right and important what she is saying, and I don't ask myself any more questions about it at the moment. Funny, I don't know myself like that.

We both pull our capes up and continue up the stairs into a large and really massive cave room. The rock is flat like a platform, but naturally shaped. The curved ceiling of the cave seems almost uniform, but just as naturally organic and wet. The whole cave has the colour of rich, dark-green seaweed. A number of creatures await us at the other end. They look at us spellbound. I feel their eyes resting on us more than I can see them clearly. In the middle sits a kind of queen - at least I think so. On each side of her chair are companions, dimly visible, larger and smaller, some more bluish, others greenish. It's only the queen whom I can see more clearly. She is a fish-headed being. In front are gills, the mouth points to the ceiling, and the eyes are turned to the sides or to us like a frog. Her henna-red hair resembles a sea fan, but it is also like a crown spreading out from the back of her head. Her clothes look like a flowing algae robe.

'Welcome!'

'Thank tha. Where are we, and who are tha, please?' I can't restrain my curiosity.

'In the Outer Hebrides, a twin town of the Orkneys.'

'We're in a city?'

'There are countless cities in the sea.'

'Sunken cities, archaeological, tha mean?'

'I mean cities where there live sea people such as ours.'

Really? Looks like nothing more than a cave to me.

'We must put an end to the land-dwellers' misconceptions about mermaids and mermen, Neptune and Nereus. The oceans are not inhabited by solitary treacherous or horrid creatures. Highly developed water people live here. You, Lucia, shall learn who we are. You will be able to see, hear and feel with your own eyes and then apply this knowledge. This is our offer to you.'

I am speechless for a moment. I look at NÃO; she nods at me. 'Thank tha, what an honour,' I am finally able to reply.

'No one knows the seas better than we do. We know everything that goes on here. And we can no longer tolerate the way the land-dwellers treat us.'

I look at NÃO, seek confirmation.

'This is your chaperone. Without her you have no access to our world. We must be careful. Land-dwellers are the cruelest creatures on Earth.'

'I assure tha, I will not harm anyone here.'

'Your heart is pure. But you cannot know when you will harm us. You do not know us or our habitat. Nor do you know our laws or what it takes to keep everything here in balance.'

She's right. I'm interested in all this, but I don't really have a clue. 'Please, pardon my naivety.'

'You have been announced to us by SANAT KUMARA. The spiritual hierarchy is a guarantor for your truthfulness. Nevertheless, you will make mistakes and we have to make sure that we notice it immediately in order to keep any damage as minimal as possible.'

'I understand that.'

'You will come to us regularly. We will teach you who the sea people are. We will teach you how we live and how mankind could use the seas and the sea bed without destroying them.'

'Why are tha teaching this to *me*? I mean, there are enough specialised scientists who are just dying to understand this ecosystem better and who have the whole day to do it.'

'We have become extremely careful about who else we let in and with whom we share our secrets. We observe individual land-dwellers. We give them tasks that are of no use to them at all and see if and how they carry them out. We first want to find out their real concern for us. We look deep into the recesses of their heart, examine the intention of their soul. Only after years of experience with them do we slowly open up.'

'But what have *I* done to make tha trust me?'

'You've been working for five years now on the largest water-purification project for the Earth that has ever existed.'

'I don't understand.'

'Remember when that old man with the tousled hair came to you in the Nete meadows and gave you a daisy?'

'Yeah, he had a wonderfully soft voice and told me about the animals and the flowers.'

'Others would have run away, taking him for a tramp. But you were open to him, listened to him.'

'Yeah, that's right. He asked me to put the daisy in a crystal vase with lots of water and the next day to drink it and tell him about it.'

'He came back.'

'Yes, and the water tasted softer and sweeter than any water I have ever drunk in my life. Then he told me how I should multiply the water and asked me to drink it, to give it to the plants and animals and to pour a bottle of it every day into rivers, lakes, sewage or the sea.'

'And so you did.'

'Yes, I promised him, and I always have the impression that water, plants and animals gratefully accept it.'

'What you call daisy water, we call DEVA water. It serves the renewal of the Earth and has the power to transform all water into its original, pure state.'

'Tha can do that? Without chemicals and technology?'

'Of course. The water, the sea, is the cradle of the land-dwellers, and if they want to survive, they must learn to know and respect our secrets. We are ready to share our knowledge with them. But first they must prove that we can trust them again. Nothing that land-dwellers today know comes close to what we know, nor will it be enough to survive.'

'Tha speak of land-dwellers and water people as if they were one.'

'So they are! They're both human.'

'Then tha define human beings differently.'

'A human being is an aspect of a human soul with a vehicle for it. The aspect is incarnated to express the divine qualities of his or her soul. The vehicle is the body. A human being does not necessarily have to have eyes where the land-dwellers have them. Nor does it need legs to stand or move about.'

A hand shakes me. 'Ms. Peeters, wake up. You've fallen asleep.'

My head hurts. I lift it. No wonder. It was lying on the tabletop next to my laptop. David's father is standing next to me. 'I must have dozed off,' I reply. I have a memory of a seaweed-green grotto, sea people, a queen, a request, formulated as a warning instruction.

'You need a break. Don't you want to go to the kitchen and cook? David will probably come home every minute and be hungry too. I'll come down when you've finished cooking.' Then he leaves the room.

I shake myself, seek to come to my senses, get up, get a glass of daisy water - no, DEVA water - and drink it all in one go. I won't let him interrupt me, even less cook for him. I am curious, I want to know now. Did I just dream that, or is there more? Back at the laptop, I research sea people, mermen, mermaids. But first, I go out of the guest room into the corridor and say out loud towards his home office: 'I'm not finished yet. Why don't tha start cooking, and I'll join tha later?'

'I can't cook.'

'SAM will probably order tha a pizza.'

Who does he think I am, his servant? I delve into the standard online dictionary of folklore, mythology and legends. Sea people (mermaids and mermen) are supernatural beings who live mainly in the sea. Ovid writes that mermaids were born from the burning galleys of the Trojans by transforming the wood into the flesh and blood of the 'green daughters of the sea'. The Irish say that mermaids are ancient pagan women who were transformed by St. Patrick and banished from the Earth. A Livonian fairy tale tells that they are the drowned children of an unknown pharaoh who experience their fate in the depths of the Red Sea. There are countless stories and eyewitness accounts from different centuries, most of them from places next to the sea or rivers where mermaids are said to have been seen repeatedly. Mermaids are described as beautiful women from the waist up and as fish-like from the waist down. They turn men's heads with their appearance, their singing and the musical instruments they play. The Sirens also tried to defeat Ulysses as well as Jason and his Argonauts with their singing. The voice of the mermaid Lorelei on the Rhine River is said to have enchanted sailors so much that they listened only to her singing and smashed their ships against the rocks. Although they spend most of their time under water, mermaids are said to be able to take on human form, go ashore and mingle with people.

Depending on the country and culture, sea people have many names. Sea queen, sea nymph, sirens, tritons, underwater people, water babies and water girls are just some of them. There are also specific names for water gods and spirits in the local languages: Havfrue, Havmand, Scylla, Kappa, Ningyo. I also discover names for sea gods: Amphitrite, Atargatis, Lir, Mami Wata, Nereus, Njord, Poseidon, Rân, Sedna, Rusalka and Wodjanoi. The Dogon tribe in Mali, who live in caves, believe they have contact with a fish god. The water spirit called Nummu, who was amphibious, is said to have come from another planet in a spaceship. Around the time of Alexander the Great, Berosus, a Chaldean priest of Bel in Babylon who was familiar with both astronomy and the history of antiquity, writes his *Babyloniaca* and describes Babylon's history of creation and the appearance of a fish-man from space who taught art and science.

My head is buzzing, then it goes 'click, click'. I've been to the Louvre several times with Elizabeth and Dad, and there's a stele made of diorite, black deep rock in the shape of an index finger, which is over seven feet tall. Engraved at the top are two men in robes, the left one standing, the right one sitting. King Hammurabi of Babylonia, 1800 B.C., speaks to a divine being and receives from him the first laws for mankind. They are neatly carved in this stone. So there must be something to it after all. What if these are not just fantasies? What if all this really exists and we are just too stupid, too arrogant, too blind for it? I need to know that now! Let's see what Wikipedia has to say about the Code of Hammurabi.

AT THE COUNCIL OF THE SEA

Chronicle time 18.762.020 - 04.02

I lie tired with burning eyes in the guest bed of the gods, but my head does not want to sleep yet. All day long I have been researching facts and figures. But over and over again the blue vase from the entrance hall of the Frei's home came to my mind. Why is it painted so conspicuously inconspicuously on the wall? Why on the wall with the archway into the actual house? The Freis seem to be too attentive to just make a joke. Let me see ... in my thoughts I stand in front of the big blue vase, ask myself where it leads to ... and in my mind I walk into the vase and ...

It's dark, but my eyes get used to it ... I am standing in front of the giant queen of the sea and some smaller creatures in the underwater cave of the Outer Hebrides. NÃO, my chaperone, is standing next to me. The queen tells us her name. ETRUTHSIA. But I'm not sure if I understood correctly and ask again. Yes, she says, ETRUTHSIA and it means 'Family of Truth'. She says she is an Anchor of Truth. Whatever that means. A picture of her name appears before my inner eye. A sword stands for the first 't'. Its tip reaches down underneath the letters. To the place where one finds truth, in the depths. The sword is made of polished silver, simple in design. Today, I also recognise ETRUTHSIA's robe more clearly. It is decorated with pearls and tufts of barnacles. The queen brings her face very close to mine: she has truly sea-green eyes. She probably wants to inspect my Afro curls and almond brown eyes.

'Follow me! We are expected,' she says. We turn into her line of sight, towards the water. The other creatures - mermen, I suppose - are about five feet tall; they have scales, some of them greenish, others blueish. On their backs they all have a shell, similar to that of a turtle, but flat like a shield. Their head is human, but where the mouth is, they have a beak and on top of their head, in the middle between the blue hairs, an opening filled with water. Their eyes sparkle red and seem to be of different sizes.

I am fascinated and amazed at the same time, feel my heart start beating faster. ETRUTHSIA, NÃO, I and the little mermen are climbing down the steps into the water. ETRUTHSIA and NÃO take me right and left by the hands. We swim out of the cave into the open sea and follow different currents. They carry us away, we go faster and faster. We swim sometimes deeper and sometimes higher. Sometimes I can see clearly, sometimes like in the twilight, waves and crystals in different colours, sometimes it is pitch dark. I am happy to be held by them. More and more mermaids and mermen join us. Some have fins, some have double fins, others have legs with feet extended by webbed feet. Still others seem to have hardly a body at all, only a head with a crown in addition to filigree threads, which seem to get lost in the water as bodies, all in dark magenta. I have never seen such beings before.

At some point a huge underwater city appears in front of us. I can see it; from above sunlight penetrates the water. The buildings have soft, organic contours and caves. We pause for a moment, probably so that I can take it all in.

'The peoples of the sea, as different as they may be, work together to care for the oceans. Here and now the Council of the Sea meets to advance our project to heal and protect coral reefs. We have decided to invite you to join us.'

I am touched and excited at the same time. We slowly swim towards a kind of entrance to a huge, elongated coral reef. In front of it is a gigantic, glassy-greenish globe on which the oceans are depicted, not the land, as on Dad's globe. Everywhere there are bigger and smaller dots with a tiny red dot right in the middle. They are probably meant to represent cities. I have to check that. The sea is as inhabited as our land. There are cities, mountain ranges and ridges, wide flat areas, valleys and ditches. I can't believe it.

Suddenly a deafening, metallically shrill noise, like I know from horror movies, when something unknown is approaching. NÃO and I cover our ears. ETRUTHSIA and the mermen and women writhe in pain. When the gruesome noise ends, we swim to the entrance of the long coral building. It looks like a snail's shell which, turning counter-clockwise, narrows more and more into a kind of round lock. In front of it on the right and left side are seaweed plants, about three feet high and fernlike, with tapioca pearls on the fronds. They remind me of fish eggs. A mermaid shovels over the plant with her flipper hand and pulls the pearls right into her mouth. Eating is so easy here.

The wall of the sluice turns clockwise from the centre of the snail shell and we swim quickly through. Now we are in a space that looks like a snail shell from the inside. The entrance opening closes, then the water is sucked out. When we are standing on the dry floor, the back wall of the snail shell sluice opens in the same way. We enter a large cavity, high and open, from which other cave spaces branch off in different directions. The floor under my feet is made of mother of pearl; underneath it shines metal. The walls are decorated with massive spiral bowl sections, and coral trees embellish the room. I cannot see if they have a function. All forms and surfaces are clearly organic.

The three of us are greeted by super-sized mermen that resemble the Tritons of ancient lore. Mighty, muscular male torsos, prominent heads with angular faces and wavy long hair. They wear tight-fitting trousers. The tail formations on which they stand have soft corners and shimmer like diamonds.

They bow before us and hand me an upper-arm bracelet of shiny gold. ETRUTHSIA helps me to put on mine. It opens along a delimited channel with a small wing- or fin-like formation on both sides. One of the Tritons says it is the Ancient Symbol of Alliances and I am now considered to be an Ambassador of Nations. As soon as it is attached to my left arm, the arm twitches and sweeps outward to discharge a burst of energy. As if that wasn't enough, the Triton hands me another miniature Triton in the form of a hairpin. He asks me to put it on as well and to keep bangle and hairpin carefully in my service bag. They are my keys to the city and to the world of the sea people.

I am confused. I feel honoured and respected. When I put the hairpin into my Afro curls, everyone around me claps their hands. I am ashamed, but ask what that horror sound was just a few moments ago. The Triton looks frustrated and replies with anger in his voice: 'The secrets of the universe are hidden in energies, frequencies and vibrations. Whoever consciously creates such sounds wants to frighten, destroy and annihilate. Most land-dwellers are not even aware of what they are doing. The cause of the sound-horror just now was probably once again a subterranean nuclear test triggered by land-dwellers. These berks call themselves scientists.'

'Please follow us now,' he says after a moment of inner contemplation. The Tritons now lead us through a long corridor, flooded with white light. We enter a kind of ballroom; large beaded ropes hang down above our heads. The light is still white, and I suspect that the ceiling material is translucent: corals or shells. There is no solid wall, only fluid organic forms as transitions. On the floor are amazing inlays of shells, perhaps abalone and mother-of-pearl with a distinct contrast of dark and light. Further ahead there is a kind of stage, a raised platform area framing the other end of the room. Huge coral trees adorned it on the right and left. I think that we are in or under a coral reef. The white light is uniform; it must come through the reef top.

One of the Tritons hands us three small mussel shells with a carbonated, orange-coloured liquid. I take a sip and immediately feel refreshed. It tastes vegetable-fruity, not fishy.

Someone is gently touching my left hand, and before I can even look around, the familiar gentle voice says *Welcome, Lucia. How do you like it here?*

That kind face, those blue eyes full of love. His hair goes down to his shoulders and he wears a purple robe that gently falls down to his feet and sandals. A white wreath of lights emanates from him.

'How did tha get here, YESHUA?'

I am a confidant of all people.

'Where are we?'

What do you think it is?

'An undersea town, but something's weird.'

Oh, what's weird?

'See the metallic glimmer underneath the floor?'

Before he can answer, two Tritons come with a plate full of interesting shapes. Delicacies to eat, I suppose. But I'll leave it alone. I want to know what's going on and look around. The hall is now filled with probably a thousand sea people. Suddenly, there is a rattling sound behind me. I quickly turn around and see how mermen who look like the ones who came with us are making fun of a Triton whose tray has fallen to the floor. They make faces at him and he looks back angrily as he picks up the tray and the shards. Then I hear music, unlike anything I have ever heard in my life. It is a kind of symphony of underwater sounds: soft, sweet, harmonious. All beings present form a circle around the centre of the hall, into which dancers step. Must be some kind of welcoming ceremony. The pairs of sea people in the middle of the circle begin to turn around each other in ever-new figures, but always in a circle with each other. They wear flowing, sarong-like robes in blue and green with golden flashes on them. When they finish their dance, they bow and everyone claps.

A fish man on stage raises his voice and asks for attention. All turn towards him and I make sure to stay close to YESHUA. I want him to answer my question.

'Dear water people, dear friends and confidants, dear alliance partners, welcome to the working sessions of the Council of the Sea on the survival of coral reefs. For us it is existential to keep the coral reefs healthy and full of life. Coral reefs are not important to land-dwellers, only to those who in some way live directly from them. Our experience in recent years is that even this group of people is not strong and consistent enough with their efforts. So we have to multiply our own efforts. With the water-restoration project of the Devas on the one hand and the reef-restoration on the other hand, we Sea People will regain strength and be better equipped to deal with land-dwellers. Although we are uncomfortable with this, we must recognise them and demand respect and cooperation. Some are beginning to understand that the oceans, their reefs and resources are not for self-service. We are already working with a very few of them, but we hope that there will be many more in the near future.'

He receives applause, half sung, half clapped.

'We thank the Ascended Masters and our Off Earth Allies for their unconditional support since we can remember. Today they have brought to us another woman whom they trust and whom we can therefore trust as well. She has selflessly proven over many years that she serves water and has shown respect for all life forms. The land-dwellers have named her Lucia, but her real name is TRUSIAN. She has just received the sign of the Alliance and the keys to this city.'

He points in my direction and everyone looks at me. I feel as if I'm turning turkey red, but I don't know whether I can do that under water. I look downward, it is mega embarrassing.

'We need not fear her. But she does not know our laws and customs, does not know what is good and right here with us. So let's be careful how we deal with her.'

I look up again. They must be able to see that I am embarrassed. Something that sounds like a sea murmur fills the whole hall, then suddenly everything shakes and I am knocked over.

The others are still standing, no idea how they did it. I quickly rise. I didn't hurt myself.

'We now want to turn our attention to our project work for the corals, and I ask everyone to do their best in the next few days so that we can implement the revitalisation concept we are developing on all coral reefs in all oceans in the near future. Please go to your project groups in the adjoining rooms now. Tonight we will meet here again for the banquet. I thank you.'

The sea people buzz and clap, then scatter, and I am happy to stand by YESHUA, ETRUTHSIA and NÃO.

'What was that?'

This? Oh, just a minor seaquake. But wait until Poseidon lets go of his pent-up anger; then the land-dwellers will feel with their own bodies what they have already done.

'They must not trust the land-dwellers - tha hear? Most of them are greedy and selfish. They will do almost anything for money and power or for fun. Please, warn them, Yeshua.'

For thousands of years, they have had the most painful experiences. The fact of how they treat you should be proof enough.

I am ashamed. Yes, I shouldn't have made that comment.

So ask me.

Right, he can read my mind. YESHUA smiles kindly at me.

'I can't explain it, but this city here underwater doesn't look like a coral reef to me.'

Really? May I ask why not?

'I went diving with Dad once on a coral reef in the Red Sea. The water was light blue, teeming with small fish of all shapes and colours. The coral reef itself was also shining in bright colours, but nowhere else was there this metallic shimmer like here in the floor. Also the entrance sluice didn't match. A snail shell, whose spiral winding serves as a sluice. It's too technical.'

YESHUA starts to laugh out loud and claps his hands with joy. Then he beckons three other beings I have not seen before. They are certainly not sea people. They are about ten feet tall like him, wearing white, gently falling robes with a blue sash around their waists. Their faces I can only see dimly: narrow eyes, small noses, the head is wide at the top and tapers towards the chin. Somehow a mixture of Caucasian and Asian head shape. All wear discreetly patterned round caps.

She saw right through you, right away, says YESHUA.

The three creatures also laugh and clap their hands with joy. Some sea creatures look around curiously at us.

HONGYSTSEE, please tell Lucia where she is here.

'HONGYETSEE - but I know him.' Judging by his clothes, he's the most important of the three. His blue sash is twice as wide as the ones of the other two. He looks old and wise. His beard, running down at a right angle from above his upper lip to his chin, is snow white. The hair on his head is hidden under the round cap.

You've blown our cover. This is indeed not a coral reef that serves as a meeting place. It is an observation station of the Off Earth Allies of the Kingdom of Servers, which also provides a meeting place for the Sea Council. We have camouflaged it with coral. But the coral cover has to be renewed, because here too the global warming caused by the land-dwellers has resulted in severe damage.

'Tha're kidding.'

Why should I?

'Spaceships fly.'

Not this one ... right now.

'I thought ... '

You can only think what you have experienced.

I am completely confused. Me, as a land-dweller, among the sea people is already a cracker, but on top of it YESHUA and Off Earth Allies from the Kingdom of Servers, who have a spaceship among the sea people, which serves as an observation station and meeting hall ... totally crass. Really crass.'

The three of us say a polite farewell to HONGYETSEE, his colleagues and YESHUA. ETRUTHSIA and NÃO want to show me more. They lead me back through the passage towards the lock entrance. Shortly before it we turn right into one of the side rooms, which is also secured by a lock door. In the room there are about twenty different kinds of sea people gathered, holding crystal rods and instruments in their hands, with which they make delicate noises to act on a pale coral. I have the feeling that they are painting symbols in the air with the crystal rods, energetically connecting them and thus healing the pale coral. In addition I hear a soft sound, like a kind of harp playing. ETRUTHSIA explains to me that my ears are not trained to perceive the variety of sounds at all. A total of twenty mixed-project groups are at work to find the best way to heal the corals in the oceans through sounds and different symbol frequencies. Each group works in a soundproof room.

I am curious, step closer and want to touch the pale coral with my hand, but NÃO pulls me back at my cape like lightning. ETRUTHSIA shakes her head and says to NÃO: 'Well done. Do not let her out of your sight for even a split second. She still doesn't understand anything about sounds and frequencies. Her ears have learned to feel the wind attentively, but they can't hear what we hear.'

'I'm so sorry. I won't be nosy like that any more, I promise.'

'You have to stay curious, but limit yourself to questions.'

We say goodbye with a bow, go outside and then into one of the neighbouring cave-like rooms. My eyes are enchanted by organic forms, pink to whitish sparkling ceiling and walls, and the floor in metallic shimmering mother-of-pearl. We sit on a kind of curved platform. A Triton is already waiting for us and hands me a tablet. I am stunned, and when he starts it, I expect symbols, music or some kind of marine law book. Instead I see pictures that tell me the story of a rebellion. Water people, fish-like with small and very flexible bodies that refuse to go ashore, not all of them, but many. The water people are slowly dying out, and some land beings are coming back to help them. But the land beings are not welcome. The water people even sabotage them. The returned land beings have to endure great hardship, many die a cruel death. They no longer remember what it takes to live and dwell in the water. Only one single merman teaches them the songs of the water people, and the DEVAS help them to build houses and grow food. After several generations in bitterly hard living conditions, the DEVAS and the returned land beings trust each other and mix together to form a new people. The original water people die out. So many sad pictures. My eyes get wet, I have to swallow. NÃO comforts me and ETRUTHSIA says we are leaving, there is more for me to understand.

In front of the entrance to this cave-like room, a large merman in a long robe of rusty colours awaits us. The robe falls to the floor like a curtain, and towards the head it merges into a high black collar that could almost serve as a hat. He bows and asks us to follow him into another room. There eleven mermen are already sitting on a circular bench, dressed like him. We climb over the seat and sit down and join them, forming a circle together. 'Welcome,' they say in chorus, but do not introduce themselves.

'Before you leave us, we want to make sure you understand something, Lucia-TRUSIAN.' They speak with one voice, as if they were all one.

'I'd love to,' I reply, but I have no idea what's coming.

'The land-dwellers must learn of the existence of the sea people. Their and our survival depends on it. If they don't treat us with respect, we will not provide them with our technologies. You, Lucia, are an extremely important ambassador for us, and we place our trust in you and in your strength.'

I am touched; I guess I'm getting red in the face again and hope they don't notice. I answer meekly: 'If there are so many sea people, why don't the land human beings see you?'

'They have broken the equal partnership with the DEVAS. They thought they were beings of higher value, more important. They cheated them and stole their technology. We have also learned from this; we hide from them.'

'How do tha do that?'

'With telepathic projection, a DEVAS technique. It allows us to go ashore and move among them without their knowledge.'

'And the technology tha speak of?'

'Hidden in bioglyphs, written by DEVAS and carefully guarded, as are many things. We have, for example, the technology to provide the world population with sufficient food.'

'I ask myself if the land-dwellers will ever come to their senses. I can see what atrocities they are already doing to Earth and how they don't care if they pollute water.'

'Whether there is a future on Earth for the human family depends on the land-dwellers. We Sea People can teach them the gentle ways, cooperation and partnership with the DEVA kingdom.'

'But will they acknowledge tha if tha show thaselves?'

'We have to take that risk. That is why we need people like you first. Look, it is the soul that makes a person, not their body or their culture.'

As I step out of the blue vase in my thoughts, I am lying in bed; but I'm wide awake and have to shake myself. I didn't dream these things up. This is real. No sooner have I showered and drunk DEVA water than I am sitting at my laptop again, pondering and researching. How am I supposed to make a meaningful contribution? Who can help me?

RÜSCHLIKON, 10 APRIL 2020

David and I see Miéko and Reto once a day now. David is working with Reto on the SAM-ILSA connection. I enjoy time with Miéko, even if I only watch her at work. David's Pa is annoying. He's always asking for something and their housekeeper hasn't come back yet. Yesterday he tried to fry steaks himself. It went horribly wrong, burnt black on the outside and still completely blood-soaked red on the inside, plus the disgusting smell all over the house. I refused to fry or clean. I cook vegan, vegetarian at most, but nothing with eyes, and I'm not his maid. He raved, and I demonstratively talked to my Dad on the phone.

In Miéko's studio it smells wonderfully of wood shavings, various types of paper, black and coloured ink. Along the window front facing Lake Zurich stands her elongated worktop: tidy, I estimate 25 feet long, with workstations for calligraphy, woodcut production and printing. Her tools at each station are neatly arranged: round wooden vats, woodcarving knives and chisels, brushes and leather stamps. At the ink station, brushes of various sizes hang on loops in stands so that the brushes dry with the hair down. Next to them are two ink stones, liquid ink and ink bars for rubbing, white ceramic bowls and pots for water, inking and mixing. If I weren't so afraid of painting or drawing myself, her studio would be a Disneyland to try out.

Miéko paints landscapes, twigs, bamboo, birds, the sea, waterfalls, fish, gods, legendary figures, all in shades of black ink on white paper. Sumi-e is what the Japanese call this. And she makes woodblock prints of spiritual themes, which she then prints in colour on paper like Hokusai and Hiroshige once did. She makes large series at low prices for everyone and small series for collectors and enthusiasts all over the world as well as super-expensive unique pieces. David told me that his father had to pay 50,000 Swiss Francs for the two woodblock prints of the Shinto sun goddess Amaterasu in his home office. Cool, really cool.

On the wall opposite Lake Zurich there are worn-out, shiny, waist-high wooden cupboards, at the top a high desk with an inclined shelf and below it elongated drawers only a few inches high. On a shelf lies the picture folder *One Hundred Famous Views of Edo* by Hiroshige spread out. The edges of the individual pictures are worn away, as if Miéko were constantly leafing through them for inspiration. In the drawers, several of which are open, there are different kinds of paper, and in one of them there are half-finished works of art, but I'm not so sure, because I don't understand anything about the woodblock printmaking art that the Japanese call Ukiyoe. I only know this famous *Wave,* which everybody has seen before, blue-white-black, by Hokusai. In the foreground, a huge, probably deadly wave breaks over sailors in their narrow wooden boats from the left, while in the background, the holy Mount Fuji is almost small and insignificant.

On the wall above the wooden cupboards hang framed works of art in ink, small scenes brought to life with just a few strokes of the brush: a frog jumping into the water, the stem of a flower that has bloomed, which fascinates me incredibly, and I don't know why. Then my breath stops: a merman. He looks just like those who accompanied ETRUTHSIA, NÃO and me to the meeting of the Council of the Sea, where they sneered at the Triton. I look at Miéko, want to know immediately how she came to it, but she is sitting highly concentrated over an ink work. I have to wait, sit down on one of her chairs at the free workstation for carving the woodblock prints and watch her carefully. Miéko is absorbed within herself. Every movement is fluid and controlled, a calm, steady rhythm of breathing, like meditation. Every stroke of her ink brush is precise. Nothing is superfluous, everything looks harmonious and intentional. Not a gram of energy wasted. When the mountain landscape is finished, her face lights up, like a little child who has accomplished something. She places the brush on a porcelain stand with troughs, which holds the brush hairs away from the clean wooden worktop. Then she stands up as if in slow motion, steps back and looks at her work again from a little further away. The corners of her mouth become even wider.

'What do you think?' she asks quietly.

I stand next to her. My heart leaps: so beautiful, so clear, so pure. A mountain slope, sparsely wooded, in lines in black and grey, thick and thin, on white rice paper. 'I'm overwhelmed, Miéko.'

'Then let's have tea so the sheet can dry in peace.'

'I have to ask tha something, Miéko.' I point to the ink drawing of the merman.

'In a moment; first we'll make some very good tea, Gyokuro, as a reward, then we'll sit upstairs and talk.'

On the outside wall of the studio, which connects the two long sides, a wooden spiral staircase leads to the floor above. On the other, short side opposite, near the entrance to the studio from the residential building right at the window front, there is a small station for making tea. Everything has its place at there, too. A crystal carafe with fresh water, a kettle, two teapots, a large and a small one, both made of the finest porcelain, and several identical tins with tea leaves, each with characters written on them. Miéko prepares us this green Gyokuro tea from loose leaves in the small pot as in a ritual. She takes some pastry from a small cupboard under the worktop and hands me the plate.

'Where are the teacups?'

'Upstairs.' She points with her head towards the spiral staircase. 'In my sanctuary. And there are very few people on Earth who have ever set foot there.'

A surge of emotion runs through my body. She takes the teapot, I take the small plate with light green mini cakes. I look again at the ink drawing of the merman, but hold back and wait until we are upstairs. There, I look at an elongated wooden shelf with books, artistic vases, small pictures and sculptures with large spaces in between. Everything has its place as if in a composition. In front of it, looking out over Lake Zurich, are two armchairs made of medium brown wood, seat and backrest covered with sea-green fabric. Between them is a round side table, on top of which are two small tea cups made of white-blue porcelain with a lotus flower. We sit down and keep silent. Miéko pours tea. We take a sip and still look wordlessly at the lake down in the valley. The tea is wonderfully mild, not as bitter as I know green tea. Then I can't stand it any longer. I finally have to ask.

'Miéko, down there on the wall, the dandelion, overwhelming. But the merman, I've seen him before, I mean, lots of them.'

'We Japanese call them KAPPA.'

Miéko turns to the side and points to a small ink drawing in an oval, gilded metal frame. I get up, stand in front of it and look at it more closely. My breath stops again. It is the symbol that the Sea People have given me as a Sign of Alliance. I look again carefully, look at Miéko and then again at the symbol. No doubt, that's it. My lower jaw sinks until my mouth is open ... I can't explain it to myself. Slowly I sit down again, take another sip of the mild tea and try to formulate a question for Miéko. I need to know ...

'Kappacho, the head of KAPPA, has once again misbehaved. It was indecent to trip a Triton while serving and then to laugh gloatingly with his people about how the tray including the goblets fell to the ground. It's lucky that the Triton remained so restrained.'

'How did tha know ...'

'I was there too.'

'So I'm not crazy?'

'Our ancestors were much more spiritually and technologically advanced than we are today. But certain information was and still is suppressed, so that the masses of people can't develop mentally but instead remain available to the economic system as willing servants. There would be so much to know, to learn and then to use to lead our planet and the human family into a golden age.'

'What is the meaning of all this? What does it have to do with tha, what does it have to do with me?'

'You are a symbol reader, a light-bridge builder, an energy renewer and a connector. I am a symbol writer. In my ink drawings and woodblock prints, I work with cosmic symbols. Pointing fingers for those who search or at least want to see. In all my works, whether they can be bought a thousand times by the masses for little money, expensively in small editions or as unique pieces for the rich who see art first and foremost as an investment - I reach them all.'

'How did tha ... why are tha telling me this?'

'We have tasks that are interrelated. More than that, we both belong to the Kingdom of the Keepers of Knowledge. Don't look so disbelieving and confused. I can prove it to the thirster after knowledge in you.'

She rises, stands in front of me and invites me to get up too. I rise insecurely and curiously at the same time. She takes a step back, pushes up with her right hand the left sleeve of her blue Japanese house jacket, and I see ... this can't be. She lets the sleeve of the jacket fall back down again and takes me by the hands. 'Only the mindful can find. Others see flowers that seem to bloom and die, see mystical beings carried into our time by sailors' yarns and children's stories; but we both see a larger, much more mysterious world.'

I push up the left sleeve of my dress, show her my birthmark. Miéko laughs at me.

'David has one just like it,' I say, agitated.

'But he doesn't see yet.'

'Has he been up here too?'

'No, he still works in the basement.'

I have to smile, sit down in my armchair again, have another sip of this divinely delicious tea. Should I tell her or does Miéko already know?

'You can choose between truth and delusion, Lucia.'

'Truth - what does truth mean?'

'For you and me: a life with many changes, ever new and exhausting tasks and growing insights.'

'But tha lead a steady life here on Lake Zurich.'

'Your eyes won't show you the slightest glimmer of truth. They lead you astray. Only a handful of insiders know what is going on in this house. Reto and I also led a steady life in Japan, but when David moved here with his parents, we were asked to pack up our things in Tokyo and move to Rüschlikon.'

'This is connected?'

'Of course.'

'Why am *I* here?'

'Your task is to bring the Earth and the human family back on the course of the divine plan. You must play a visible role in this world. The Sea People know this, and the Stone People know this too.'

'Miéko ... it's a bit much to ask.'

'Another illusion. You were born into this land-dweller body twenty years ago. But how do you explain that you have such abilities?'

'I was always studying and reading, watching nature, being alone with myself.'

'Your soul gives you your consciousness and your soul is eons old. I returned to the white pyramid for you to help prepare you for life in a physical body. For any Off Earth Ally, Earth is a much greater challenge than any human soul can imagine. Except the OBLAN; but that is a different matter.'

'So we're not treated like human souls?'

'No, you must first learn what masculine and feminine on Earth means, what matter is, dense and ethereal.'

'Miéko, do tha know what happened to me back then?'

'Your birth was scheduled for the 5th of January 2000, and then suddenly it had to happen very quickly. When your mother was shot, we had exactly two hours to let you incarnate into the growing life in her womb. It was very painful for you. Actually, you should have had a few more weeks to prepare yourself.'

I am even more confused than before, looking at her with my mouth open.

'Earth is a realm, Lucia, not a planet.'

'What does that mean?'

'She is not an object, therefore she has no edge. The Earth is a systemic environment, a multidimensional reality. And all those who learn to read symbols, parables and allegories, who learn to meditate, who are familiar with sounds and their effects or who can work absorbed in themselves will come to sense this realm.'

'I always saw animals in the clouds in the meadows along the river Nete in Lier. A white stallion storming towards me in the blue sky, for example.'

'If you retrain your conditioned thinking, you can grasp the One, the Unlimited.'

'So I'm not crazy?'

'You belong to those who are just learning to recognise and use their abilities. Let's have a drink to celebrate that.'

I reach for my tea cup, but Miéko stands up and takes a small white jug with characters and a cork stop from a cupboard on the shelf. In her second hand she is holding two small bowls the size of a shot glass.

'This is my best sake.'

'I don't drink alcohol.'

'I have been drinking for years to numb myself. It hurts to see so many blind and deaf people around me.'

'We are celebrating. Why do you want to numb yourself?'

'It takes a great deal of strength and courage to go down this road. You still have both in abundance, simply marvelling at the wonders on the other side of the veil and looking up at those who already know and understand them better. But as the years go by, it can be very frustrating to deal with all the weaknesses of those closest to you, those you love ... My life is not as perfect as the outside world would like to paint it.' She shakes uncontrollably for a moment. 'What am I saying, Lucia ... Now is not the time for this subject. Now is the time for real confrontation.'

'Real confrontation?'

'It is necessary in order to have the experiences that your life plan foresees as a path of knowledge.'

'I should confront myself and the world with all that I have now seen and learned? Is that what tha're trying to tell me?'

'Accept your true purpose and the spiritual hierarchy of the world will be with you, no matter who is fighting against you. And if you are frustrated and discouraged, come to me. My life story tastes of unreasonableness, aberration, dream and delusion, like the life of all people who learn to see. I drink to your health, and to the hope that you bring us.'

FAMILY COUNCIL SO

Chronicle time 18.762.020 - 03.16

We are delighted to have you with us again, Avidya-SOLAS. Please tell us how this Earth life went from your point of view.

I have been back home again with my soul family for a while now; I could recover from the transition and enjoy the reunion with SOLAS. But the joy was short. My consciousness fills me completely again. I remember the tasks I took on and compare them bitterly with what Avidya did and especially with what he *did not dare to do*. My Avidya aspect is inconsolable; his older incarnations, which were extremely successful, are no reason to cheer up.

As you are still thinking back and forth, let us begin as the Council of Elders. For this incarnation, you had asked to be allowed to perform three tasks that would contribute to the unity of the human family on Earth, and you chose two tasks for yourself to further your own development.

Yes, that's correct, I reply and bow to the elders of my soul family. *In order to promote the unity of the human family, I wanted to start my own company to mine metals and minerals in an ethically responsible way and let all people involved share fairly in their benefits and profits. I wanted to be a role model for the raw materials industry worldwide, a shining torch to help end the exploitation of mankind and Earth with all its consequences. I wanted to be elected to the highest offices of the industry associations in order to exert even more influence on a change towards good for all and the unity of the human family. And I wanted to pave the way for Thomas-THEODAR to continue my work and, more importantly, to give Lucia-TRUSLAN the foundation she needs to begin her great work for the human family.*

You have not fulfilled any of these tasks, although SOLAS and we had given you all the support you needed and kept nudging you to return to the path you had chosen. Please tell us what happened from the Avidya aspect of your soul.

Since my birth in Bombay, I fought for survival. My English father left my mother shortly before my birth and went back to his homeland. My mother was not abandoned by her family, but she and I brought shame on the Moha family. Out of my anger at my father, I was motivated to go to England myself, to make something of myself and then take revenge on him.

The soul of my earthly father steps beside me and puts its hand on my shoulder in a soothing way. *I shouldn't have abandoned you, Avidya-SOLAS. I'm so sorry. To make up for this, the elders and I agreed that one aspect of my soul's spark would immediately reincarnate and lead the life of a child abandoned by his father in Mumbai. The child meditated, so I could reach and guide him. He developed into a person living in inner peace and united with the others in the city.*

The words of my earthly father's soul don't comfort me.

You will remember that we chose India and a Hindu-influenced, neighbouring soul family for you, so that you could learn from childhood a way to be and stay in contact with your incarnated soul aspect in your inner being as soon as the overly intellectual school education started.

Yes, I learned early on to meditate and follow my inner voice. My mother always attached great importance to that.

But you stopped doing so when you arrived in England and concentrated only on survival and making money.

In the first few years, I had to do extremely menial work, usually sixteen hours a day. I slept on a damp mattress in a rotten cellar hole, all my belongings in a duffel bag. I saved every penny; at some point I could buy vegetables and fruit instead of just rice and bread, then a clean shirt, at some point a new pair of shoes. Those were six hard years. I worked my way up doggedly and adapted.

Your development plan envisioned difficult early years in London, including a lowly background. How else would you develop compassion for the poor and weak from the beginning, remain inclined towards them and stand up for them? But SOLAS could no longer reach Avidya. Avidya no longer took time for inner reflection and mindfulness in order to receive the guidance of his soul spark.

I look down in shame and continue. *My personal development goals included becoming the head of a family and being a kind, caring and loving father to everyone. A king who provides and guarantees order. When I was twenty-five years old, I made friends in London with the brothers Sahadeva and Nakula Kumar and fell in love with their younger sister Titiksha. They lived like me in the Hounselow district. It was the happiest time of my life. Then I met the rich widow Amal Ali while exploring London on a Sunday in Edgware Road among the Lebanese. I thought I would be able to realise my professional ambitions better and above all faster if I married her and not Titiksha.*

You made it a thousand times harder for yourself and everyone else.

I look down in shame again.

Shame is not appropriate, Avidya, aspect of SOLAS, because SOLAS has learned, albeit with serious consequences.

Yes, I reply and look up. It doesn't become easier for me as the Council of Elders continues. *Titiksha was your wife in previous incarnations and you had agreed to use this close bond and understanding.*

I married Amal, made her late husband's metal trade flourish and wanted to take care of her two sons. But I didn't manage to do so amid all the work. Amal and I also had two children, Pritha and Maya, but that wasn't good for business, and only Pritha developed as I imagined she would, became an Ayurvedic doctor and a respected person, albeit with a social flaw.

We do not need to go into that here. Just this much: Pritha has no blemishes and she is not your daughter.

Don't pull my leg.

Back to you.

Yes ... I kept the money in the business. Amal didn't like that at first; she wanted to buy a stately house in Chelsea and beautiful clothes as soon as possible. But I wanted to develop the company into a powerful player, I wanted to own raw material mines myself and save taxes just like the big mine operators with holding structures and letterbox companies around the world.

Are you being honest with yourself here, Avidya-SOLAS?

Maybe not quite. Above all, I wanted to finally belong there with them, to be respected and no longer vulnerable. I lost the strength to resist all the humiliations. I bought the mining concession in Kolwezi and others in other countries, mostly in South America. But business was always most difficult in the Congo. Then I met Thomas there. It was immediately clear to me that I had to tie him to the Vijay Group and my family. He was obsessed with standing up to the Chinese in the commodities market, and that bite and determination was much needed.

Now another soul approaches me. I immediately recognise the energies of THEODAR. He embraces me lovingly and says: *I have lost contact with Thomas since he is no longer under the influence of his indigenous mother Jin Jin. I therefore agreed to change his original incarnation plan in order to still have a chance to make our necessary contribution to TRUSIAN's task. Lucia needs help from Thomas, although now in a different manner than planned prior to the incarnation.*

Yes, I reply without really understanding. *In any case, Thomas was having a love affair when I met him in Kolwezi, and I had to end it, not only to lure him to London with the well-paid job, but also to keep him there.*

And how did you do that?

Giacomo Aringhe-Rosse told me that I should give out the command 'Plus Ultra' to the guards at the gate. They would then know what to do to scare away the demonstrating women once and for all. So Thomas was no longer able to gather information for his doctoral thesis about the resistance of the population, nor could he meet his girlfriend.

And you accepted that they shot unarmed women?

I did not order it, but I did not care what they would do.

Did you realise what happened when the protests ended abruptly?

No, I never asked about it. I was just relieved that Thomas was at some point concentrating only on the business and my daughter.

But now you know what happened!

Partly. SOLAS has witnessed many things, but no single soul knows as much as you Elders. I now know again that Thomas is Lucia's earthly father and his help is needed to fulfil her task.

At that time we discussed with SANAT KUMARA what to do. One aspect of EDEL's soul has incarnated again to assist Lucia. But to solve this problem we had to make use of a soul split.

I'm so sorry that I messed everything up, I'm really very sorry.

Your suffering maintains the darkness. That helps no one. We have to compensate. But you could have known all this and much more if you had made the effort to be in touch with your soul spark in your innermost being and had followed its inspirations. You could have avoided all the consequences if you had not given in to your control-obsessed fear and your purely self-absorbed thoughts.

My light-shape collapses, it only flickers; yet immediately all aspects of SOLAS catch and comfort me.

Please tell us what else happened from your point of view, dear brother, says the Chairman of the Council of Elders.

Thomas, I timidly begin again, *was the son I always wanted and needed to further expand the business. I supported him, he followed my wishes. Also my suggestion to marry Maya, because she was very fond of him. She understood immediately that he would always be able to offer her a life of prosperity and prestige. All I had to do was to make sure that the letters he wrote to his love in Congo in the beginning were never sent.*

And you felt entitled to do that?

Thomas is a doubter, a brilliant mind, a hard worker; but he remains a doubter who lacks the courage to go all the way to the bottom of things. I knew he would give up if she did not answer right away.

How did you manage to dispel his doubts about marriage to Maya?'

I promised him that on my death he would inherit shares in the company. And since he was so eager to outdo his own father in his career, he let go of his doubts and took Maya as his wife.

But you knew that Amal would not agree to your promise. The condition for marrying her was that she, and later her two sons, would inherit your shares in the company, so that the property would again be exclusively in the hands of the Ali family.

Yes, but I was hoping to convince her that the most capable person must run the whole thing so that everyone could continue to live in great prosperity. I had convinced her, she showed insight. Why she did not allow me to change my will in favour of Thomas and David at the last moment, I don't know.

Would you like to know?

Yes!

Amal found out your secret.

That isn't possible.

Oh, yes. She found out that you still loved Titiksha and that you continued to meet with her regularly after your wedding. Titiksha's soul had agreed to wait for you for many more years because there was still a chance that you would accept your task together with her. This meant a great and painful sacrifice for Titiksha, for which we are very grateful to her soul. Nevertheless, her sacrifice was in vain.

How did Amal find out?

People in dense matter call it coincidence. A tender letter from Titiksha to you was stuck unnoticed for years in the inside pocket of one of your jackets. An employee found it when she wanted to finally have the jacket cleaned and handed it to Amal.

Tell me one more thing. It was planned that I would leave the Earth again when I was 75 years old, but it was not planned that this would happen so painfully and quickly because of pancreatic cancer.

This cancer was the direct result of your dominant thoughts and feelings for almost the entire incarnation. First powerless anger towards your father, then deep fear of what was to come in London, and finally no confidence in your own self and the constant manipulation of events. Over the years you became more and more unstable and insecure; for fear of failing and falling, you clung more and more to things, to matter. The frequencies of pain and sadness overgrew your whole self and SOLAS had no chance.

I couldn't have described my inner life better myself.

We regard your incarnation as Avidya as failed, SOLAS. You have not fulfilled any of your tasks. Do you see it the same way?
Yes, I answer as Avidya-SOLAS sadly.

Where and how do you trust yourself to compensate for the many and serious causes that your actions have set in motion and that you yourself now recognise?

I have been thinking about this since I became one with SOLAS again. I am deeply ashamed to have failed so badly, to have damaged the plan for Earth and endangered the rise of our soul family.

We will also add this to your list of tasks to be learned: self-mortification, guilt and shame do not belong to a healthy development of consciousness of the soul.

Yes, I understand ... There is too much to balance, I can't do it alone. I guess I haven't matured enough to make sure that the balance is right either. And I suspect that I don't know in the slightest way what the consequences of operating the mine in Kolwezi will be for tens of thousands of people there, perhaps in the whole province. I won't even talk about the mines in other countries.

We agree, the Council of Elders responds with one voice. *One aspect of EDEL and a soul split are already dealing with the compensation that concerns Lucia-TRUSIAN. But everything else can only be decided in the planning session for the next incarnation, when the PERGAMENT of FILATERATES is available as well.*

The chain of my wrong decisions probably began with the fact that I wanted to win the respect of those who exploited and disregarded me as a poor guy from India. Instead of presenting myself to them as an example of human family unity and responsible behaviour, I celebrated them, their manners and whatever prestige has to offer. Perhaps I could repeat such a reincarnation.

We are convinced that you should first learn to free yourself from your material delusions so that they do not stand in your way in later incarnations.

The delusion that it is all about me? The deception that I have nothing to do with others? The deception that the Earth is there to be used by man?

These are just a few of them. We are convinced that it would be good for you to return to Earth as soon as possible. There is much to do.

And what about killing the incarnations of Shaira-EDEL and Amaike-MOISTARA?

You are not strong enough or careful enough to balance the murders. Or to change industrial mining either. Two souls from our Council of Elders have already voluntarily accepted this balancing challenge in alteration of their incarnation plan.

And the rise of our soul family on the way back to the Creator?
Is not possible at the moment after the development of your incarnation. We must first learn to serve better.

What about Titiksha?

There is reason to rejoice with her soul family. In spite of the fact that Titiksha did not fulfil that part of her incarnation task which was to found a family with you in neighbourly help and to support you in your tasks, she patiently took everything upon herself. She also supported her earthly and spiritual brothers unreservedly. Together Sahadeva, Nakula and Titiksha Kumar have helped their soul family to expand their consciousness and thus to further ascend on the way back to the Creator. All thirty members of their soul family have already made their ascent, and we rejoice heartily with them. May we also succeed in doing so in the next teacher-learning-loop. And now go, rest well. Afterwards we'll prepare for your next incarnation together with the others in the planning room.

RÜSCHLIKON, 28 MAY 2020

The test result has arrived. We really don't know how to deal with it. And, what is worse, David's Pa is no longer bearable. Every minute, he's moving heaven and earth to find a top job somewhere in deep sea mining. As soon as one of Thomas' business contacts is in the media, SAM plays the news over loudspeakers and the flat screens at the workstations and in the kitchen. It can be press information on a company's own websites, news from TV stations, reports and commentaries from newspapers, online service notes or social media news. The constant SAM chatter is annoying, and it hasn't helped him one little bit. So David's Pa is just making phone calls around the world, friendly blah-blah, which I have to listen to from his home office all the way here to the guest room. Closing my door doesn't help for more than half an hour, then he comes running in again, telling me some nonsense he's just heard from someone and I'm supposed to include in my project work.

In order to create news balance in the house, David programmed SAM to summarise once a day the worldwide news about COVID19 and also all #blacklivesmatter and Congo news. In fact, we are working now under constant noisiness. Thanks to Spirit, we have Bea. She lies here next to me at the chair, so that I can stroke her over the head. It's good not only for her, but for me as well.

David comes in with his phablet in his hand. 'Look at this, Lucia.'

But it doesn't get that far, because he stares at my screen as if spellbound.

'Green fluorescent alien spaceships in a galactic sandstorm? Haha.'

David points to the photo on my laptop and fantasises, while Thomas comes in curiously as well.

'No, microbes in deep sea sludge under the microscope of an American marine microbiologist.'

'Sod it, aliens and UFOs would suit me much better.'

'Tha're not gonna say that anymore, David if tha hear what this is about.'

'Let's hear it then, Ms. Peeters,' commands his Pa.

'Researchers have had such samples from the deep sea since 2002.'

'So what?'

'Despite all efforts, no laboratory in the world has so far succeeded in reproducing them in Petri dishes, the small round glass things in which everything that can be rapidly multiplied, such as ...'

'Mold, foot fungus, corona viruses ...' jokes David.

'Bollocks! We cannot reproduce them, even though we have offered them all the food they have in the deep sea.'

'Well, I guess they didn't have that cool energy drink we have in the fridge.'

'They had what we busybody human beings do not have: time, a lot of time to exist and live.'

'You're crazy. Why would they want that?'

'To supply a human being with energy for a day, tha need 100 watts. Such a microbe needs only 1 zepto-watt of energy.'

'Sure, it's much smaller.' David takes his phablet and probably wants to check the zepto-watt unit.

'Zepto-watt is 10^{-21} watts.'

'I can't imagine that. Give me an image, Lucia.'

'A zepto-watt of energy is when tha take a single grain of sand, and then tha imagine a pellet that is only a thousandth of the mass of the grain of sand, and then tha drop it a nanometer. A nanometre is a millionth of a millimetre. And tha have to drop the thousandth of a grain of sand only once the millionth part of a millimetre. That is enough energy. That's all these microbes need to exist.'

'And how often does a grain of sand like that have to fall for me?' Thomas wants to know.

'For humans we need a pineapple. A real one. If tha drop it on the floor from hip height 881632 times a day and link the released energy into a turbine, it will produce 100 watts and can supply an adult man with energy for a day.'

'I won't do that, guaranteed: too strenuous and sticky.'

'Think about it! The land mass of the deep sea is more than twice as large as the land mass above sea level. In the deep sea there is no light, no oxygen and hardly any food. Life in the deep sea follows different laws than those we know here. We know sun, oxygen, photosynthesis, rapidly growing ...'

'At all costs, if Pa has his way.' As David says this, he pushes his elbow hard into the ribs of his father, who he twitches.

'Ouch, that hurts. Stop it!'

'Human cells die after days, weeks, months, and human beings die after eighty, maybe soon a hundred years, but then that's it. These microbes are thousands, hundreds of thousands, millions of years old. But that is also mega-short, if tha think of the time that the Earth has existed: at least 4.6 billion years, most scientists agree. Sunlight, photosynthesis, day and night cycles ... all these make us fast and short-lived. But not the microbes. *We are the problem of the Earth!* There are at least two completely different circulatory systems on Earth, and the human system is the weaker one. *We* are the short-lived, and *we* also destroy the long-lived. If the age of the Earth were a twenty-four hour day, in two thousandths of a second we would destroy what has already existed for 23 hours, 59 minutes, 59 seconds and 998 thousandths of a second.' I get up, turn to David's Pa and say, 'Have tha understood now? Instead of exploiting the deep sea for further growth here on land, we should better study and understand this cycle of life, and transfer its mechanisms and capabilities to our short-lived, all-consuming world, so that we humans and the Earth live longer.'

'Cool! You are simply brilliant,' David cheers, embraces me, almost crushes me.

His Pa looks at us silently with open mouth.

Shortly afterwards, the three of us sit at the kitchen island and have dinner. I made tacos with guacamole, hummus, mixed salad and fresh fruit. Thomas still had to have scrambled eggs with bacon. What he stirred together in the pan seems as depressed as he is. David now also eats vegan. We chew silently, the air crackles with tension between Thomas and us. David is still thinking about when is the best time to tackle the matter and has not yet found an answer.

'It doesn't look as good as expected, David,' his Pa begins timidly. 'The commodities industry is shocked by events in Hong Kong. The Chinese security law that has been imposed is taking the breath away from entrepreneurial freedom. I have been asked to resign my mandate at the London Metal Exchange. China does not like the fact that ... '

'Do what you want, Pa, and go where you want. I'll stay here with Bea, study and develop SAM.'

'It's not that simple. Either I stay in classic mining, but there is no top job that interests me. Or I accept Giacomo's offer and have to move to the USA. Or, third option, I go back to Vancouver and become managing director of a small company that focuses on the deep sea.'

'The corona crisis will certainly bring new opportunities.'

'I can't sit around here idly making small talk on the phone or in the business club in Zurich. I need a real job again.'

'Ah, that's how it is, old man.'

'Don't call me old, David. I'll be only fifty in a few days. That's the best age for a man.'

'Midlife crisis, then.'

'Nonsense.'

'Can't you see you're pissing us off?'

'That's enough, David! Who takes care of all this?'

'Do you really think that's what this is about?'

'Of course it's about that, just that.'

David rolls his eyes.

'Be that as it may, I will probably accept Giacomo's offer. All I have to do is sign. I will learn to deal with the less pleasant things like working in the USA. At the moment the USA is almost at a standstill because of Corona anyway. Maybe that's why Giacomo is still thinking about it and will accept my Swiss proposal after all. The corona death rates in the USA are going to dizzying heights with that idiot Trump. As CEO of a newly emerging company, I certainly have all the options.'

'Are you sure about that, Pa?'

Before Thomas can respond, SAM gets in touch. 'Message on CNN about Giacomo Aringhe-Rosse. Now playing on all screens.'

'Hang on, SAM, I'm going up to my home office first to take notes.'

Thomas grabs his smartphone, slips hastily from the bar stool, leaves food and beer behind and runs up the stairs.

David rolls his eyes. 'Something must be done, Lucia. It really can't go on like this,' he says quietly to me. Then he waits a moment until he thinks his father is in the home office and instructs SAM: 'Start, SAM.' He's about to use the remote control to mute the screen in the kitchen so we don't have to listen to it, but the first words of the CNN newsreader hit us like a bomb.

One of the most influential men in the international mining industry, Giacomo Aringhe-Rosse, an Italian citizen with a green card, has just been handcuffed and taken from his suite at a hotel at Central Park in Manhattan to a detention centre in Brooklyn. According to the FBI, he was arrested on strong suspicion of multiple counts of incitement to murder, fraud, money laundering, tax evasion and sexual abuse of minors. Aringhe-Rosse is considered a confidant and henchman of some of the richest men in the world. He has been under round-the-clock surveillance by the FBI for months. The prosecutor responsible will shortly provide the press with further details. Aringhe-Rosse's lawyer, when asked, indicated that he would cooperate with investigators and prosecutors on behalf of his client.

We look at each other for a moment with open eyes and open mouths.

'Blimey!'

'I don't believe it, David!'

'I wonder if they'll interrogate Pa once he gets back to the States.' David blushes. 'I feel hot, Lucia.'

'Do tha think he knew?'

'No, I didn't, Ms. Peeters!' Thomas stands chalk-pale in the doorway of the kitchen. 'Don't look at me like that. I didn't know what Giacomo was up to. He never allowed anyone to look at his cards. 'Don't ask me about my business,' he said to me the other day in New York.'

'And you didn't run out on that remark?'

'Don't talk nonsense. It can mean everything and nothing.'

'That is *the sentence of* the godfather. Don't you watch classic movies?'

Thomas remains silent.

'At least tell me *what* you knew, Pa.'

Thomas Müller comes two steps closer.

'Giacomo provides the super-rich with opportunities to invest money long-term and with high returns. He is active in all resource-rich countries and maintains contacts with local elites. I also knew that he optimises his tax burden. After all, we all do. But I didn't know anything about criminal activities, and I'm not involved in that kind of thing: you know that.'

David and I look at each other. My rage is boiling in my veins. It's over, it can't last a moment longer. I jump off the bar stool. 'Mr. Müller, I quit. I'll pack my things first thing in the morning and I'll be gone.'

David remains calm. We had already talked about it and he understands me. His head is red and hot. I get a cloth napkin from the drawer, run cold water over it and hand it to him to cool his face.

Thomas rumbles back. 'First you take advantage of me, and then you want to run away from me. Impertinent and arrogant, I call that, Ms. Peeters. Come down off your high horse. You're no better or worse than I am.'

'News concerning Giacomo Aringhe-Rosse,' SAM reports before I can reply.

'Let's hear it, SAM,' David says calmly. Thomas comes all the way back into the kitchen to hear better.

The New York Times is reporting as breaking news on its online portal that, together with Giacomo Aringhe-Rosse, his bodyguard Vito Puzo was arrested. Puzo is a former commander of a paramilitary special unit who has been in hiding for years, using a fake identity and passport. Vito Puzo is accused of multiple murders as well as arms and human trafficking and has been wanted by Interpol for years. After a face-lift, he worked as a bodyguard for Giacomo Aringhe-Rosse under the name of Enzo Morello.
I have found a photo of the arrest and I am sending it to all screens.

On the flat screen in the kitchen appears the image of a muscle-bound, bald man with bulging lips in a black shirt and suit, surrounded and restrained by four FBI agents.

'Do you know him, Pa?'

'I ... what?'

'I want to know if you have anything to do with this guy.'

'No.'

Thomas has become as white as a sheet of paper. David and I look at each other. Somehow neither of us believes him. Thomas goes to the bar cupboard, gets a bottle of whisky out, leaves the kitchen and goes up the stairs.

SAM speaks up again via loudspeaker. *I found a CNN breaking news story, not a minute old.*

'Let's hear it, SAM,' instructs David.

Giacomo Aringhe-Rosse's bodyguard Vito Puzo has managed to escape from prison. It could be that he had helpers. A large-scale manhunt has been launched.

I go up the stairs into Thomas' home office and knock on the frame of the open door. He sits in his office chair, swings it around with a nudge from his foot, looks at me absent-mindedly, with a full whisky glass in his hand.

'Yeah?'

'I don't want thar money. I don't want anything from tha. I'm gonna pack up and go right now.'

'You make it too easy on yourself, Ms. Peeters. Just so you know, I'm not a bad person!'

'Tha want to be a ruler on a corporate throne and think the world outside is none of thar business. I'm terrified of people like tha.'

'You're just being snooty.'

I've had it. I turn around and want to go to the guest room, but at that moment the bell rings at the front door. The door buzzer goes off without any further inquiry.

'Lucia,' David calls from the entrance hall. 'Reto is here for you.'

With moist eyes I go down the stairs and towards Reto. He takes me in his arms, holds me tight and says: 'I'm here to fetch you. This is not the right place for you.'

RÜSCHLIKON, 7 JUNE 2020

'A bizarre reception committee for my fiftieth birthday, isn't it? ... I never expected to see *you* again, Ms. Peeters.'

David and I have been sitting next to each other on the sofa in the living room since early morning, waiting for his Pa to come down the stairs. David wanted it that way.

'Happy birthday, Pa.'

Thomas Müller opens his arms, probably waiting for David to stand up and hug him. But David remains sitting next to me and instead says: 'We are waiting for answers.'

'What is this nonsense about, David? And that on my birthday! And as for *you*, Ms. Peeters, please leave my house at once.'

'*She* stays as long as *I* stay.'

'Have you gone crazy too, son?'

David points with a movement of his head to a large envelope with a ribbon, which lies between us and Thomas Müller on the coffee table. Thomas takes it in an unsettled state, opens it, pulls out the test report of the Swiss DNA laboratory and reads aloud:

The two test subjects are half siblings with a 99.9 percent probability.

'Explain that to us, Pa. No fussing around.'

Thomas turns red and remains silent.

'Time to come clean, Pa! Lucia has already left this house, and I wonder if I have to leave too.'

Thomas looks as if he has been hit by a truck and gasps for air.

'We're waiting, Pa.'

David does this very well; I can't do it like this, I'm still too dazed. When the test report arrived, we hugged each other and cried, overwhelmed with joy. But the fact that his Pa lied to us makes us mega angry.

Thomas sits down on the armchair opposite us. His lips move, but at first no sound comes out. Then he begins in a stammering manner: 'During my doctoral thesis on industrial mining in Third World countries ... at the RWTH ... I received a scholarship to conduct research in the Congo. At protest meetings I met Amaike Keita ... I immediately fell in love with this brave, clever and beautiful woman. We were very happy for several months ... at least I was. Then Avidya offered me to continue my research with him in London ... paid and then a permanent position as manager as soon as I had submitted my doctoral thesis. He simply took me with him ... from one day to the next .... I couldn't even say goodbye.'

'Tha abandoned my mother and me!' I'm trembling, would like to get up and wring his neck, but I can't.

'No! I didn't know ... that she was pregnant. I never would have gone with Avidya if I had known ... I always wanted children. David, you know how much I love children ... I always wanted you to have several siblings, didn't I?'

'Anyway, tha bought yourself a son with Avidya.'

'I did not! That's a vicious allegation!'

'How could you ever marry Maya, Pa?'

'They ...'

'She is a calculating woman who loves only herself, if she can love anyone at all. She never paid attention to me, never held me, never caressed me like a mother does. I was just an accessory, part of your show of a happy family.'

'No, she ...'

'Come on, spit it out ...'

'She's not a mother and never wanted to be. I forced her to.'

'Just keeps getting better.'

'You wouldn't know anything about that.'

'You're just talking yourself deeper and deeper into it.'

'This is really not my fault.'

'I don't believe a word you say anymore. Your actions speak louder than words. Can't you see that Lucia and I know you're hiding something, that you're lying like hell?'

Silence. He rubs his hands, gets up, walks up and down, looks at us and then immediately down again. David reaches for my hand.

'All right. There's something you should know, David ... Maya was ...'

'Was what?'

'My cover ... '

'And on top of everything else, you're supposed to be an agent!'

'We'll talk about that when you get older, maybe in ten years.'

'Either you come straight with us here and now and make peace with me and Lucia, or there won't be any "in ten years". Do you get it? You're adding insult to injury.'

Thomas exhales deeply several times. Beads of sweat cover his forehead. He pulls out a fresh handkerchief as usual and dabs them. 'The team leader brought Ms. Peeters from Aachen, I didn't even know her name. Then we met in the corridor on the day I handed the CEO position over to Ismael. She looks like her mother, only her skin is lighter. She wears the same ring as she ... she talks like her, she looks at me like her, she laughs like her. I have never loved another woman as I loved Amaike.'

I don't believe a word he says anymore. 'And it never occurred to tha that tha might be my father?'

'No! I was just fascinated by you, and when the team leader told me you were a talent of the century, I spontaneously decided to hold on to you.'

'Bloody liar.'

'Your story has a nasty beauty mark, Pa.'

'No! No, goddamn it. I really didn't know that ... Amaike was pregnant, and if I had known ... I would have stayed with her. You know how much I adore you, how much I like children ...'

'I know how much you like your status, your prestige, your Porsche ...'

'Why did tha tell my mother thar name was Adam?'

He touches his heart, staggers and then sits down dazed again on the individual armchair opposite us.

'Please, try to understand and don't judge me.'

'We want the truth, the bloody truth. Lucia more than me. Do you have the slightest idea of the life you've thrown her into?'

'No ... yes ... perhaps ... oh, I don't know.'

'You're just getting a taste of your own medicine.'

'Adam ... Adam is my second identity.'

'You're not a double agent!'

'Adam is the being that still lives inside me. I am ... I ... am bisexual ... predisposed ... I am so ashamed of it. Once a year, when I go fishing in Quebec, I live it up. With Adam, my friend from my student days in Aachen. Adam ... is just like me. Sometimes we also meet on business trips ...'

He looks somewhat relieved, but there is something fishy about the story. 'And what was my mother to believe?'

'When she asked my name ... I answered 'Adam' spontaneously ... it just came out like that. I guess I wanted to warn her ... about the monster inside me. Afterwards I didn't have the courage to tell her my real name. I was afraid she'd leave me if I confessed I'd lied to her.'

'I don't believe a word tha say. Tha used my mother through and through. Tha sounded her out along with the other women for thar doctorate, and on top of it had good sex for a little while. That's what I believe.'

'No, damn it, NO! I wrote her three letters from London, but never got a reply.'

'That's all? Three letters from London to Kinshasa? And tha claim she was the love of your life? That doesn't add up. Tha had her address and tha never went back?'

'I ... you ... you have to believe me, I thought she didn't want to know about me anymore.'

He cannot stand up to my gaze. I stare at him in silence. David does the same.

'What else can I say?'

'How about the whole bloody truth at last? We can take it, Pa - better late than never.'

'But I want ...'

'To manipulate me to stay in thar good graces because things happened that tha don't want to face anymore?'

'No, no, no! Ah ... You're getting me all mixed up.'

'It's as clear as it can be. Tha are my biological father. That's for sure. Tha claim tha knew nothing about my mother being pregnant. She told her mother and sister she told you. Someone is lying, and I can't figure out who is lying or who told the truth. It's that simple, isn't it?'

'No, it's not that simple. Your mother and I had a wonderful time together. I've never loved another woman as much as I love her.'

'Tha left her and married someone else shortly afterwards. Sort of a contradiction, or am I wrong?'

'I had to ...'

'Think about thar own future? Career and making money? Already understood.'

'No. It wasn't that simple. My father would never have accepted Amaike.'

'Why don't I believe tha?'

'You don't know my father.'

'David says he was an asshole.'

'What?'

'A bitter, arrogant asshole he was, Pa, plain and simple. Why do you think I only ever wanted to visit Grandma Jin Jin?'

'Then you can understand ...'

'Why tha betrayed the love of my mother and me along with it? No, we can't. Don't tha have any human values? What kind of a pathetic coward are tha?'

'You cannot imagine what it would have taken at that time to stay with your mother.'

'Tha said that tha did not know she was pregnant. Do tha notice anything? Tha're embroiled in new lies.'

He remains silent and looks down.

'Tha want David to love tha and don't realise that won't work if tha soften the truth depending on which of us tha talk to.'

Again he is silent, kneading his hands so hard that his ankles turn white.

'I'll make it easy for tha. I accept that tha are my biological father, and ask no further questions. David is my brother, and that's good for both of us.'

'That takes a load off my shoulders.'

'I hear that, Pa. But I'm not finished. You want to get to know Lucia better, take care of her, be there for her?'

'That's right, David; you understand me.'

'Tha lie. Tha want a new job as CEO, in a company that is about to exploit the resources in the deep sea without first understanding what that means for the ecosystem. My skills, my knowledge and my diligence were useful to tha. That's what it looks like.'

'Yes, but you mustn't think of it that way.'

'If tha want to prove to me that tha want to be my father, change sides now.'

'Change sides?'

'Tha fight with me and David to preserve the oceans in their natural state.'

'But I have to earn my living.'

'Don't mind if tha do. But if tha want me to call tha father one day, then take David's and my side professionally.'

'You are insane!'

'Tha know all the tricks of the trade in industrial mining, don't tha?'

He remains silent while his face says: '*Of course I know everything that goes on.*

'It's time, Pa, to start thinking about *our* future.'

'What do you mean, David?'

'You help uncover what needs to change as quickly as possible - with no ifs, ands or buts.'

'If I do that, I'm a dead man in this business.'

'So far tha are a destroyer of nature and a despiser of humanity. Tha are one of those who, for two hundred years, have been destroying the Earth and rendering it inanimate faster than it has been in billions of years'.

'It's not that black and white! Don't be naive. Who is responsible for the prosperity of the Western world?'

'Fine, I'll make it easier for tha. Tha write an article about everything tha know about the cobalt mine in Kolwezi and we will publish and distribute it on the internet'.

'Are you insane? Nobody'll want me for top billing then.'

'I am clearer in my mind than tha are. If my mother's life meant a thousandth of what tha claim, that is a matter of honour.'

'What does that have to do with anything?'

'The guards at the mine in Kolwezi shot my mother in the back, my grandmother too, and that I am alive today is a miracle.'

'That ...'

I get up to go back to Miéko and Reto.

'You can't treat me like this, especially not when you are my daughter. You owe me respect and consideration too.'

'Enough. Stop pretending to be the prudent, virtuous one. Tha lie, tha exploit, tha do what is necessary to get the money tha want, for tharself, for thar glory, for thar progress. Tha serve even bigger liars, exploiters and killers. Tha pretend to exist separately from others and have thar own code of work and success. Tha pretend that something in thar way of doing business makes up for the horrors tha cause to people and nature, in Kolwezi and I don't know where else in the world. But this horror, this cold-heartedness is part of tha. And it will never disappear by itself.'

'That's not true, and I'm gonna prove it to you.'

'Where, in the next top job for a commodity company?'

He pulls a bitter face that collapses like a house of cards as David adds: 'I'll give you twenty-four hours to tell Granny Jin Jin yourself.'

HUMANITY LOG

Chronicle time 18.762.020 - 06.10
Project: *Let there be light*
Giacomo Aringhe-Rosse (aspect of ALANOS) and Clemente
Chigioni (aspect of ALANI)
Located 40° 39' 0.374" N 73° 56' 58.496" W

'You have twenty minutes,' explains the smaller of the two prison guards to Clemente Chigioni in a sharp tone of voice and, while closing the heavy iron door behind him, says quietly to his colleague: 'The more criminal the prisoner, the more exalted the confessor.'

The small visitors' room of the prison is bare, stone-grey and bathed in cold neon light. It smells of disinfectant. Giacomo sits slumped down in brown prisoner's clothing with folded hands in handcuffs at the shabby table. Clemente goes to the visitor's chair. Two surveillance cameras follow him, the chubby mid-seventy years old in a cassock with sun-kissed skin, hairless as an egg, perfumed and with rimless glasses on his hooked nose. They are not allowed to listen in on a confession. Clemente places his mouth-nose mask, Bible and a small box with communion wafers one after the other on the table with his thin, highly veined right hand, dominated by the massive gold ring with the crucifixion of Jesus. He sits down; his heart is bitter.

A soft, wilting scent of sweat emanates from Giacomo as he says in an unusually rattling voice: 'They treat me like cattle.'

'I know how you feel.'

'My lawyer says the FBI has evidence that'll put me away for life ... But when I name names ... '

'Omertà!'

Giacomo shrugs and lowers his head.

'Secrets with blood on them remain our most precious possession.'

Giacomo remains silent.

'The Schild want to liquidate you. *They* helped Vito escape.'

'I see,' says Giacomo, more hopeless than composed. 'Violence is a service like any other.'

'From Vito I know that Schild's men will hang you in the cell and make it look like suicide. They don't think you're a man of honour.'

Giacomo grabs his throat.

'Two of his men have already infiltrated the detention centre.'

'Can't the family do anything for me?' he begs Clemente with wet eyes.

Clemente grabs the box and opens it: 'I will give you a final communion. The poison works within thirty minutes and is undetectable.'

Giacomo's eyes open wide and stare at the hosts. A tear runs down his cheek.

'This is all the family can do for you.'

Giacomo swallows, looks piercingly at Clemente and asks: 'How will the lemon crop be this year?'

'*You* must protect the family now.'

Giacomo nods. Tears roll down from his eyes. He clumsily folds his hands. 'Begin,' it rattles meekly from his throat.

Clemente says a long prayer in Latin. Then they both rise. Clemente crosses himself and blesses Giacomo, says another prayer in Italian. With the 'Amen' he takes the top host out of the box and puts it on Giacomo's tongue. He retracts his tongue to allow the host to melt in his mouth and crosses himself. After a few moments he nods. Clemente gives him his right hand and Giacomo kisses the ring. Then Clemente leans forward, kisses him on the forehead and whispers: 'May God forgive us ... I'm supposed to tell you from Vito that the artichoke is paying for this with its heart.'

There is something like satisfaction on Giacomo's face.

Clemente turns his upper body towards the door and waves for the cameras to send in the guard. Then he puts the mouth-and-nose mask back on, takes the Bible and host box and walks leisurely to the door. It opens and the two guards enter. The taller of the two asks in surprise: 'Have you taken confession yet, Your Eminence?'

'Yes, my son. Mr. Aringhe-Rosse has cleared his conscience.'

'I suppose he had quite a lot to confess, didn't he?'

'God moves in mysterious ways, my son.' Then Clemente turns to Giacomo one last time, bathed in tears and stammering the Lord's Prayer.

RÜSCHLIKON, 15 JUNE 2020

I write the last pages of my Bachelor's thesis, follow the lectures online, which are actually no longer lectures, and deliver my assignments to my professor. I'll have completed my Bachelor's degree in August, and I don't know what will happen then. But for the first time in my life, I feel like I'm at home. Like the whole house, my room at the Frei's has a sandstone floor, a desk and chair made of light-coloured wood, a reading chair, a French bed, and a simple wardrobe built into the wall. Nothing fancy. The coolest thing is the ceiling, or rather the ceiling painting. A big blue vase, like the one in the entrance hall. I haven't told Miéko what I did with the blue vase in my mind, but I'm sure there'll be a good opportunity soon.

In this house nothing is just there, everything has a function, a task. I'm glad that I've left the show-off house of Thomas Müller behind me. Next to my guest room is a small Japanese bathroom with a wooden tub and shower and a small washbasin. The bathroom I share with the occupant of the other guest room, and that is David. He and Bea live here now as well. We also share the toilet in the guest corridor to these two rooms, a Japanese one that flushes your bottom with warm water, cool. This thing has so many buttons and settings that I can't see through it. Reto joked he will issue a sitters license once I have master this loo.

David and Reto have managed to link SAM and ILSA to SAMILSA. Together we are thinking about how we can make faster progress. The data to be collected and processed is simply too complex. We need to systematise better. Scientists have been doing research for years to suggest what should and shouldn't be allowed by the UN's International Seabed Authority drafting the Mining Code for the deep sea. But they are all still in the very early stages; they know far too little and work isolated in their specific fields of expertise. Countries and companies on the other side are putting pressure, wanting to access the treasures of the oceans now and quickly. This is precisely why we need to make progress with SAMILSA, to make projections and visualise future scenarios. We know little about the animals and microbes, how long they live, how slowly they need to grow, how they connect with each other. We do not know how tolerant they are of changes in their habitat. We do not know how much more widespread the effects of deep sea mining are in relation to the pure mining area itself and how long the effects will last. Oceanographers measure the currents on the bottom and their influence on the bottom sediments. Other are measuring the turbidity of sediment plumes that are formed in the water after the deposits have been whirled up by external influences such as sampling. Geologists study the composition of the sediments. Biologists study the different sizes of fauna and flora, ranging from meso- to megafauna, from small animals to giant octopuses. They have been trying for decades to get to know the animal and plant world, not to mention the life of microbes. Little has come out of it. Geochemists are trying to make long-term statements on the formation and development of the deep sea. Every day all these scientists find something new: new creatures, new habitats, new living conditions. All of this has to be collected, connected and analysed. David has now provided SAMILSA with a search and evaluation algorithm. SAMILSA searches on the Internet alone and also links alone. I only have to look at the results and conclusions and can start thinking about a strategy to wake up the world.

'Lucia, are you coming?' asks Miéko.

I lost track of time again. We both wanted to go to the garden right behind the house to harvest fresh lettuce and vegetables and then cook together at noon today. So far I've only watched Miéko cook Japanese food, but I want to learn it too. Miéko has offered for me to stay here and do my Master's degree in

Switzerland. She and Reto think it's good for my development and also for David's. David thinks it's a mega cool idea and has already pulled out all the stops at the ETH Zurich. My professor at the RWTH in Aachen wants me to stay and has offered me a part time research position. And, luckily for me, there's radio silence with Thomas Müller. David goes down the hill to see him briefly once a day and checks that everything's all right. David thinks he can't survive on his own. Thanks to Spirit their housekeeper Fee is back, otherwise he would become even more depressed. But he has come up with a new strategy to get a top job. After the summer, he wants to do an MBA at Harvard to use their alumni network and image for his career. I don't think he'll get that far. His whole life is just big fat play.

The doorbell rings at the front door, and brings my thoughts back to the here and now. The artificially intelligent voice, the new male voice of SAMILSA, calls for David.

'Can you identify the person, SAMILSA?' I hear David ask in the room next door.

'A young man, Asian, wearing a mouth-nose-mask. Just a moment ... he is taking it off ... Just a moment please ... Mr. Robin Ong.'

I jump up in horror. 'What? How do tha know him, SAMILSA?'

'His picture is among the deleted files on your laptop's hard drive, Lucia. My facial-recognition software says there's no doubt.'

'Tha snooping through my deleted files?'

'You gave SAM access to your laptop yourself.'

'But only for deep sea research.'

'Then you should have been more specific.'

'Open the door, SAMILSA.'

'He is standing in front of the other house. Should I open it anyway?'

'Yeah, let him in. I'll call Pa on the smartphone; tell him to say hello, we'll be right there.'

'I'm not going, David.'

'You bet you will, Lucia. Or do you think he's come to shake hands with Dr. Thomas Müller?'

When David and I arrive, Robin is standing in the entrance hall talking to Thomas. I have a lump in my throat and jelly in my knees. My heart is racing. Robin's face is sunken and pale, his black hair is more tousled than usual. Only trainers, jeans, white shirt and blazer show him as I know him. In his right hand he is holding a bouquet of red roses, which he stretches out to me when he sees me. His eyes light up. With his left hand he is holding on to the drawstring of his carry-on luggage.

'How do tha know where I am?'

'From Dimitri.'

'How did tha get here?'

'With Singapore Airlines, landed at 8:15 a.m., filled out the Corona form, was checked for a fever, showered in the arrival terminal, bought flowers and got into a taxi.'

David pulls Thomas by the sleeve and tells him to go upstairs with him. I accept the roses and ask Robin to come into the kitchen with me. 'Shall I make us some tea?'

'Yes, that would be lovely.'

I take a pot and tea from the cupboard, and put the kettle on. I invite Robin to have a seat at the kitchen island and serve him a glass of water and fresh fruit. Then I look for a vase for the roses, fill it with water, arrange the flowers in it, smell their beguilingly delicate scent for a moment and put them on the kitchen island as well. Robin watches me with every step. I pour the hot water on the tea leaves in the pot, take two tea cups and sit down next to him. The green tea still has to brew. Robin turns to me on his bar stool and takes my right hand, looks spellbound at my snake ring and then into my eyes.

'I didn't want all of this to happen. You must believe me, I didn't want this.'

'Why are tha here?'

'I can't live without you.'

'I haven't heard a word from tha since March, when we last met at Café Dom in Aachen.'

'It was impossible to be in touch.'

'Don't tell me tha can't talk or text anymore.'

'There was no hope.'

'And where are tha going to get it now?'

'Guan Yin saved me.'

'Since when has the Goddess of Mercy been involved in commodity trading?'

'My mother saved me.'

'Since when does she wear the trousers?'

'The Chinese government saved me.'

'Oh, have they conquered Singapore now, and is thar family on the run too? The only thing on the news is that they have started to squeeze the last of the freedoms out of Hong Kong with their National Security Act.'

'You know about that?'

'The whole world is talking about what's going on in Hong Kong. Beijing is taking away by the back door the special status promised to the Hong Kong Chinese for fifty years: rights to free speech, assembly, democracy and an independent judiciary based on the rule of law. With wishy-washy wording, they can take down anyone who does, says or writes anything that doesn't suit the Chinese leadership. They can take anyone to China to their detention centres and have them tried by their special courts in mock trials. Just as it suits their agenda.'

'Then you understand what saved me.'

'Don't talk in riddles again, please. Cut to the chase.'

I pull my hand out of his, pour us green tea, slowly, but my hand is shaking. When I put the pot down again, he immediately grabs it again and strokes it. With his thumb he keeps touching the snake's head of the ring and mumbles *lóng*. Then he looks at me with wet eyes: 'I prayed to Guan Yin every day, got sick, lay in bed for days. The Chinese doctor told my parents that my heart was weak and would not recover. My mother understood immediately. My father did not. He had me checked in Alexandra Hospital with Western medicine. They found nothing organic and I told my mother everything.'

'So you finally avoided beating around the bush?'

'She consulted the I Ching a few months ago about my prospects for a happy marriage. *Creation has a sublime effect on success, and through perseverance.* She said she must interpret differently if there is a woman in my heart ... Every day we both went to the temple praying to Guan Yin.'

'And that helps?'

'Conny Wong was arrested during demonstrations in Hong Kong. She is friends with the student activist Joshua Wong. My father was shocked. It's not good for business, he said. He waited until she was free, then told her father it must never happen again.'

'And he accepted that?'

'He grounded Conny. It wasn't good for his business either. You don't mess with the power elite in Beijing, it's not good for business.'

'And a goddess does that ...?'

'Conny's father defended China's new security bill for Hong Kong.'

'And Guan Yin did this too?'

'When that happened, my father was shocked, ended the business relationship and broke off the engagement. We Singaporeans appreciate what freedom means.'

'Tha're still not on a plane back to Europe. Tha told me tharself, tha owe obedience to your father.'

'I told my father about my business idea, about the company *Ong Origin*, which will trace and certify the origin and supply chains of all metals and minerals to the end customer. Then I told him that I carry a woman in my heart whom I love more than anything else ... Father cried and asked me to forgive him. Then the whole family went to the temple to thank Guan Yin.'

Before I can make a reply, Thomas comes into the kitchen, David follows and with gestures and facial expressions signals to me that he could no longer hold him back.

Robin, however wants to spill the beans. He gets out of the chair, stands in front of me and takes both my hands. 'I'm here to take you away, Lucia.'

'Do what?' I don't believe what he says and I look at him confusedly.

'Nobody is going to take away my daughter that quickly,' Thomas Müller interferes.

'Thomas, stay out of this. Get yourself an espresso, and then we'll go back to the home office. We're interrupting. SAMILSA, make a double espresso.'

Robin looks as if he has been hit by a truck and twists his eyes. I don't know whether it's because of Thomas' behaviour or because the coffee machine is brewing espresso as if by magic. Thomas takes his espresso and the two of them disappear again thanks to David.

'That man said *daughter*. Is he... is *he* your father?'

'Yeah, but he abandoned my pregnant mother back in the Congo. He doesn't deserve for me to call him father; all he did was sire me. But David is my younger brother, and we get along brilliantly.'

'And who is your family now?'

'My Dad and Tilly in Belgium. I am here in Switzerland because our professor helped me to an internship in deep sea mining; and guess what, I ended up with the company that owned the mine in Kolwezi, which my mother was shot for. Crass, totally crass.'

'And now you're going back to Aachen?'

'No, David and his neighbour have built an artificially intelligent computer that we want to use to make scientific predictions about how deep sea mining will change, disrupt and probably destroy the ecosystem and thus also destroy the basis of human life ... But that's another story.'

'You must come with me, Lucia.'

'Where to?'

'My parents want to meet you.'

'I ...'

'I already have a plane ticket for you in my pocket.'

'Do they know that I'm milk chocolate brown with an Afro curly hair, wearing dresses with a flight jacket and calf-high lace-up boots?'

'I showed them all the pictures of us.'

'And thar father has no objection?'

'He ...'

The doorbell rings and the door opener hums at the same moment.

'Who does that?' Robin asks in astonishment.

'SAMILSA, the artificial intelligence.'

'Just like that?'

'Facial recognition.'

'And me, how did it recognise me?'

'SAMILSA used a photo of tha on my laptop to identify tha.'

'So you do love me after all.' A tear rolls from the corner of his eye.

Bea and Dante come running in. Robin gets up on the bar stool in shock and pulls his legs up. Dogs are not his thing, especially not big ones. I lead them away towards the entrance hall and ask Miéko and Reto to come into the kitchen. Thomas comes down the stairs as well, David follows, and shortly afterwards they are all together in the kitchen staring at Robin. That's how I felt when I arrived at RWTH as a female freshmen. I introduce Robin Ong from Singapore to everyone once again.

Thomas questions him. 'And who are your parents, young man?'

'Typical Thomas, as if that matters. Better ask about his character, Pa.'

'My father is O. K. Ong and my mother Zai Intan.'

'The owner of Ong Raw Materials International?'

'Yes indeed, sir.'

'Stop it, Pa! Robin's not here for you.'

I think so too. I don't like the way Thomas Müller puts on his father role like a jacket when its suits him. But he is just getting started. He takes his smartphone out of his pocket, lets it dial a number, turns it up to loud and puts it on the kitchen island for all to see.

'Wei?' it says on the other end of the line.

'Dear Mr. Ong, Dr. Thomas Müller here from Switzerland, former board member of the London Metal Exchange, former CEO of Vijay ... Perhaps you remember me,' says Thomas.

'Ah, Mister Doctor Muller. Yes, yes, good day, good day.'

You can hear in his voice that he half bows on the other side.

'I just wanted to let you know that your son Robin has arrived safely at my house in Zurich with my daughter. I'm passing you over so you can have a brief word with him yourself.'

Robin is shocked, can't make a sound at the first moment. 'Father? ... Yes ... it's me.' He tilts his head and torso forward. 'I'm at Lucia's ... 这比我想的要复杂，现在无法解释.'

'Yes, Mr. Ong, it is a little more complicated than your son can explain at the moment. But I can explain it, Mr. Ong, I can,' Thomas interferes again without being asked.

Silence at the other end of the line. I've had enough of this. 'Mr. Ong? This is Lucia speaking. I thank tha for sending Robin and I am delighted to follow thar invitation.'

'Aijaaa. We are happy, we are happy.'

'With your permission, Mr. Ong, I'll join you in Singapore as well to discuss business.'

'Are you out of your mind?' whispers David and pushes his elbow into Thomas' ribs. 'It's none of your business.'

Thomas writhes with a painfully distorted face.

'Mr. Ong, here's Lucia again. I look forward to visiting tha together with Robin. First please give us a few days on our own.'

'Yes, yes, yes, Missis Lucia, we are very pleased.'

Then I end the conversation and the embarrassment is over. I would love to disappear into the ground in shame. What does this Thomas Müller actually think?

Reto takes a step forward, looks at Miéko and says: '家に連れて帰ろう 同意しますか？' Miéko nods, winks at me, and Robin's face lights up. Apparently he understands Japanese. I only suspect something.

'As long as Doctor Müller still needs time and rest to reorganise his business affairs, we would be pleased to welcome you as a guest in our house.'

Robin walks up to them both, bows a little and shakes their hands. He looks at me confused. I can't blame him. 'I gladly accept your kind invitation,' he replies.

'And what about me? I do have something to say about that too,' protests Thomas.

'We would be delighted if you would drop by for dinner today, Doctor Müller, at least if your condition allows for it. At seven o'clock, if that is convenient for you. I'll get the barbecue going.'

But Thomas replies with bitterness in his voice: 'No, thank you, Mr. Frei. I get on fine by myself.' He *has* to get on fine by himself, because his mother has had to learn from David that she is a double grandmother.

EQUIPPED

Chronicle time 18.762.020 - 06.17

'We have a visit to make,' says Miéko, takes me by the hand and walks towards the entrance hall of her house. I have no idea where we're are going. I don't know anyone here except David, Thomas and them. When we get to the entrance hall, I reach for the cupboard door, take off my slippers and exchange them for the sneakers. 'Do I need a jacket? It's raining.'

'Where we are going, you don't need this. Sturdy shoes will do.' She grabs me with her left hand and turns us both towards the mural of the big blue vase. Now I know what she is up to.

'I went through the vase once on my own, Miéko, in my mind, and I ended up ... '

'At ETRUTHSIA's cave in the DEVA Kingdom. I know. Close your eyes and walk with me in your thoughts. You'll see what happens today.' Soon after, I feel someone holding my right hand too. I open my eyes and see NÃO smiling at me. I let my eyes wander. We are standing together in the big green cave on the Outer Hebrides. Behind us the steps lead into the sea, which claps against them. In front of us, at the back of the cave, ETRUTHSIA is sitting on her throne. She holds the handle of a shiny silver sword with both hands. The tip of the sword rests between her legs on the wet stone.

To her right and left are some of the mermen and -women I met at the Council of the Sea, Tritons, Kappas and many more.

'Welcome. Come on in.'

Together we walk hand in hand towards them. When we are fifteen feet in front of her, Miéko and NÃO let go of me and with looks in their eyes tell me that I have to walk the last bit alone. I feel warm, especially as ETRUTHSIA rises and now looks down on me from almost 10 feet. I take two more steps and look her in the eyes.

A Triton approaches me from the right and presents me with a leather, amber-orange hip bag, as people used to wear centuries ago on their belt or over their kilt. I open the tightened ribbon, which closes with eyelets around the opening to form a bow. In the bag I find my hairpin and my upper arm band from the Council of the Sea. The Triton says that more *keys* will be added over time. I should always carry them with me.

ETRUTHSIA grasps her sword with her left hand alone, turns it and holds the tip up.

'This is the sword of truth, as I bear it in my name.'

I remember when she wrote down her name for me at our first meeting; I could clearly see that the first t in her name was not a real letter, but a shiny silver sword.

'You have proven yourself worthy of the truth and of your being. As of now you carry the sword of truth in your name as well, visible to all on Earth. She touches both my shoulders with the tip of the sword, then the head and finally, extremely gently, my chest in front of the heart. She pulls the sword back, grasps it again with both hands, says something I cannot hear, and all of a sudden the sword doubles. Then she hands me the left one.

'*Lucia-TRUSIAN, she who puts the truth on the table*, take now your sword in hand and name and become one with it.'

Ashamed, I look down and only up again after a moment. First I have to comprehend all this. ETRUTHSIA points with the tip of her sword to the walls of the grotto, and there the name TRUSIAN shines in golden letters, only that the T is a silver sword and its handle extends above the horizontal stroke of the letter, where I can clearly see a ruby and an emerald, just like in my mother's ring. I am touched, my eyes become moist. The People of the Sea sing a wonderfully melodious song that I do not know. When they have finished, everyone claps.

'Bring the dragon amour,' orders ETRUTHSIA. From behind, Miéko and NÃO come with a kind of samurai armour in amber-orange leather and put it on me. Helmet, chest, back and arm armour. The leather is arranged in small, overlapping panels and bars which seem to be sewn together flexibly. In any case, I can move easily in them. This armour is heavy nevertheless. I pass my hand over it, feel how soft the leather is, and also rough stones on the breastplate. I look closer and detect a collection of uncut gems, arranged as a star cluster, just like on my left forearm. I have to take a deep breath, pause, and then look at NÃO. She is wearing a leather armour just like this now as well. We look like identical twins. But before I can think, we are already moving on. Miéko and NÃO take my hands again and ETRUTHSIA asks everyone to follow her.

ETRUTHSIA walks ahead into an opening at the back of the cave, the three of us behind, followed by Tritons, Kappa, mermaids and I don't know who else. We walk through a dark shaft, damp but not unpleasant. I don't know how long it takes, but finally we are standing in another big cave with an octagonal lake or waterhole of blue-greenish water. We walk up to about fifteen feet towards its shore stones and ETRUTHSIA shouts: 'SILVIAR'I'A, we are ready.' Then she quickly takes two steps back and we instinctively do the same. The water becomes restless, higher and higher waves move powerfully from the centre to the edges. Suddenly a huge scaly amber-orange dragon emerges.

He catapults himself onto the stones of the cave. The water splashes. I flinch while all the others stand still as if it were the most natural thing in the world.

The dragon lowers his head towards me and sniffs at me. I am very calm inside. We know each other. SILVIAR'I'A: yes, the name says something to me, feels familiar. The huge creature is parading up and down in front of me. Head, teeth, mouth, wings and legs are clearly dragon-like. Two wings, a mighty body on four legs with five-linked feet and flippers in between. Except for wings and webs, the dragon is covered with golden-pink-amber-orange scales. Colours and physique also make me think of a seahorse. The animal sparkles towards me from light green eyes. Instinctively I stretch out my flat right hand towards his head and want to touch it. The dragon's head comes even closer, sniffs directly at my hand, sniffs at the sword in my left, then pulls its head back, snorts and emits fire towards the grotto ceiling. The eyes of all the sea people are fixed on me. I feel safe; I am calm inside, and obviously the dragon feels that too. Again he tilts his head, this time towards ETRUTHSIA, who delicately places her hand between the two nostrils. She turns her head to me and says: 'Lucia-TRUSIAN, this is the link you were missing. SILVIAR'I'A is your dragon companion. Awakened now is your inner conquest and duty. *The truth is coming!* Let us celebrate.' ETRUTHSIA bows to both of us and SILVIAR'I'A - a she, not a he - sniffs at me again. Miéko joins me and hands me a Japanese-looking scabbard for my sword with a long leather strap, which she artfully fastens around my waist. Now I have both hands free again. And immediately SILVIAR'I'A grabs me gently with her mouth and puts me down on her neck in front of her wings. She places NÃO behind me in the same manner. All others gather in front of us in a semicircle and ETRUTHSIA sings elatedly:

You are honoured, for your words are true.
We are comforted, the truth is near.
The fire of the air,
The fire of the earth,
The fire of the seas,
The fire of the stars,
May the Dragon Rider
Succeed with great deeds.

Everyone claps and starts singing a song again, another one I don't know. It sounds like hope and confidence in what is to come.

Then follows a strong jerk. SILVIAR'I'A pushes herself off the bottom of the cave and jumps back into the blue-green water. I hold on as tight as I can. At first we are in a mighty whirlpool created by her immersion. But now it goes down for minutes at great speed. At some point the water becomes dark grey, I suspect we are now in the open sea. SILVIAR'I'A lets herself drift skilfully with the different currents, a kind of underwater street system - at least I can see and feel different currents. The water layers are sometimes warmer and sometimes colder, but they are becoming lighter now. She carries NÃO and me to a sunken city. Some mighty buildings and columns are still standing upright; others lie overturned or already broken into cairns on the ground, partly overgrown. In front of them, looking at us, a huge Triton with long grey hair, thick beard and a golden trident in his hand is waiting for us. SILVIAR'I'A puts her legs up and bends her head towards him. It seems to me like bowing to the ruler of the water, because that's what he seems to me, so tall, strong and wise he looks. He does not say a word, but the two of them seem to be communicating. He pushes himself off the seabed and swims away, SILVIAR'I'A follows him.

What comes next is overwhelming. We swim towards a gigantic underwater farm and then over it. Below us, mermen and -women care for different kinds of plants. They caress them, they sing to them, they make music for them. Others use round sickles to cut larger plants and tie them into bundles. In between, smaller sea children play. Wow. The area we are swimming over must surely measure tens of thousands of football fields. I can't get enough of it. I would like to get off my dragon companion and feel it for myself and see it up close. So I tap SILVIAR'I'A on the neck and point my finger down. She expels yellowish air through her nostrils. Air bubbles rise. The Triton turns to me and shakes his head. Understood, I have to keep my fingers off.

This is the mega version of something I read years ago, *Nemo's Garden*. An Italian grows fruit and vegetables in underwater greenhouses off the coast of southern Italy.

The Triton and SILVIAR'I'A pause. The Triton comes close, face to face and says to me in a deep thundering voice: *The secrets of the sea and all our technologies lie in vibrations and sounds. We share them with those who have shown us that they respect us, our habitat and our knowledge. Make this clear to the land-dwellers, or they will perish by drought, fire and flood. Tell them that I and the dragons are getting angrier every day. They should not be surprised if the sea quakes more and more often, if more and more dams burst, if more and more rivers burst their banks every day and drag land and people with them. They must not be surprised when the land is on fire and devours their houses. Enough is enough! Make that clear to them.*

'I have seen and understood. I promise tha, I will do my utmost to convince people that the oceans can provide life for them too.'

We trust you. If you need us, come through the blue vase.

He nods at NAÕ and me again, and before I can say goodbye, SILVIAR'I'A hurries with us towards the water surface. I feel an ever increasing vortex of air, I see people, buildings, trees and mountains disappearing beneath us. SILVIAR'I'A constantly increases her speed. We penetrate several cloud layers. At some point a gigantic space station comes into sight. On its underside I recognise numerous smaller and larger spaceships, round and longish, docked to a kind of landing zone. Wow, what a sight. But we are landing on a kind of dragon deck right behind it. About fifty different-looking dragons are gathered there. SILVIAR'I'A lands gently on her four legs in a free position. A dragon with red scale armour, four legs, long tail and huge wings blows fire at us as soon as we touch down. He seems to be an unfriendly fellow. SILVIAR'I'A remains unimpressed and walks a few steps to another free spot right next to a waterhole; it could also be a pool for water dragons. To the right of us a rather pelican-like dragon, much smaller than SILVIAR'I'A, is standing and is blowing fiery air out of his nostrils. SILVIAR'I'A replies. To our left is a snake-like dragon, dozing away, his four legs with three claw-like toes each and his ultra-long tail stretched out far from him. SILVIAR'I'A lifts us from her neck and then points with her head to a shiny metal gate barely fifty yards further. Apparently we are supposed to go there. We both set off in our samurai armour. It occurs to me that either other dragon riders wear something like that too, or we look completely out-of-place.

After barely ten yards, a small golden dragon appears in our path, looking like the one on the blue Ishtar Gate from Babylon in the Pergamon Museum in Berlin. He walks on four legs like a dog and has a long neck that ends in a snake-like head with two large eyes and a flat mouth-opening. He touches me with his split tongue. The upper body, including the tail, is covered with scales. The two front legs have lion paws; the two back legs show the claws of an eagle. One claw extends away to the back, three to the front. I stand still and let myself be felt. This takes a moment, then the little dragon runs away. Probably not interesting enough. We continue walking towards the entrance to the space station. Suddenly there is a ruckus behind us. We turn around. SILVIAR'I'A and the pelican-like dragon romp around like two young dogs. I have to smile and we continue on our way. On the right in front of us is a tail feather snake shining from afar. This one is bluish and covered from top to bottom with bright red and yellow feathers. The Toltecs, Aztecs and Maya worshipped such beings as a deity. When I was in the highlands of Mexico once with my Dad, I heard about them during a guided tour. They call them Quetzalcoatl. This one looks mega cool and I enjoy her sight for a brief moment. We continue walking towards the entrance. I'm curious why SILVIAR'I'A brought us to this space station, or whatever it is.

When we step in front of the metal entrance door, it remains closed. NÃO points to a kind of scanner. She takes her upper arm bracelet out of her service bag and motions to me to do the same. Together we hold them against the scanner, and indeed the metal door opens. In front of us stands - I can't believe it - YESHUA. A feeling of happiness rushes through my body from head to toe.

Welcome to the Mothership, you two!

We hug.

'How nice to see tha again, YESHUA.'

We are expected, you, Lucia-TRUSLAN, more than NÃO and me.

'By whom?'

By SANAT KUMARA of course and some of the Ascended Masters ... in the reception room, right next to the Bridge. Let us go.

We walk along a wide corridor, pass three smaller lifts and now stand in front of a large one whose sensor scans us from top to bottom.

We only take this one so that you can satisfy your curiosity, comments YESHUA and winks at me.

NÃO giggles. I don't think that's funny.

As the door opens, thousands of tiny creatures stream towards us, no larger than a tiny lentil, transparent. They roar and rage in confusion like a horde of wild schoolchildren after being forced to sit still for too long. At the very end, a cairn, which reaches to my ankle, apologises for the behaviour of his *Elementals* and follows them towards an exit marked *DEVA Kingdom*. What was that?

We get into the big round lift. A beam of light scans us again and YESHUA says: *Bridge*. We dash up, at least that's what I suspect from the light indicator. The lift stops and three male light beings, about ten feet tall, get in. They are laughingly engrossed in conversation and don't notice us. The first one looks like an elderly Tibetan monk from a Lama monastery. He has a roundish, benevolent face, shaved hair, an upper lip beard and a pointed grey goatee. He is wrapped in a floor-length greenish light robe, and in his left hand he plays with a mala made of wooden beads. The second one seems younger. He has shoulder-length brown hair and a full beard. On his head he wears a shawl slung into a kind of turban, and he is wrapped in a royal blue robe. The third seems even younger, with long blond hair, bright blue eyes and a full beard. He is wearing a golden robe.

The lift announces 'conference rooms'. The door opens and the three of them get out into a wide, bright corridor and pass out of sight to the right. I stretch my head behind and see a whole range of beings, men and women in floor-length robes of different colours, all with a radiant aura. Approaching from the left are beings that I have never seen before. Also about ten feet tall, waxy greenish-blue shimmering heads, round at the top, tapering at the chin, huge eyes, two small nostrils and a tiny mouth, more a line than a mouth. They wear fluorescent robes in various colours decorated with ornaments and symbols. Their hands are long and narrow, their fingers are delicate. Two look at me. Suddenly someone pulls me back into the lift by my sword.

What about the lack of curiosity?

YESHUA should understand that I have to get to the bottom of things. When the lift door is already closed again, it opens once more. A man and a woman enter and eye me from top to bottom, but lovingly.

Hello. May I introduce Lucia-TRUSIAN and NÃO, MOTHER MARY and LORD MAITREYA.

The woman seems to me the embodiment of pure light, love and compassion. She is considerably taller than me, with a radiant, delicate face, blue eyes, blonde hair, and she wears a white robe with a headscarf, over it a blue robe with purple cuffs. Her aura shines golden and white from her chest upwards and then down to the floor: first green, then yellow, orange and finally red. The man is dressed from top to bottom in a white light robe, headgear like an Arab, but in white, and the headband that holds it is in a bright blue. Dark hair, dark beard and brown eyes; the skin colour is similar to mine, maybe a little lighter. They smile at NÃO and me. The lift continues to rush upwards and soon comes to a halt. 'Bridge', announces the loudspeaker of the lift. We get out behind them. They walk along an equally bright but slightly narrower passage to the left. YESHUA points with his hand to the right.

We go this way ... Come on, go ahead and ask, Lucia-TRUSIAN.

'Yeah, I want to know a lot of things. First of all, these little transparent, mega-excited little fellows, YESHUA ... '

They must come from the Nikola Tesla deck. We call them Elementals, a single-purpose life form. United as a group, they contribute with their whole being to the purpose for which they were created. They are master builders on the smallest level. The DEVAs have to tame them and keep them connected, otherwise they will be up and away God knows where. These were relatively large; most of them do not have a size beyond the microscopic level and go into other dimensions. The land-dweller scientists are right on their heels with their up-quarks and down-quarks. But they have not yet figured out what is really behind them. The Elementals live from vibration and frequency. Every field in particle physics, such as the one that land-dwellers call the Higgs field, is the vibration of a category of Elementals.*

'Wow. And the three men: I've seen them before, but I can't remember their names or what they do.'

NÃO, we'll have to perform some more memory work with her - what do you think?

I am afraid so too, YESHUA.

'Don't make fun of me. Tha're acting as if I don't know on purpose ...' Embarrassing situations always make me blush with shame.

The three gentlemen, Lucia-TRUSIAN, form a group of Universal World Teachers. They are known as MASTER DJWAHL KHUL, also called the Tibetan Master, MASTER MORYA and MASTER KUTHUMI. All of them reached the fifth initiation at some point and then decided to follow the career path of an Ascended Master. First they dictated messages to Helena Blavatsky and then to Alice Bailey for the land-dwellers. Unfortunately, the land-dwellers elevated the two ladies to cult status. The three world teachers fell into oblivion because of this. Since 2019 they have been providing the human family with up-to-date knowledge for the 21st century through the book series Ageless Wisdom Evolving, received and edited by a lady in Minnesota. I call the three also the Teachers of Teachers. They are extremely busy and do not allow themselves any rest from turning things on Earth to the good after all. Do not blame them for not even noticing us. I suspect they mistook you both for team members of MIYAMOTO MUSASHI, the great samurai.

'There is something royal about the Master in the blue robe; and the one who seems to me the youngest, Master KUTHUMI: he must have been a highly praised teacher long ago.'

YESHUA laughs lovingly.

How quickly you see through everyone. MASTER MORYA *has indeed had a remarkable career on Earth. He led, among others, the lives known to land-dwellers as Abraham, King Melchior, King Arthur, Grand Mogul Akbar and Thomas Moore the poet.*

'And MASTER KUTHUMI?'

Lucia got to know a fraction of his teachings at school, as Pythagoras, but did not learn there what he taught on the spiritual background of numbers and geometry. That is why Tilly taught you what Pythagoras left the land-dwellers in terms of spiritual wisdom about numbers. MASTER KUTHUMI *led the lives of King Balthazar, Saint Francis of Assisi and Shah Jahan, who had the Taj Mahal built in Agra.*

'So tha've known them both since tha were in the manger?'

He laughs out loud. *You can see it that way. But I too have lived not only the life that Christians describe as that of Jesus of Nazareth. They don't want to know about my time in India. But on the way back to the Creator one always meets three to five times, as we usually joke here on the Mothership.*

We have reached the end of the corridor. Straight ahead is the 'Bridge', says a sign to the right of a metal door that probably opens electrically as well. YESHUA and NÃO have stopped in front of the room with the sign 'Reception Room'. But I go on and hope the door to the bridge opens. I eagerly want to know what it looks like there. But nothing happens, the door stays closed. YESHUA laughs out loud at me.

I turn around and say, 'Only those who go too far can look around properly.'

*Right, but not right now. In here, please, Lucia-*TRUSIAN.

ON THE MOTHER SHIP

Chronicle time 18.7602.020 - 06.17

You're late.

I beg your indulgence, Lord of the World; our fighter constantly asks and explores what she can whenever she gets the slightest chance.

Very forgivable. SANAT KUMARA and the other four at the table laugh.

Do you now believe, Lucia-TRUSLAN, that you are not alone and that your task is worth taking on?

'Yes, SANAT KUMARA, and I want to tell tha from the bottom of my heart: I am ready.'

That's what I wanted to hear! Take your seats, please.

It is a modern meeting room, rounded walls with an oval table and eight seats. The three on the long side facing us are still free. SANAT KUMARA is sitting at the right head end. I do not know the other gentlemen. SANAT KUMARA smiles at me as I stand before him in the dragon armour. YESHUA sits in the middle, I on the right side, right next to SANAT KUMARA and NÃO on the left of YESHUA. Opposite me sits a youthful-looking African, small black curls, like mine, but cut short as is suitable for a man, large bright brown eyes, broad nose and strikingly beautifully shaped round lips. He wears earrings with small diamonds in both earlobes. Around his head shines a violet aura that merges into royal blue. He also wears a yellow-golden cape with a round symbol embroidered with gold threads, which I do not know yet.

I also welcome you, Lucia-TRUSLAN and NÃO. I am brother AFRO, one of the Ascended Masters of Africa. My task is to guard and spread the knowledge of the African tribes in its original form from all ages and to connect with my brothers and sisters of other indigenous peoples on Earth.

'I greet tha too, brother AFRO. I can't believe there's someone who looks like me.'

Everyone else laughs heartily, but not the two of us. He will probably have had similar experiences on Earth as I have.

'Can tha tell me what knowledge tha hold?'

For the time being only this much, because we are here for another reason. The African tribes were once sublime peoples. We spoke the language of the stars. Gloria, whom you met in Kolwezi, still speaks it today. Your grandmother Shaira and your mother Amaike spoke it, and your aunt Walikia speaks it too.

I have to pause, my eyes become moist as images of the day I spent with Gloria and Walikia in Kolwezi rise up in me. Brother AFRO senses this and gives me a moment to catch myself.

Are you okay?

'Yes.'

We indigenous people are able to grasp the truth intuitively and can translate it into conscious thought. In the past, when we came to Earth from the stars as seeds, we had a dark purple-blue skin colour. As you can see, this has had to change due to the intense sunlight in Africa.

He points with his finger at his nose and smiles. I smile back.

We feel connected with all beings and life forms, no matter whether they are plants, animals, humans, angels, elves, devas, dragons, conrees, Ascended Masters or our brothers and sisters from other stars. We feel and know the sounds, noises and rhythms, the heartbeat, the pulse, the melodies of wind, clouds, water, fire and all life, everywhere. More than in any other material on Earth, the echo of the music of the spheres is alive in water, just as are the unspeakably stupid deeds of the land-dwellers. We indigenous people are at the same time connected to all planets and intelligences. My brothers and sisters would say the same thing, whether they originate from North America, or from Australia, New Zealand, Polynesia and the Arctic Circle. All indigenous peoples and their descendants are capable of this.

His words resonate within me as if I had always known this. I have lived it, in the meadows along the river Nete, with the animals, trees, grasses and stones. AFRO looks at me intently, all the others do too. It is probably time to say what I have understood. They seem to be waiting for it. I take a deep breath.

'I understand now that ZONCRIET is a Great Being, a Great Soul manifesting as the body of the Earth, and humans are only a single organ of this body in different dimensions. And because the land-dwellers of dense matter do not want to understand that they are only a part of something much bigger and not the most important thing, the whole organ is sick. That makes the other organs sick, too, and so the whole body is sick. Land-dwellers are destroying the human organ and thus the whole body. What has developed over billions of years and is supervised by SANAT KUMARA and many who help him is sick, seriously sick. It is sick because the land-dwellers are sick in the head and almost dead in the heart.'

The white man caused the disease and spreads it daily, says the elderly Indian chief with the eyes of an eagle and the face with the map of life, sitting to the left of brother AFRO. His long grey hair is held up by a light blue headband with a single eagle feather in it. *They call me WHITE EAGLE. I am glad that I can now count on you and your team.*

The human family is indeed an indispensable organ in ZONCRIET's body, and ZONCRIET's condition continues to deteriorate. You, your team and many more are needed to heal the organ. This healing process will have to reveal the full extent of the disease and will cause even more stress than it already does in the whole body. The spiritual land-dweller disease will also affect other vital organs, the kingdom of animals and plants. Therefore, you must not only help to heal the human organ but also be prepared to add essential nutrients and trace elements to the whole body. Entrust yourself to the guidance of YESHUA and his team, of brother AFRO, WHITE EAGLE and theirs as well as MOHAMMED and SAINT GERMAIN.

To the left of WHITE EAGLE, on the other side of the table, sits, or should I better say floats, a cloudy being, in its centre a green-gold-red symbol, which is more of a work of art with breathtakingly beautiful, filigree written golden Arabic letters.

I see the amazement in your eyes and I take it as a compliment.

'Yes, tha are unique and utterly beautiful.'

I stand for faith. So that you too can receive clearly the messages of the Creator, of God, you must purify yourself again and again and also keep yourself pure. Then you can best grasp the faith in what is true and real and also spread the knowledge about it. I will help you with this.

'Thank tha. How do I know they're messages from tha?'

Whenever your soul is calm and your heart is at peace. Do not do evil and do not repay evil with evil, however hard this may be for you, especially when you think of the people who have done or will do evil to you and others.

'But who stops evil? Who provides justice?'

No one escapes what he has sown. Follow your task and your destiny; be courageous and truthful.

I must look rather questioning, because the man on the left headboard is now also starting to talk. He looks young and fresh, around forty, full brown hair, combed back and a full beard. His robe of light shines in royal purple, just like the iris of his eyes.

You allow me to introduce myself. I am known as MASTER SAINT GERMAIN. Some also call me Count Rakoczi after my last incarnation in the dense physical. I come from the constellation Cygnus. I am the guide of the seventh, violet ray and will take over your guidance as soon as you have returned to Aachen.

'Should I?'

You'll work from Aachen, even if it's still a mystery to you how exactly. You will learn everything in its time.

I am amazed and touched at the same time. But my whole body vibrates warmly and harmoniously ... Interesting. Before I can thank everyone, the door opens behind me and I turn around. A radiant woman with long blonde hair and blue eyes comes in, wrapped in a robe with royal blue headgear. Her aura shines in white at least three feet above her body. All rise and bow, I do the same.

This, Lucia-TRUSLAN, is the Planetary Guardian, her name is IMMACULATA. She guards the pure plan for the Earth and the pure concept of the soul ZONCRIET, says SANAT KUMARA and bows to her again.

Remember me?

'No, IMMACULATA, I'm really sorry.'

You wanted to go to the Bridge, but the way was still denied you.

'Yes,' I reply. Whatever I say, think, do, really everything, is known here.

Now your time has come. Follow me and you will see what you and your team need to work towards.

She turns to the door and then to the right, we all join her. The door to the Bridge opens, and I'm looking forward to a kind of command headquarters like the one I know from the *Star Trek* movies. But I was mistaken. She can probably read my disappointment from my face.

Do you honestly believe that highly developed beings work with a technology that comes from the imagination of land-dwellers with limited consciousness?

I've never thought about it that way before. She probably doesn't expect an answer and continues. *This is the Bridge to the Plan for Earth, and thus to the Creator's plan for our solar system and our galaxy. Everything is interdependent; everything conditions and influences each other.* She steps aside. In front of a huge window front out into space, a freely suspended globe of about seven feet in diameter is rotating. *Here you can see what the Earth has to be transformed into, so that it once again corresponds to the Plan and can fulfil its task for the solar system, the Milky Way and the cosmos.*

I can clearly see the continents, endless woodlands and green spaces, mountain ranges and oceans, hardly any deserts, but above all no megacities. Instead, many small and medium-sized cities, judging by the circles, all around a shining tiny red dot. I point my finger at one of them and IMMACULATA smiles.

Portals, some also call them Stargates. Every town and settlement has one or will have one around it. They don't need to be built. They are all already there. They were given to Earth by other star races when it began its service in the fabric of the whole. Here, look ... She points to New Delhi, touches the surface, and the image of a stele appears. I have seen it before. *This stargate is a gift from Andromeda. You stood in front of it when you visited India with your adoptive parents.*

'The Iron Column in the courtyard of the Quwwat-ul-Islam Mosque, do tha mean this one? No one can explain why it is so corrosion-resistant.'

When the time comes for this part of your tasks, you will find many Stargates, put some back into operation and with your team teach the land-dwellers how they work. This is also part of your tasks.

I pause. IMMACULATA, SANAT KUMARA, YESHUA and all the others look at me piercingly. It is as if suddenly a limiting layer in me bursts and I know again.

The Earth and everything that belongs to it should be an attractive, joyful place of meeting, learning and exchange for this part of the cosmos, a kind of galactic university.

MORE

You, dear readers, can expect the next volume to come around in one-and-a half-years from now, depending on how much of my time is taken up by other duties. Until then, however, I will shorten the waiting time for all those who are eagerly awaiting it. The blog on my homepage www.drmartinaviolettajung.com will keep you informed about the next volume and where to meet me for readings and discussions, also online.

In a monthly *Letter of Secrets* especially for fans I also answer readers' questions about my writing, what books I read and how I learn, also letting you see more sketches and watercolours I have made of the characters and their experiences in other dimensions. For this purpose please register with me via the e-mail chrosanatkumara@icloud.com. I look forward to our dialogue!

Yours
Martina Violetta Jung

Room For Your Notes

Printed in Great Britain
by Amazon